The ɓ

of Natchez

Published by David J Publishing 2018
Copyright © Colin McAlpin

This book is a work of fiction and as such names, characters, places and incidents either are products of the author's imagination or are used fictitiously. Any resemblance to actual events or locales or persons
living or dead is entirely coincidental.

The right of Colin McAlpin to be identified as the author of this work
has been asserted by him in accordance with the
Copyright, Designs and Patents Act of 1988.

All rights reserved, including right to reproduce this book
or portions thereof in any form whatsoever.

First David J Publishing paperback edition 2018
www.davidjpublishing.com

Cover Design: Copyright © Jacqueline Stokes
www.yannadesignstudio.co.uk

A CIP catalogue record for this book is available from the British Library
ISBN: 978-0-9957057-4-6

Also By Colin McAlpin

Julia
Santa Fe Sisters
The Midnight Star

The Rachel Andrews Mysteries:
A is for Murder
Holy Murder
Dead Line

Dedication

With much love, to my daughter Heidi and her wonderful family:
husband Ray, daughter Scarlett and son Freddie.

With thanks to a great friend, advisor and researcher, Angela Lubbock; to a much missed friend, supporter and editor, David Culbert; to the always helpful people in the Louisiana Office of Tourism, The Mississippi Tourism Association, the Natchez Visitor Center and the countless others along the Mississippi who offered kindness and information.

The Belle of Natchez

by

Colin McAlpin

Colin McAlpin

For Amy, - A genuine Southern Belle.

DAVID J PUBLISHING

Chapter 1

SHE STOOD IN THE CLASSROOM and listened to the children playing outside in the small, flag-stoned yard. From beyond the white-painted wooden fence she could hear the sounds of the riverside drifting across the town in the shimmering afternoon heat. She heard the shouts of the men as they busied themselves on the jetty with the bales of white cotton and bags of raw, brown tobacco leaves.

The children, adding their own commotion, were playing chase-and-catch or throwing a ball around a circle while a piggy-in-the-middle tried vainly to catch it. Four small boys were standing along the fence watching the horses and carts rumbling past along the cobbled street that ran down to the river and the landing.

A small crowd of expectant citizens had either gathered at or were making their way to the jetty, to greet visitors or to embark on the approaching riverboat.

She caught the first notes of the calliope, booming and echoing across the water, and presently saw the stern-wheeled paddle-steamer, billowing gray-white smoke from its stack, ease its way around the sandy island where the river turned gently towards the town. Several of the ladies waiting in carriages lined along the jetty and river bank were waving silk and linen handkerchiefs in excited greeting, their male companions standing beside the carriages and raising their hats in salute.

She turned from the window as a small girl tugged at her dress.

"May we go out to play, Miss Dubois?"

She smiled and nodded and the child and her friends raced from the classroom to join the others in the playground.

Erin Dubois was the unlikeliest of school ma'ams. She was, it was true, unmarried and at the age of twenty-seven even she considered herself unlikely to be otherwise. Not that she had never been asked for she had turned down several proposals from otherwise quite suitable young men of wealth and good standing, scions indeed of society. She simply considered all her suitors as vain and shallow creatures and, anyway, she did not love them.

As she cleared away the books scattered on the desks and on her table she fingered a straying strand of auburn hair behind her ear. Erin Dubois was, by almost everyone else's judgement, a beautiful woman. She was tall – 5ft 9ins – and slender and her gray eyes held secrets and promised mysteries and captivated all who knew her.

She was, too, unconventional and strong-willed, as the men who sat on the town's Board of Education had often enough and to their chagrin discovered. Her approach to the education of the young was free-spirited – more often than not conducted along the banks of the river or on what she called 'great adventures' in the woods that circled the town than in the confines of a hot and stuffy classroom.

And what particularly exasperated the gentlemen of the Board of Education was that Miss Dubois was utterly loved by her pupils and by their parents.

Erin had lived in Northville Landing, the small Louisiana town that hugged the western bank of the Mississippi River, all her life. It was not a prepossessing place for it had only one main street and that had a scattering of warehouses, stores, offices and houses on only one side since the other side sloped down to the levee.

Attempts had been made to expand the town and thus several side streets ran half-heartedly to nowhere. The town had started life as a refuelling stop for the riverboats and there had once been a ferry across the river, until it was realized there was nothing worth visiting on the opposite bank.

Still, Northville Landing had survived, somehow, and was as thriving a location as could be seen given that what Southerners referred to as the War Between the States or the War of Northern Aggression or, for those of a more gentile disposition, the Recent Unpleasantness had ended a mere two years ago – it was now 1867 - and it had left the South destitute.

The citizens of Northville Landing even had a boast about their town: there was no Eastville, no Southville, no Westville … there was just Northville, and that made it unique.

Erin's father, Sebastian, had been a gambler on the riverboats, a spendthrift whose frequent money-making schemes yielded only misery and poverty, by which time he was off chasing a new dream. He was, people said of him by way of head-shaking mitigation, French, and they all knew what a rogue and a cad a French riverboat gambler could be.

All of which Sebastian Dubois undoubtedly was: a rogue, a cad, a bounder … and Erin loved him and cherished the memory of every moment they had spent together. And however "not received" he was in polite society Erin's Irish mother, Orla, loved him.

Orla McMaster had come to America as a young girl. She had been orphaned at the age of six and had spent the next nine years in the cold arms of the Sisters of the Redemption in a miserable and barren corner of County Donegal in Ireland before escaping to a new life in Louisiana.

There she met, fell in love with, married and lived life gloriously if uncertainly on the edge with her handsome Sebastian. She would have wished it no other way.

Erin was, though, not so enamoured with her sister, Olivia Julianne. Olivia Julianne appeared to have turned her pert little nose up even as she lay in her crib and continued to disapprove of everything about her family until she married the wealthy and successful businessman Orell Windom Hamelin Thynne – the Third, no less – and was whisked off to supervise the social elite of Natchez, doubtless with her upturned nose.

OWH Thynne – the Third, which he always insisted upon – had made his fortune in the provision of goods, mostly of a shoddy and unreliable nature, to the Government and Army of the Confederate States until Confederate money became useless – it was said that at the start of the conflict you took your money to market in your wallet and brought the goods home in a cart, and at the end of the conflict you took your money to market in a cart and brought the goods home in your wallet – and OWH Thynne III switched to providing the Union Army with goods.

He was, in Erin's opinion, a tall, miserable, cheapskate of a man and he and her disapproving sister were ideally suited to one another. Others, curiously, would have informed her differently had they been aware of her unfavourable impression. However, Erin told herself, a man who calls himself Orell Windom Hamelin Thynne – the Third, no less – simply had to be the most stuffed of shirts. Plain Erin was good enough for any lady to be called.

Erin's mother had been the one who insisted on the sisters obtaining a good education, and she worked to the point of exhaustion, at several jobs, to raise the money to this end. Erin had proved herself an intelligent student at her college in New Orleans, forever asking questions and not resting till she had obtained a satisfactory answer.

Olivia Julianne, on the other hand, sought only answers relating to the newest fashions, the location of the next ball and the names of the most handsome and wealthy young men.

After seeing the children safely on their way, Erin bustled around the one-room school preparing it for the following day's lessons. She wiped the blackboard and shook the chalk from the cloth out of the window. She laid out the books the children would need. She saw her pupils delivered safely into the arms of their families and locked the door.

She stood at the gate and watched the riverboat churn its way free of the jetty, the passengers lined along the decks to wave farewell to their families and friends. She walked to the edge of the town, along the riverbank pathway in step with the boat. She stopped to watch the great paddles gather power and waited until the boat had passed the sand island and had disappeared from view.

Erin unlatched the gate and walked along the gravel path to her house. The path was fringed by trees dripping Spanish moss and behind them there was a small, square garden filled with flowers. The house, a two-storey building, was painted white, though in places it required refreshing, and it had been the one good deed her father had managed to provide. He had won it, fair and square, in a card game and had even obtained, again by fair and square means, enough money to allow Erin and her mother to live comfortably.

Her parents were now dead and she lived alone, quite contentedly so, except for a black companion, Jessie, who ran the house with a warm-hearted efficiency. Jessie did, however, have one abiding obsession and that was to see Erin graced by the state of matrimony. To this end she took every opportunity to encourage Erin to hold dinner parties to which suitable potential beaux might be invited … it was, in Jessie's oft-stated opinion, the duty of a young lady of Erin's stature and intelligence to be happily and fruitfully embraced in the arms of marriage.

Erin certainly held dinner parties, many of them, and certainly invited males, the brothers, cousins and friends of her female friends, and certainly many of them were smitten by her … they all departed in disappointment. If, Erin said, she was ever to marry, which was highly unlikely, unwanted even, she would do the selecting of a mate herself. Jessie, at this point, would merely knit her brows, narrow her eyes and mumble … and then plan her next campaign.

Jessie was two years younger than Erin and had come with the house, which proved a blessing for Erin since she was not; she was the first to acknowledge, of a domesticated nature. Erin and Jessie came to a mutually beneficial understanding: the school ma'am would teach her pupil how to read and write and would instantly release her from bondage, even pay her a small allowance, and the pupil would continue to take care of both the teacher and the house.

It was an arrangement that caused no end of scandal throughout the town and the wider Northville Parish but greatly delighted and amused Erin, particularly since it was another irritant for the Board of Education to suffer. In time, of course, matters of a more pressing nature – like a war and enemy occupation – gave the citizens something new to worry about.

Inside, the house was thankfully cool. To combat the heat of high summer, Jesse had opened the windows and the double doors that led from the side of the drawing-room to a back garden. Delicate lace curtains fluttered and billowed in the light breeze.

Erin stood at the door and looked across the garden, to where it dipped towards the road and the river, and smiled.

"Thank you, papa," she whispered, "I love you."

She strolled around the garden, fluffing the flowers, smelling their sweet scent, turning her face to the sun in a blue, cloudless sky. Behind her she heard the rattle of crystal glasses and turned to see Jessie prepare their daily ritual.

As they did every afternoon when she returned from the school, the two friends sat on the porch and exchanged the news and gossip they had picked up while in town.

Erin sat at the wooden table on the shaded porch as Jessie poured them a freshly squeezed drink of tangy orange. They sat quietly and listened to the birdsong.

Jessie suddenly remembered the letter and took it from her apron. She reached it across the table and Erin took it.

"A young gentleman delivered it after you had gone to the school," Jessie explained.

Erin tore the envelope and removed the single sheet of paper. She read the copperplate writing, read it again and looked up at Jessie.

"Gracious me," Erin said, reading the letter for a third time, "it seems that lawyer Joshua Abernethy wishes to see me as quickly as possible; he has, he writes, something to tell me that might be to my advantage. How very mysterious," she handed the letter to Jessie, "What do you make of this, Jessie?"

Jessie read the letter, twice.

"It appears to me, Miss Erin, that Mr Abernethy wishes to see you as quickly as possible and he has something to tell you that might be to your advantage."

"Then to Mr Abernethy I shall go, this very instant."

"It appears to me, Miss Erin, that would be a fine idea."

Erin got up and went inside the house to fetch a bonnet and, on her way out, to select a parasol from the hallway stand. She walked back into Northville Landing, past the still busy jetty, past the school, past the red-brick St Mary and all the Saints, along the main street to the offices of Lawyer Joshua Abernethy.

Inside the dark wood-panelled office she approached a young man who was deep in thought over a large, open ledger. Erin coughed and the young man raised his head.

"Why, Miss Dubois," he said.

"Indeed it is, William," she said, he having been one of her pupils, "I have come, as quickly as possible, to see Mr Abernethy. Might he be in?"

"Of course, Miss Dubois, I shall inform him you are here. Please take a seat."

Erin had not the time to sit down for instantly William had returned to usher her into Mr Abernethy's office. There, at his bidding for he drew a chair up to his desk, she sat.

"Your letter," she said, "was most intriguing … and mysterious. I could not contain my curiosity … so here I am."

Mr Abernethy took from a desk drawer a small bundle of papers tied with a red ribbon and opened the documents in front of her. He sifted through them until he found a particular one.

"This, Miss Dubois," he began, holding up the document for her to see, "is the last will and testament of a gentleman by the name of Daniel Riparian …"

"I have never met …"

Mr Abernethy held up a hand to stop her.

"I know you have never met this Mr Riparian, nor I suspect have you ever heard of him until this moment. However, if I may continue …"

Erin nodded and he continued, adjusting his spectacles at the tip of his nose.

"Mr Riparian was, apparently, done a great service many years ago by your late father, the precise details of which he did not specify. However, in his will, Mr Riparian states he wishes to repay that great service, feeling it would be in the nature of a debt of honour.

"Mr Riparian knew your father had died but he also knew about you and your sister, Olivia Julianne, and knew that she was now married and that you had remained a ... er ... um ... a ..."

"A spinster of this parish," Erin said, smiling.

"Quite, quite. Thus, you being a ... well, Mr Riparian felt you would benefit more than your sister if his debt was repaid to you."

"Gracious me," Erin said.

"Indeed. Your benefactor has, it appears, left you ..."

Erin leaned across the desk, in a state of growing excitement.

"He has left you ... a riverboat."

Erin wondered if she heard Mr Abernethy correctly. She stared at him then at the document he held.

"I beg your pardon, Mr Abernethy; did you say this gentleman has left me a paddle-steamer?"

Mr Abernethy nodded silently. Erin sat back in her chair.

"Was this Mr Riparian of a confused and demented mind?"

"No," Mr Abernethy said, "he was, by all accounts, a successful businessman in Natchez and was certainly quite sane. It states quite categorically here that he has left you a riverboat ... it lies in Natchez and goes by the name of the River Queen."

He handed the document across the desk and she quickly read it.

"Gracious me," Erin said at length, "Mr Riparian has also left me a sum of money: $6.000."

"And it is Union money, not that of the late Confederacy," he said.

"Even better," Erin said.

The lawyer waited for her to say something more.

"What on earth would I do with a paddle-steamer, Mr Abernethy? I am a school teacher and I have been only once in my life aboard a paddle-steamer. I know absolutely nothing about paddle-steamers ... what would I do with this River Queen?"

"Well, Miss Dubois, you could, indeed you should, sell it. Doubtless the money would be a pleasing addition. If you like, I could make enquiries among colleagues up and down the river and seek a purchaser. I realise this has come as a surprise and you are a mere wom …"

And in that ill-prepared sentence Mr Abernethy touched a nerve in Erin's very being. He meant well, but Erin Dubois was not a mere woman. She might be a mere school ma'am, but she was a school ma'am who was now the owner of a Mississippi stern-wheel paddle-steamer. The least she could do, she instantly determined, was to travel to Natchez and see the River Queen. She might also pay a call on the other River Queen, her sister, Olivia Julianne.

She thanked Mr Abernethy for his kind offer and rose, gathering the documents from his desk.

He got up and followed her to the door of his office.

"What do you propose doing, Miss Dubois?"

"I propose, Mr Abernethy, to go to Natchez and see my riverboat."

Clutching the documents, Erin hurried back through the town with a thousand thoughts and unanswered questions tumbling through her mind. Who was the mysterious Mr Riparian and why had her father done him a great service … and what was that service? Why had the mysterious Mr Riparian left her, of all things, a riverboat? And what could she possibly do with such a ridiculous gift, except, as Mr Abernethy had suggested, sell it?

She arrived home with only one thing resolved: the answers, if any there be, were to be found in Natchez so to there she must, clearly, go. She had no idea of what she would find in Natchez, apart from the riverboat, but she felt she could not do otherwise; she was too sensible a person to believe in such a nebulous thing as fate, but if it did exist then it was drawing her to Natchez.

When she had settled at the small, roll-top desk in the drawing-room, Erin untied the documents, several of which she had not had the opportunity to examine fully in the lawyer's office, and began reading them.

There was no additional information about her benefactor – she could not, in truth, accept that he was anything of the kind, aside for the comfortable sum of money he had also bequeathed her – and much about the River Queen. She did not understand all the technical details of the paddle-steamer, its size, what its engines and boilers were like, how many passengers and how much freight it was capable of carrying, what crew was required to man her. All of this, she felt, was irrelevant.

She did, however, come across a letter headed with the name and address in Natchez of another law firm. In her haste to avoid any undue unpleasantness following Mr Abernethy's thoughtless remark about her being a mere woman, Erin had not given him the opportunity to provide all the information he possessed. She resolved to apologise for her tardiness.

She did, though, have another source of information in the Natchez law office and, though she hated to admit it, she felt that her sister's husband, the Third, might have known Mr Riparian, they both being successful businessmen in the same city.

Erin and Jessie discussed the surprising events of the afternoon and pored constantly over the documents until the evening drifted into night and they had to light candles and lamps to allow them to continue.

Erin had to arrange for someone to take over her teaching duties while she was away in Natchez – that would please the Board of Education if not the pupils and their parents – and she would have to send a telegraph to Olivia Julianne to let her know of her visit. She would have to arrange passage – on a paddle-steamer, how ironic – from Northville Landing to Natchez and Jessie would have to remain to take care of the house.

This last decision was reached with great reluctance on Jessie's part since she lived life beset with concerns about Erin's free spirit. It was not at all fitting that a lady should undertake such a journey on her own, she should at the very least have a female companion by her side. The decision was, however, made and Jessie knitted her brows and narrowed her eyes and muttered her disapproval and reluctantly conceded that she should remain and look after the house.

As she lay in bed that night, Erin could not sleep nor banish the questions and the thousand thoughts … but she knew she must go to Natchez.

Chapter 2

THE NEXT MORNING ERIN WALKED to the jetty and into the red-brick building that was the office of the elaborately-named Mississippi Steamboat Passenger and Freight Company of New Orleans, Northville Landing and Natchez and purchased a passage on the Delta Pride, arriving at Northville Landing on the coming Wednesday from New Orleans on its regular service to Natchez, five days away.

As she was standing at the ticket desk examining a plan of the Delta Pride's available cabins – she had decided, now that she had sufficient finances at her disposal, to treat herself to the most luxurious cabin the riverboat had available – Erin was joined by a distinguished, gray-haired gentleman and a pretty young girl of seventeen years. The gentleman touched his right hand to his hat, lifted it and bowed.

"Miss Dubois," he said, "I see you are about to book passage."

"Why, Colonel Sinclair, how nice to see you. Yes, indeed I am travelling to Natchez to see my sister Olivia Julianne," Erin decided not to mention her other business in Natchez, "And Amelia, how pretty you look, are you also travelling on the Delta Pride?"

Amelia smiled and embraced Erin, who had been her teacher.

"Yes," Amelia said excitedly, "Papa has business to conduct in Natchez and has promised to take me to a ball there; it will be my first proper, grown-up ball."

"And you will be its belle and you will surely break many a young man's heart with your beauty," Erin said.

Amelia blushed contentedly and relished such a heady prospect.

Colonel James Reid Sinclair, a tall, whip-thin man of fifty-seven, had built a formidable reputation in the Army of the Confederacy during the recent conflict. He had fought with distinction throughout the Virginia campaign and with Kirby Smith in the Trans Mississippi and upon the ending of the war had turned his energy to restoring his family home and business. He was now one of Northville Landing's most prominent citizens, guiding the town, indeed the South, towards better times.

The exact nature of his business in Natchez he kept to himself since it involved a group of fellow former Confederates determined to rid the South of the Northern carpetbaggers, greedy and ruthless speculators who had thronged into the beaten States to obtain, largely by dubious and criminal means, property and business that the impoverished owners could not hope to retain.

He was a consummate gentleman and thus it was no great surprise to Erin that he immediately took upon himself the task of acting as her protector on the journey. She did not object.

"If you are travelling alone," Colonel Sinclair said, "then you must allow Amelia and me to act as your guardians, you must book a cabin next to ours. We live in troubled times and while I do not wish to alarm you Miss Dubois, a lady travelling on her own might find herself in need of protection."

Erin nodded in agreement, thinking of how Jessie would have agreed with the colonel.

"That is very kind of you, Colonel Sinclair," she said, "I would be more than happy to be accompanied by yourself and Miss Amelia," she winked at the girl, "We can plan your grand entrance to the ball."

Amelia blushed contentedly and relished such a heady prospect.

Colonel Sinclair took on the task of arranging the two cabins and booking a table for dinner on board for the coming journey, while Erin and Amelia talked of ball gowns, dances and dashing young men whose hearts were about to be broken.

The colonel further offered to have his carriage pick up Erin and her luggage on the coming Wednesday and convey her to the landing. She did not object, indeed she felt quite excited about the venture upon which she was about to embark.

The days leading to Erin's departure for Natchez were a whirl of activity and preparation that chiefly involved the selection, rejection and reselection of dresses she could wear during the journey and while staying with her sister … the latter decisions resting upon her desire not to look quite like the dowdy, spinster school ma'am Olivia Julianne never tired of hinting she was.

Well, Erin determined, she was not married to a successful businessman – with a dubious past – and was not the social Queen of Northville Landing let alone Natchez but she was not quite the hopeless case her sister considered her to be. She was possessed of gray cells that, unlike her sister, were at least on speaking terms and she was determined not to be dismissed as either dowdy or spinsterish … she was proud of being a school ma'am, so that jibe did not merit consideration.

Sisters can be such infuriating creatures.

On the Wednesday in the early afternoon, she and Jessie were conveyed to the jetty landing in Colonel Sinclair's carriage. When they arrived at the already crowded riverside, the colonel and Amelia were waiting to greet her and organize the loading of her luggage.

Erin embraced Jessie, who still harboured reservations about the journey, and when her friend had returned home she waited for the arrival of the Delta Pride.

Erin watched, as she had done so often from the school, the people around her, the passengers and those waiting to greet arriving passengers. She watched the men collecting the luggage and tagging it with the cabins it would be taken to. She watched the men taking large wooden crates and bales from the wagons lined along the jetty. She listened to the excited chatter of the people around her.

Amelia, still in a happy daze thinking of all the handsome young gentlemen awaiting her in Natchez, stood beside her and Erin could not help smiling as she saw that the girl was dancing, actually dancing on the spot with her feet tapping at the thrill of the future.

Colonel Sinclair was some way off talking to a group of men, Erin assumed they were also going to Natchez, and she noticed that one of them was watching her closely. So closely was he studying her that she felt a blush burn her cheeks and she looked away.

The man, she guessed him to be in his thirties, was fashionably dressed and wore a white fedora on his sandy hair. He was certainly handsome, she allowed, but she wished he would not keep looking at her.

She had a disconcerting feeling that he was examining her very soul ... gracious, she told herself, do think of something more ladylike and appropriate.

The colonel finished his conversation and moved from the group to join Erin and Amelia. And Erin stole a shy glance at the man and saw him smile and raise his hat. Gracious!

The excitement grew around her as the crowd heard the calliope of the approaching Delta Pride, heard shortly after the swish-swish of the paddle and saw the riverboat slow and churn its way towards the landing.

The vessel was small in comparison with some that plied the Mississippi. Neither was it as grand as some Erin had seen or been told about by friends who had travelled on them.

The Delta Pride was a wooden vessel, painted in blue and red; it was 70ft by 135ft long and 10ft by 20ft wide and had a draft of 2ft. It had a crew of ten and carried 150 passengers in cabins that were comfortable though more functional than ornate.

She wondered what her vessel would be like and found herself still in a state of astonishment that she actually owned a paddle-steamer. She still could not quite grasp the fact.

The people on the landing watched the passengers disembark, watched the greetings of joy and the tearful reunions.

When all those getting off at Northville had departed the luggage was carried up the gangway to the cabins, the crates and bales were lifted aboard and stacked in the holds. And it was then the turn of the passengers to board.

A young boy was holding a slip of paper at the top of the gangway, checking names against cabin numbers and directing the passengers in the right direction. Colonel Sinclair obviously knew the layout of the Delta Pride for when the boy had ticked their names he directed his daughter and Erin along the deck to a stairway. They climbed to an upper level and walked along, past a row of cabins until the colonel stopped and opened the door of one.

"This is your cabin, Miss Dubois," he said, stepping aside to allow Erin to enter. "My daughter and I are occupying the next cabin. Please settle in and join us in the lounge for a coffee when you are ready."

Erin took the key from him and thanked him for his kindness. She stepped into the cabin and found that her luggage had already been delivered. The cabin was small, but clean. It contained a small dressing table with a mirror in front of which was a white and blue delph basin in which there was a matching jug with hot water in it.

Against the far wall, which had a square, curtained window, there was a bunk covered with a blue and red quilt. Two fluffy towels and a small bar of scented soap lay on the quilt. There was a stuffed, leather chair and a small wardrobe. To the left of the dressing table there was a small room containing a bath.

Erin spent the next half-hour hanging several dresses in the wardrobe, to minimise their creasing, and arranging her toiletries beside the basin.

She sat on the bunk bed and bounced on it. She passed it as soft and comfortable.

She washed her face and smoothed her hair with water. The vessel was still alongside the jetty and she listened as the last of the passengers came aboard and found their accommodation. She heard the shouts of the crew and the rattling chains as they were pulled onto the boat and presently she felt the Delta Pride sway gently and the engines thumping into life to turn the great stern wheel.

She selected a bonnet, draped a shawl around her shoulders and went outside to see the vessel move from the jetty and glide slowly up the river, past the town.

As she turned from the rail to call upon Colonel Sinclair and Amelia, Erin saw the man some way along the deck. He turned towards her and smiled.

She offered him as indifferent a greeting as she could muster, thinking him altogether too forward while at the same time thinking him quite handsome … and intriguing. She came to the conclusion that he must almost certainly be a Yankee and quickly turned to knock on the door of the cabin occupied by Colonel Sinclair and his daughter.

They returned to the lower deck and walked to the lounge. The room's interior was richly decorated in red and blue velvet drapes and had tables placed about a polished wood floor with deep red leather chairs around them. Above their heads there hung crystal chandeliers in which candles flickered and curled strands of smoke up to a polished wooden ceiling.

Colonel Sinclair directed Erin and Amelia to a table at an open window and pulled out a chair for Erin while his daughter stood at the window to watch the riverbank glide past.

A light afternoon breeze drifted into the lounge and Erin listened to the sound of the water lapping along the side of the vessel.

A young black boy came to the table and the colonel requested a pot of coffee and some sweet cakes be brought. The boy departed and Amelia was persuaded to join them.

"I trust you find your accommodation to your satisfaction, Miss Dubois," the colonel said, lifting a linen napkin from the table and placing it across his knee. "The Delta Pride is an old boat but a fine one, I know it well and use it for my visits to Natchez but sometimes I find fellow travellers who do not know her think her a tad on the inadequate side, compared to many of the other vessels."

"No, indeed I find my cabin to be quite charming and comfortable, with everything I might require for the journey. You were very kind to organise it for me."

Amelia said she would like very much to explore the vessel.

"May I, Papa?" she asked. "May Miss Dubois and I look around, I expect there is much for us to see and explore."

"Well, my dear," her father said, knowing that she was determined to do so anyway, "only if Miss Dubois does not mind and provided you do not get in the crew's way."

"Thank you, Papa," Amelia said and turned to Erin, "We might begin our exploration first thing in the morning ... if you do not mind."

Erin smiled and assured her young companion that she, too, would love to see around the Delta Pride.

The boy returned with the coffee. He carried it on a silver tray and set the delicate china cups and saucers in front of them, the cream and sugar in matching containers in the centre of the table. The colonel thanked the boy and gave him several coins.

Erin lifted the silver pot and, a finger on the lid, poured the coffee.

"You are, I believe you said, travelling to see your sister in Natchez," the colonel said.

"Yes, I do not see Olivia Julianne as often as I should," Erin said. "I also have some business to conduct when I get there, but mostly my journey is to allow me to see my sister."

She remained reluctant to discuss in detail the nature of her business, largely because she was unsure of its exact nature. Was, indeed, there any business worthy of discussion awaiting her in Natchez?

"Tonight," the colonel said, "I have reserved a table for dinner; you must accompany Amelia and me as our guest. The food is quite famous on board the Delta Pride and we would be delighted if you joined us."

"Oh do say you will, Miss Dubois," Amelia pleaded. "We could discuss the ball and perhaps you could help me think of a pretty dress."

Erin nodded and said she would be delighted to join them for dinner. She did not, anyway, relish dining alone, as a single lady quite possibly in her cabin if such a service were available, and Colonel Sinclair and Amelia were excellent companions. She was on an adventure of her own and did not wish to miss a single opportunity to see and hear and experience every emotion, every moment of what it had to offer.

They sipped their coffee in comfortable contentment and watched their fellow passengers arrive in the lounge.

Erin saw the man standing in the doorway. He was scanning the tables and when he saw her he smiled – that annoyingly knowing smile, she thought – and began making his way through the gathering crowd towards their table. Erin concentrated on spooning sugar into her cup and pretending she had not taken a whit of interest in him.

"My dear Masterson," the colonel said, holding out a hand for the man to take. "Why don't you join us, I see most of the other tables are fully occupied."

The man smiled and sat down. The colonel made the introductions.

"This," he said, indicating Erin, "is Miss Erin Dubois and, of course, you know my daughter, Amelia. This is Mr Brent Masterson, a business acquaintance of mine. He is, like us, travelling to Natchez."

Brent Masterson bowed and reached across the table to rescue Erin's hand from the sugar bowl. He lifted it to his lips and hovered a kiss above it. Erin gifted him a shy, chaste smile and decided her coffee required more cream. She prayed he did not detect her blushing confusion, which was out of character since she had been similarly treated in the past.

She listened as he talked with Amelia about the coming ball, which he would also be attending, and detected a Northern twang. He looked up at her capturing her eyes on him, though she quickly looked away in an attempt to remain aloof. Yet she found herself watching him with a growing interest she found disconcerting.

Brent Masterson, she allowed, was a handsome man. Lines at the corners of his blue eyes hinted at laughter long lost from his life for he now had a more serious look.

There was a deeper truth in her assessment than Erin knew for he was, indeed, from Boston, by way of Baltimore in Maryland. He was a wealthy man, owner of a hotel in Lynchburg, Virginia, and was currently considering the purchase of one in New Orleans and one in Natchez.

He had supported, though did not fight for, the Union during the war but the conflict had touched him, brought him tragedy with the death of his wife and son.

Erin did not at first hear him address her.

"Amelia tells me you are travelling to Natchez to visit your sister, Miss Dubois."

Erin realised the comment was addressed to her and agreed that it was so.

"My sister is married to a Mr Thynne …"

"Orell," Brent said. "Why, I know him well, we have done business together. I had no idea that Mrs Thynne had such a charming sister."

"I suspect that is because Olivia Julianne has never considered me charming. We seldom have the opportunity to meet; we live quite independent lives in two greatly different worlds. I would not be surprised to learn that my sister has not spoken of me to many people."

The conversation petered out into an awkward silence and eventually the little company finished its coffee and cakes and stood to leave the lounge.

"I have arranged a table for dinner this evening," Colonel Sinclair said. "Perhaps you would like to join us, Brent."

Brent considered the invitation and looked at Erin.

"That is most kind of you," he said. "I would be delighted to join you, if Miss Dubois has no objection."

"I have no objection," Erin said. "I am a guest myself."

"Then it is settled," the colonel said. "Shall we meet at 7.30? Dinner has been ordered for 8pm."

As she walked back to their cabins with the colonel and Amelia, Erin conceded she had absolutely no objection. She also enquired of a porter if hot water might be delivered to her cabin at 6.15.

Amelia slipped her arm into Erin's and grinned broadly.

"I think Mr Masterson has been greatly taken, Miss Dubois, greatly taken."

"Gracious me," Erin said. "I think you are greatly mistaken on that account. He scarcely knows anything about me, and I know even less about him."

Chapter 3

ERIN CLOSED THE DRAPES IN her cabin and lay on the bunk to rest, and to gather her thoughts since she had many of them racing through her mind: her business in Natchez and what she was going to do with a paddle-steamer, the reunion with her sister ... the intriguing – and handsome – Mr Masterson.

She dozed fitfully and awoke at 6pm. She rose and began to sort through her dresses in search of something suitable for dinner. She wondered why it mattered so much. As she was choosing and placing her choices on the bunk, a knock on the cabin door signalled the arrival of the hot water for her bath. It was carried into the room by three young black boys and poured into the bath, sending a swirl of white steam billowing around them.

She had chosen a green dress, trimmed with delicate, embroidered white flowers and she brushed her hair and tied it into a fashionable bun, securing it with a comb that allowed two fine strands to frame her face.

She could hear the excited, if muted, chatter of Amelia in the next cabin and eventually she heard the cabin door being closed and the knock on her own cabin. She swung a cape around her shoulders and opened the door.

"Oh, Miss Dubois, you do look very pretty," Amelia said when Erin stepped out to the deck.

"And so do you," Erin returned the compliment for Amelia wore a white dress and had draped a yellow shawl around her shoulders. And accompanied by Colonel Sinclair they walked along the deck, down the stairs and to the dining-room.

Brent Masterson was waiting for them just inside the dining-room, seated in a leather chair. As they entered he stood up and shook Colonel Sinclair's hand, smiled warmly at Amelia, took Erin's hand and kissed it.

"I think, Colonel," he said, "that we are already the envy of every other gentleman on board the Pride to have the company of two such beautiful ladies."

The colonel smiled and winked at Erin.

"And I think Mr Masterson is altogether too attentive," he said warmly for he considered his friend a most delightful man. "He should be watched and treated with caution."

"Then I am well and truly warned, Colonel. I shall follow your instructions to the letter," Erin said, though she made no objection to Brent taking her arm and leading her to their table.

The dining-room was the most magnificent of the Delta Pride's passenger services. Like the lounge in which they had taken coffee, it was decorated in red and blue velvet drapes and white Irish damask linen table clothes.

Windows ran along the left side of the room looking onto the bank and to the countryside that passed. There were around thirty tables lined along the polished wooden floor in three rows of ten and on each table there was a lamp of richly coloured glass in which a large red candle flickered and danced its light across the fine china plates – in red and blue – and silver knives, forks and spoons. A crystal glass at every placing held a white linen napkin.

At the far end of the room there was a small, round platform with chairs arranged in two rows behind music stands for an orchestra that would, so a printed announcement left in every cabin declared, be providing entertainment from the following evening until the vessel reached Natchez.

Chandeliers of hanging crystal strands provided more romantic candlelight and white coated waiters bustled efficiently around the tables with meals carried on large, round silver trays.

Each table place had a printed menu in a pretty wire holder and offered a range of soups, meat, chicken and fish dishes to be followed by a good selection of sweet cakes and jellies.

Over dinner the four enjoyed an interesting conversation during which Brent outlined his plans for his hotels in New Orleans and Natchez and about the one he already owned in Lynchburg. He did not exclude Amelia from his attention for he discussed the ball she was to attend in Natchez, adding that she would undoubtedly be its shining star.

"Will you also be attending the ball, Miss Dubois?" he enquired.

"I have not been invited to it," Erin said. "I knew of it only when Miss Sinclair mentioned it recently."

"Then you must come," Brent said. "I would be greatly honoured if you attended as my guest. It is a significant event in the social life of Natchez; indeed I know that your sister and her husband are to attend. So of course you must also be there."

"Yes, Miss Dubois, oh do say you will come," Amelia said.

"Well, in that case, how could I possibly refuse?"

Brent explained that while in Natchez he would be staying at The Briars, one of the city's most fashionable establishments.

"I know it, though I have never been inside it," Erin said. "It was where our late President Mr Jefferson Davis married his wife Varina Howell."

"You told us all about the wedding in school, Miss Dubois, it was in 1845," Amelia said.

Erin laughed.

"It was indeed. I am delighted to know that at least one of my pupils paid attention in class."

Colonel Sinclair raised his glass.

"A toast," he declared, "to President Davis and to the glorious Lost Cause."

They concluded their meal and the colonel asked if he might be excused as he had seen some gentlemen at another table he wished to speak to. He asked Brent and Erin if they would be kind enough to escort Amelia safely to her cabin.

Amelia asked if she might be permitted to stroll around the

deck before retiring for the night and Erin said she, too, would like to take a walk. Brent asked if he might be permitted to accompany the ladies.

The evening was still warm and a light, refreshing breeze blew from the river. Erin drew her cape around her shoulders and tied it as they walked to the stern of the Delta Pride to watch the great paddle churn and foam them to Natchez. Across to the banks of the river they could see the lights of small hamlets glide by and above them a full, white moon danced serenely through small, fluffy, red-tinted clouds.

Presently they turned and walked back along the deck and climbed the stairway to their cabins. Brent thanked Amelia for her company and at the door of her cabin wished her a pleasant night. He accompanied Erin to her cabin and kissed her hand before seeing her safely inside.

Miss Erin Dubois, he thought, as he walked back to his own cabin, was a most interesting lady.

Erin sat at her dressing-table and looked at her reflection in the mirror. Mr Brent Masterson, she thought, was a most interesting man. She poured some water into the basin and washed her face. She undressed and lay in her bunk listening to the sounds of the boat ... and had a most pleasant night.

For Erin the remaining days of the journey were an emotional mixture of confusion and wonderment: Brent was constantly and tenderly attentive and she wondered quite why while trying to concentrate her thoughts on her reason for going to Natchez.

The 'why' sprang from her comparisons between her own position – a school ma'am, spinster of the Parish, as she had herself reminded the lawyer Abernethy – and that of a man such as Brent Masterson. Why, she pondered, would he be so clearly interested in her?

Her attention ought, she knew, to be directed towards what she might discover about her mysterious benefactor, Mr Riparian; how her father had assisted him, why she was the owner of a riverboat ... and, always, what on Earth she could possibly do with it.

She knew that she would meet Brent on at least one more occasion for she had accepted his invitation to the ball. Indeed, on several of their deck promenades that had become a small but significant ritual after dinner he had spoken of his desire to see her in Natchez. He had even, without being told what it was, offered to be of whatever service she required concerning her business.

She even worried about telling Olivia Julianne about her inheritance for she had a feeling the news would elevate her sister's pert and dismissive nose even further. She could hear the tone of disapproval already. Erin, more than once, considered returning immediately to the safety of her well-ordered life in Northville Landing and asking lawyer Abernethy to find a purchaser for the River Queen. A Mississippi paddle-steamer she did not need.

And yet … and yet …

Chapter 4

THE PASSENGERS WHO HAD GATHERED along the decks watched as the Delta Pride approached the landing. It was just after noon and the vessel had made good time, losing just two hours on the journey from Northville Landing.

The wheel slowed and began to churn in reverse as the steamer, hissing white clouds into the warmth of the day, manoeuvred towards the jetty where men waited to grab the ropes thrown to them for securing.

Brent had joined Colonel Sinclair, Amelia and Erin at the rail and they viewed the frantic activity on the jetty until the vessel gently bumped and slid and swayed to a standstill and the crew began pushing out gangplanks.

"Well, Miss Dubois," Brent said, "we have arrived safely in Natchez, after a most pleasant journey. I have a carriage arranged to pick me up, may I offer you a ride to your sister's home? I know where it is."

"That is very kind of you," Erin said, "but I trust Olivia Julianne received word of my arrival and will have sent her carriage to collect me."

"Then," Brent said, "I wish you a safe journey and hope to meet you soon. I will, of course, make arrangements to collect you for the ball," he turned now to the colonel and his daughter,

"Colonel, it was good to meet you again. And Miss Sinclair, I await your entrance to the ball, you will be magnificent."

Amelia dipped him a shy curtsey and blushed.

They waited until most of the disembarking passengers had vacated the vessel and made their way along the deck to the gangplank and the jetty.

"I see my carriage waiting," Brent said and took Erin's hand in his.

Erin watched as he walked through the crowd of people and reached his carriage. She was somewhat disappointed to see it was already occupied by a beautiful young woman, and even more so to see Brent climb into the seat beside her and kiss her on the cheek. She did her best to dismiss the cameo as of no great consequence to her and searched about for her sister.

The colonel and Amelia, met by a gentleman, were escorted to a carriage and with promises of meeting her at the ball, if not before it, they too departed.

Left alone on the landing, Erin wondered if her message had been received by Olivia Julianne or, if it had, if her sister had forgotten to come to collect her. Presently, however, she heard above the still noisy commotion of the jetty the affected – with her sister everything was affected – drawl of Olivia Julianne calling her name.

A crew member carried her luggage to the waiting carriage and Erin, following, took a deep breath, arranged her face into as warm an expression as she could muster and went to embrace her sister.

Natchez was built on a bluff overlooking the Mississippi River. It was an elegant city, the oldest settlement on the river and named after its original inhabitants, the Natchez Indians. It had been taken by Union Flag Officer, David Glasgow Farragut, in 1862, which did not entirely endear him to the citizens since he was himself a Southerner, married to a Southern wife.

The capture had, though, helped Natchez in many ways for it had escaped the ravages and destructions that had been visited upon other Confederate cities. It had been, and was becoming again, a place of trade and commerce inhabited by many wealthy families who occupied great mansions. Orell Windom Hamelin Thynne – the Third – and his disapproving wife considered they, indeed were, among the upper echelons of Natchez society.

It had, in the aftermath of the war, become even more of a Confederate stronghold, a staunch bastion of the Lost Cause. During the occupation the Catholic Bishop, William Henry Elder, had actually been arrested and briefly jailed by the Union authorities for refusing, in 1864, to urge his flock to pray for the President of the United States. Many citizens remained unconvinced that the President of the United States was deserving of the kindness and grace of the Good Lord.

Natchez clung to the memory of the Old South and fostered that memory with the formation of several often clandestine societies and organisations.

The drive through the busy streets was conducted in an anxious silence for Erin awaited what she feared would be her sister's litany of remarks about how she was dressed, how she remained unmarried, how much more of an effort she should make. It was ever thus when they got together, Olivia Julianne enjoying every aspect of the superiority she felt. She was the glamorous sister, the fashionable leader of Natchez society; the married sister with the wealthy and influential husband … Erin was, well, Erin was the spinster school ma'am.

There was no doubting, Erin had to concede, that Olivia Julianne was all of these things and all of these things were once again manifested when the landau, pulled by two prancing horses whose coats were more magnificent than anything Erin could ever hope to wear, drove through the ornate iron gates and travelled along the tree-lined gravel driveway.

The trees presently ended, in a well controlled circle, and revealed the white painted mansion with its Doric pillars, its balcony that ran around the first floor that contained no less than eight large bedrooms.

Erin's heart both soared and sank: soared at the grandeur of the building, at the splashing fountains and the bobbing flowers and shrubs and sank at what she knew was to come.

The carriage came to a halt at the bottom of the wide steps

leading up to the oak double doors and a small gang of servants spilled from the hallway and descended upon the sisters, assisting them down and taking charge of Erin's luggage, such as it was.

Inside the hallway, with its light wood panelling and row of tables on which sat vases of fresh flowers, Olivia Julianne directed a battery of commands to three maids who scurried off to fetch tea and sweet cakes. Erin reflected that had several of the Confederate Generals barked their commands with half as much authority as her sister the war would have been won.

She was ushered along the hallway and into a sitting room of such enormous proportions that Erin could have fitted her entire home in one corner and still have room left over to hold a ball. A fire, even though it was unnecessary since the afternoon was hot and cloudless, crackled in a black grate.

The room contained three leather settees ranged in front of the fire in a U shape, with a long, glass table in the middle. Other deep leather chairs formed islands of comfort and ease around the room and on the walls were portraits of Olivia Julianne and Orell Windom Hamelin Thynne – the Third – and oil paintings of scenes of the Mississippi River. Olivia Julianne was childless, which she secretly regretted but publicly declared a blessing since it allowed her to devote all her time to OWH, his business interests and the house.

Erin settled herself in one of the settees while her sister completed the 'orders of the day' and, on its delivery, the pouring of the tea and distribution of the cakes. Finally, she sat down opposite Erin, crooked her little finger and sipped at her drink.

"My dear Erin," Olivia Julianne began and Erin steeled herself, "I simply must introduce you to my dressmaker, your clothes are …," she sought the appropriate word, "… so old-fashioned, dowdy even. We cannot have you spend your time as our guest looking like a ragamuffin from the poor house. Orell has important friends calling regularly, they might see you."

"I hardly think I am hideous enough to have them screaming in disgust and mortal terror," Erin said. "I have several very presentable dresses in my luggage so you need not concern yourself as to my appearance. When Orell's important friends do call I can always run and hide in a dark cupboard. I expect you have organised several for such an emergency."

"You are impossible, Erin, I do declare you are impossible!"

They drank their tea in continuing awkward silence. Erin judged she had acquitted herself quite well in the conflict's opening skirmish.

"I have, by the way, been invited to a ball," Erin said, and smiled at the look on her sister's face, "Apparently it is a very important event in Natchez."

"You do not mean the Delafield Ball?"

"I do not know what it is called, only that it is a ball and I have been invited to it ... by an extremely pleasant gentleman."

"Gracious me," Olivia Julianne said, "and who might this extremely pleasant gentleman be?"

"A Mr Brent Masterson. I travelled in the company of Colonel Sinclair and his daughter Amelia ... and we were joined for dinner by Mr Masterson. He asked if I would be gracious enough to be his guest at the ball."

"Brent Masterson!" Olivia Julianne said, astonished that anyone would ask Erin to a ball, let alone Brent Masterson.

"That is certainly what he called himself. He did mention that he knew you and Orell."

"He is one of the wealthiest men in Louisiana ... are you certain it was Brent Masterson?"

"Unless he was a demented deck hand masquerading as Mr Masterson I can only assume he was who he claimed to be."

Olivia Julianne sipped at her tea and Erin judged a victory won in the second skirmish. She was quite enjoying herself.

To combat the onset of another silence, Erin got up and walked around the room to look at the paintings. She also wondered how best she might broach the subject of the exact nature of her visit since such meetings with her sister were distributed as seldom as she could muster throughout the year.

Finally she returned to the settee and reached for another cake.

Olivia Julianne then asked the obvious question.

"It is not," she began, "that I am displeased to see you again, dear sister, we meet so seldom, but is there a particular reason for you coming now? Has anything happened?"

Erin arranged her thoughts and explained why she had come to Natchez. She recounted the mysterious letter from Mr Abernethy and how he had revealed the good deed by their father that had resulted in a Mr Riparian leaving her in his will a sum of money and a riverboat paddle-steamer by the name of the River Queen.

Olivia Julianne listened to all of this in amazed silence though she quickly gathered her curiosity to ask how much the sum of money amounted to. She was content to discover that it was not a great amount; she spent as much in the local shops in a single month.

"But this Mr Riparian, who on earth was he? I have never heard of him, and the thought that our father did him a great service is a surprise to me … I am astonished to learn that father ever did anyone a service, with the exception of the owners of every gaming house along the river."

"Papa was a better man than you ever allowed," Erin said. "But I have no real notion of who my benefactor is, other than he was apparently a successful businessman here in Natchez. I thought Orell might know something about him."

"I have never once heard his name mentioned. Have you any contact in Natchez who might be of assistance?"

Erin reached for her purse and withdrew the documents.

"Only the law office here from where the news was dispatched to Mr Abernethy. I have come to speak to them and to see what the riverboat looks like."

"What would you possibly do with such a thing as a riverboat?" Olivia Julianne said, and Erin thought she detected that irritating nose wrinkle in disapproval.

"Mr Abernethy said he could seek potential purchasers if it was what I wished."

"It must surely be what you wish," Olivia Julianne said. "You could not possibly think of any other action. Orell would, I am sure, be only too willing to assist in the matter."

"Perhaps," Erin said, "but I think I should like to see the River Queen for myself before I make any decision. It is really quite exciting being, for however a short space of time, the owner of a paddle-steamer. It is moored here, somewhere, in Natchez and I intend to discover where from the law office."

Olivia Julianne was outraged at the very idea.

"I cannot allow you to go traipsing around the river in search of this boat, you have no idea how dangerous the riverside haunts can be, how inhabited with rough and uncouth men it is. I simply will not permit such foolishness."

"My dear sister, I intend to complete my mission and will not be swayed from it."

Erin placated her sister by promising to search for the River Queen after discussing all the other details with the law firm.

The sisters dined alone that evening since Orell was engaged in business meetings and Erin was shown to her room where she took out the documents and checked the name and address of the law firm she planned to visit the following day. She had survived the first day with her sister and felt sufficiently buoyed to face what information might come her way.

Chapter 5

OLIVIA JULIANNE HAD THE LANDAU prepared for Erin's visit to the Natchez lawyers – Thomas McCutcheon, Jordan and Coates, Commissioners of Oaths – largely on the grounds that her sister ought not to be allowed to arrive on foot but in a more impressive manner.

Driven and delivered for her meeting in a landau by a liveried coachman would, she insisted forcefully, be more fitting. Impression was paramount.

Erin, who would not have minded walking through Natchez, the better to gather her thoughts, quietly agreed on the grounds that it was too early in the morning to suffer another skirmish.

On the drive Erin felt quite grand and allowed that Olivia Julianne had been right to insist on the carriage. However, she decided not to admit it.

The office she sought was housed in a two-storey, grey stone building in a busy street that was lined with stores, banks and other offices. Erin was assisted from the landau by the coachman and she opened the door and stepped inside. The coachman said he would, as instructed by the Mistress, wait for her.

She approached a desk at which a young man, in an almost exact replica of the office of Mr Abernethy in Northville Landing, was scribbling in a large ledger. The young man looked up, placed his pen in a crystal inkwell and smiled a toothy greeting.

"My name is Erin Dubois and I have come from Northville Landing on business. I am not certain who might be of assistance but you could mention the name of Mr Abernethy of that town."

The young man directed her to a chair beside which there was a small round table with periodicals neatly placed upon it. He said he would make the necessary enquiries and return presently. Erin thanked him and reached for a periodical ... it was a full year old but she flicked absently through the pages.

The young man returned and requested she accompany him, along a corridor to the office of Mr McCutcheon.

Mr McCutcheon was a man in his late forties, a squat man with a red, friendly face and grey hair brushed behind his ears. He was standing at a desk that was covered in papers and documents and when Erin crossed the room to him he came to meet her with a firm handshake. He drew a chair to the desk and asked her to be seated.

He returned behind his desk and asked the young man to bring them some coffee.

"Miss Dubois," Mr McCutcheon said, unwrapping the red ribbon from a roll of papers, "I am so pleased to finally make your acquaintance, Mr Riparian spoke highly of your father."

"I must confess you have the advantage of me in the matter of Mr Riparian," Erin said. "I never knew him, nor that he ever existed until Mr Abernethy brought him to my attention. I have, in addition, no notion of what service my father rendered to him."

"Your father, quite simply, saved Mr Riparian's life and, furthermore, he set Mr Riparian on the path to becoming a wealthy and successful businessman."

"Gracious me," Erin said. "I cannot think how my father achieved all this ... you do know what sort of man my father was? I loved him dearly but he was something of a, shall I say, something of a wild spirit."

Mr McCutcheon nodded and laughed. "Yes, Miss Dubois, I know what your father was ... but he was also, in many regards, a most remarkable and generously warm-hearted man."

"But how did he do Mr Riparian such a great service?"

Mr McCutcheon settled himself back in his chair while the young man poured them a cup of coffee and departed.

"Some eleven years ago," Mr McCutcheon began, "your father first encountered Mr Riparian, standing in what might only be described as quiet desperation on a levee of the river.

"Mr Riparian was contemplating suicide for he had been made bankrupt by an unsavoury business associate who had stolen the company profits and absconded to New Orleans and, I believe, from there to South America.

"To make matters worse, Mr Riparian subsequently lost his wife and young son, when she abandoned him and went to live in San Francisco. When your father came upon him he was, you might well understand, in a poor way. However, your father gently directed him from the river and took him to a refuge for the destitute where he paid for a bed and two meals a day ... and returned daily to see how Mr Riparian was keeping.

"They became friends; I believe it was during their conversations that your father spoke of you and your sister. Anyway, several weeks later your father won an extremely large sum of money at the card tables and, knowing that Mr Riparian had once been a successful, albeit unfortunate, businessman, he offered it to him to start afresh. Mr Riparian offered to make your father his partner but the offer was refused. The life of a businessman behind a desk would not have suited your father, not at all.

"Mr Riparian went on to establish a most successful business but always vowed to repay your father's kindness. He began to search for your father and for you and your sister, without initial success. He also tried to find his son only to discover he had died of a fever in California. Eventually, he learned where you were living and intended to visit you. Alas, he died of a heart disease before he could achieve this.

"My firm acted as Mr Riparian's legal advisors and while going through his papers we discovered a will, with the notes relating to yourself."

Erin had listened to the story in rapt silence and did not grasp that Mr McCutcheon had stopped.

"Miss Dubois!"

Erin shook her head.

"Gracious, what a remarkable tale," she said. "A novel would not do such a narrative justice."

"There is more, by way of a further document I discovered after sending what I thought was the complete information to Mr Abernethy. Mr Riparian, in addition to the River Queen and the sum of money you already know of, left you a boatyard and a further sum of $25,000. You are now, Miss Dubois, an extremely wealthy young woman."

He handed the document across the desk and Erin read it.

"Miss Dubois, are you feeling unwell, you have turned quite pale? Shall I fetch you a glass of water?"

"No, thank you, no. I am not sure what I am feeling at the moment. I have been left a large sum of money, a riverboat and a boatyard … it is all rather overwhelming, I confess. I left Northville Landing as a school teacher and now … and now, I own a boat and a boatyard. If I feel anything it is confusion."

The lawyer rose and came around his desk, sitting on it, fearing she was about to fall into a faint.

"Can you tell me something about the River Queen, and the boatyard?" Erin asked.

"Well, I do know that the yard was once one of the finest in Natchez. Mr Riparian purchased it as a thriving concern and expanded it further. It once employed some thirty men, many of them skilled craftsmen and engineers. The yard, it was known as the Natchez Mississippi Construction Company, specialised in the building of some of the finest paddle-steamer interiors to be found on the river. It even built a number of quite excellent smaller work vessels."

"You speak of it in the past tense, Mr McCutcheon. Does it no longer exist?"

"It does exist, though it has not been in business since the death of Mr Riparian, some six months past. I believe all of the men have been laid off, save for a few who remained to protect the machinery. It is just a few miles to the south of Natchez."

"And the River Queen, what of it?"

"I believe it lies moored at the yard. It ran regularly for many years from Natchez, up and down the river, but has not operated for some time. I confess I do not know what condition it is now in. I understand your situation, Miss Dubois, and if you wish to dispose of the boat and the yard I could handle the sales on your behalf."

"I appreciate that, Mr McCutcheon, but I would like to take at least one look at the River Queen and the boatyard. I am sure my pupils and friends in Northville Landing would be fascinated to hear all about them ... that and what you have told me about my father would make an unforgettable tale, would you not say?"

"I would indeed; it would be a most unforgettable story. Would you like me to arrange an escort to the yard for you?"

Erin gathered all the documents together and got up.

"Do not trouble yourself; you have been very kind already. I have a carriage waiting outside so if you could direct me to the yard that would be sufficient."

Mr McCutcheon escorted Erin to the front door and he approached the coachman to issue directions to the boatyard, pointing down the street, waving his hand to the left and pointing straight ahead to where she would come across the boatyard ... her boatyard.

"The man you should seek out when you get there is a Mr Joshua Gabriel Frampton; he was Mr Riparian's foreman at the yard. He will be able to provide more details of the River Queen."

He helped her into the landau and she was driven towards the Natchez Mississippi Construction Company ... her Natchez Mississippi Construction Company, her River Queen.

Chapter 6

AS THE LANDAU MADE ITS way through the busy streets the properties along the riverside turned from prosperous to derelict. The landscape was littered with the empty, lifeless shells of abandoned warehouses and broken, roofless timber constructions. Occasionally small groups of men could be seen sitting in listless idleness at the buildings and yards in which they had once been employed. Even the river seemed to meander at a slower pace as if it too had arrived at the conclusion that there was nowhere useful it could go.

Erin looked around her with a growing feeling of despondency as they approached the yard she now owned. She was, she kept telling herself, a school ma'am who knew nothing about this grim and depressing world and her only course of action was to pay the briefest of visits to the yard and the riverboat and accept the advice of both Mr Abernethy and Mr McCutcheon to find a purchaser for both.

They turned, as directed by Mr McCutcheon, from the dirt road running alongside the river onto a narrow, rutted road and bounced and swayed along it until she saw ahead the closed and locked gates above which there creaked a faded sign announcing their arrival at the Natchez Mississippi Construction Company. It looked as run-down as all the others they had passed.

The coachman stopped at the gates and suggested Erin should remain in the carriage while he went to see if anyone was beyond in the yard. As he walked cautiously towards the gates, Erin stood in the carriage and saw, moored at a broken wooden jetty, the River Queen.

The coachman walked along the high wooden fence on either side of the gates, peering into the yard. He returned to the gates and shook them, calling for someone, if someone there be, to open them and let them enter.

Receiving no answer, he returned to Erin and shrugged his shoulders.

As he was about to suggest he drive her back to her sister's home the gates creaked open and a man stared out at them.

The coachman returned to the gates and explained who they were and why they had come. The man glanced at Erin and after what she assumed was a careful consideration of the information he had received squirted a stream of brown tobacco juice at his feet and nodded.

He opened the gates to allow the landau to pass through and, closing them, followed the carriage to a wooden building boasting the title of Main Office.

The coachman assisted Erin down and the man led them into the room. The coachman decided he had better remain with his charge and took a seat in the corner of the room.

"I have just come from a meeting with Mr Thomas McCutcheon," Erin said, taking a chair at the table, "and he suggested I should seek out a Mr Joshua Gabriel Frampton who would be able to tell me about this company and the River Queen … I am Erin Dubois and I am now the owner of the Natchez Mississippi Construction Company and of the River Queen. Could you please fetch Mr Frampton, if he is on the premises?"

The man considered the request. He gave a moment to the hitching of his stained and torn trousers.

"He's on the premises and he's been fetched. I am Joshua Gabriel Frampton … ma'am."

"Then I am delighted to make your acquaintance, Mr Frampton," Erin said and offered her hand. She was somewhat uncertain how to behave in such circumstances, other than to be as ladylike and businesslike as possible.

The man looked at the extended hand then he smiled, a brown-stained, broken-toothed smile. He took from his trouser pocket an oil-smeared rag, wiped his hands and shook Erin's hand.

"You're the daughter of Mr Sebastian Dubois, then?"

"Indeed I am, Mr Frampton."

"A fine fellow your father was."

Everyone seemed to be of a similar opinion. Erin wondered if it was the father she had known. Perhaps this entire episode in her life had been a great mistake, a great legal misunderstanding, and the generosity of Mr Riparian had been intended for another Erin Dubois. Nothing would surprise her any more.

She waited for a resumption of the conversation and looked more carefully at Mr Frampton. He was a tall, whip-thin man – apparently obsessed with the chewing of tobacco for his jaws were in constant motion – with diminishing strands of red hair oiled in streaks across his head. She had noticed on arrival that he had a limp and assisted his movement with a walking stick. She also detected the remains of an accent clearly not obtained in America.

He was, as she would eventually discover, originally from Ireland, from the town of Ballymena in the County of Antrim in the Province of Ulster. He had lived in America for some thirty years, he was now in his fiftieth year, but had not quite lost his strong Ulster accent.

"Mr Frampton …," Erin began.

"You can call me Joshua or Gabriel, if you have a mind to."

"Either name is quite excellent …"

"Mother and father were partial to the Bible, strict Presbyterians all their lives."

"Well then, I shall call you Gabriel," Erin said. "My mother was Irish. You may call me …," she did not know what she should allow him to call her.

"If it's fine by you ma'am," he said, "I shall call you Miss Dubois."

"That would be most suitable. So, Gabriel, what can you tell me about the company and the River Queen?"

What the company's former foreman and present caretaker had to tell Erin was much as she had been told by Mr McCutcheon. It had been run on behalf of Mr Riparian by Gabriel as one of the foremost repair yards on the river and one which had earned a formidable reputation for designing and building the often lavish interiors of many of the paddle-steamers. The company engineers knew all that was required to know about the engines, the boilers and the smallest nuts and bolts that kept the vessels moving. And thirty-five of the best men available in Natchez were employed by the Natchez Mississippi Construction Company.

The war years and the Union capture of the Mississippi had not helped and upon the ending of the war, and of the Confederate States, times had not improved.

While Natchez had escaped the major ravages of the conflict and was now increasingly prosperous. Furthermore, since other companies were moving into those areas dominated by the NMCC the success of the latter had suffered greatly, not least because Mr Riparian had suffered from ill health.

But, Gabriel emphasised, the workshops, the tools and machinery – which, if Erin wished, he would gladly show her – remained largely intact and had, indeed, been maintained by a small number of employees who had been retained for such a purpose.

"What became of the other men?" Erin asked, assuming they had been such craftsmen as carpenters and painters.

"Some obtained employment with other companies, many of them are still around and looking for work," Gabriel said.

"And what of the River Queen?"

"She was, still could be with a lot of hard work, a fine vessel," Gabriel said. "The Yankees used her to move troops up and down the river and Mr Riparian took her back when the war ended. The Yankees, though, left her in a poor condition, not being overly enthusiastic about velvet drapes and polished wooden walls. She's been tied up for just over a year.

"The old lady, she's eight years old now, has attracted interest from at least two other companies but Mr Riparian held her in great affection and wouldn't contemplate selling her. Don't know if you're aware of it but even if she was put back in order, which she certainly could be, she'd be good for just two or three more years. These steamers usually last for around five or six years."

"Is she safe?" Erin wanted to know. "She would not sink?"

"She's tight as a nun's … beg your pardon, ma'am: she's been looked after as best we could. I could show you plans and even drawings of what she looked like when she was working the river, that is if you want to know any of the mechanical details … length, width, draft, size of the wheel, power of the engine."

"I'm afraid all of which would be a mystery to me, Gabriel. I would like to go aboard, not today but as soon as possible. I have much to consider."

"You mind if I ask you a question, ma'am? What are your intentions concerning the company and the old lady?"

Erin realised he and the men who remained at the yard had their concerns about the future and, in as much as she could, she owed them a swift decision. She simply did not have a decision formed in her head; it had all come upon her as a shock.

"I confess, I have no clear idea what I am going to do," she said, then by way of testing him she added, "Have you any thoughts on the matter, Gabriel?"

He studied her closely. He had warmed to her as soon as he had met her and saw in her something she probably did not see in herself. "It's your decision, ma'am," he said, "but if you were asking me, and I guess you are, I would open up the yard, most of the better men would come back, they were always treated well by Mr Riparian. We did the best work on the river, anybody will tell you the same, and we could make it work. Of course, ma'am, like I say: it's your decision."

"Gracious me, I had no such plans. Indeed, I have been advised to seek a buyer."

"I understand. This must all be a confusion to you; I was just flapping my gums."

Erin got up from the table and thanked him for his time. He escorted her back to the landau and watched as she was driven from the yard. He stood at the gates until the carriage had gone from his view and closed and locked the gates. He walked to the jetty and looked up at the River Queen.

"Guess we've both reached the final bend in the river, old girl. It was good while it lasted."

A jumble of confusion, as Gabriel had predicted, raced and churned through Erin's mind as she was driven back along the riverside and through the streets of Natchez. It had been quite a morning, one that had thrown her life down several paths.

She tried to make sense of what she had been told by Mr McCutcheon and Gabriel. She was now a wealthy woman, or at least one with enough money to provide her with financial security for a long time. And then there was the matter of the boatyard and the River Queen.

And what was she going to tell Olivia Julianne, and Jessie, and what would the reaction of her sister be?

But at the back of her mind, like a small and delicate seed, one thought kept a constant vigil and it brought her back to the suggestion, the briefest of passing remarks, made by Gabriel ... she could re-open the yard, possibly even restore the River Queen.

She dismissed the notion; she was a school teacher, a mere woman, as Mr Abernethy had so thoughtlessly pointed out. She had not the faintest idea about running a business.

And yet ... and yet.

Her mind was still racing when the landau turned into the driveway of her sister's home.

And yet ... and yet.

Chapter 7

ERIN FOUND THE HOUSE IN a whirl of activity when she entered. Olivia Julianne scarcely had time to acknowledge her return for she was in her most formidable Commanding Officer mode, issuing instructions and directions to the staff.

"What on earth has happened?" Erin asked of a maid she detained while the girl, laden with an armful of crisp linen, was scurrying along the hallway. "Has the war started all over again?"

"No miss," the maid said. "The Master is bringing a party of friends just arrived from New Orleans and the Mistress is getting the rooms ready."

The maid hurried off and Erin went in search of her sister. Olivia Julianne was in the dining-room overseeing the setting of the table for dinner.

"Olivia Julianne, do stop for a moment and tell me what is happening. Is the Empress of Russia coming?"

"Do not be foolish, just a group of dear Orell's business and political associates. He has been so busy that he quite forgot to inform me until barely an hour past. They are important guests and everything must be in order for their arrival."

"Gracious me," Erin said as the staff fussed and milled around her, "Is there any assistance I can render?"

"No, everything is in hand," Olivia Julianne said. "However

it would be a great help if you prepared yourself to join us for dinner. I will get one of the girls to get a bath ready for you ... and please select something appropriate to wear. Better still, I shall ask one of the girls to go to my dressing-room and select a dress that does not establish you even more as a school teacher. Now do not dawdle, Erin, go and get ready."

Erin negotiated herself through the commotion and went to her room. She could still hear Olivia Julianne and her army on manoeuvres downstairs and sat on the edge of her bed to catch her breath. When her sister entertained no imperfections could possibly be tolerated ... the slightest crease could not be allowed on the table cloth, the slightest smudge could not be allowed on the crystal glasses, the slightest petal could not be allowed to droop in its silver vase. No General ever approached a battle with as much attention and fuss as did Olivia Julianne a dinner party.

Erin wished she could stay in her room until the visit and feeding of dear Orell's business and political associates had been consigned to the pages of history. She considered having a terrible headache or an attack of the vapours, anything to escape the evening to come. But she knew she could not escape. She sighed and waited for the bath to be prepared, putting her time to use by selecting a dress. She settled upon a pretty blue dress with small white and yellow flowers embroidered at the neck and around the hem.

She finished her bath and was towelling herself dry when Olivia Julianne arrived to supervise her progress. Erin busied herself by brushing her hair as her sister stood disapprovingly at the end of the bed.

"It will not do, Erin, it simple will not do," Olivia Julianne said, picking up the dress. "Blue is simply not your colour."

Erin knew her protest would be fruitless but she offered it anyway.

"I think it is quite pretty."

"You would, but it is simply not suitable. Indeed, it is quite plain. I told you to go to my bedroom and select a dress. I have a green dress I have worn only once and green is the colour that compliments your hair. I will have it brought to you. Do finish dressing and I will bring it to you myself. And the girl will look after your hair."

Presently she returned with the green dress, carrying it like a precious treasure. Erin quietly allowed that it was a fine dress, though she also felt that she would wear a Hessian sack if it stopped her sister's litany of complaints.

"The guests will be arriving within the hour," Olivia Julianne said as she laced Erin into the dress and fluffed and fussed it into shape. "And now you look quite satisfactory, Brent will be most impressed."

"Brent?"

"Yes, Mr Masterson – your admirer – will be in the company so you do want to look your best."

"He is not my admirer," Erin protested. "I would be astonished if he even remembered who I am. Why do you imagine him to be my admirer? The very notion"

"Has he not invited you to the Delafield Ball?"

"And he has almost certainly forgotten that as well."

"You are impossible, Erin, quite impossible. Now, finish brushing your hair and join me to greet the guests."

Erin studied herself in the dressing-table mirror and wondered why she suffered her sister so easily. She could command the rapt attention of a classroom full of lively and noisy children with confident authority yet in the company of her sister she was reduced to stumbling compliance. She had not even had the opportunity of telling Olivia Julianne about her morning discoveries.

One day, she told her reflection, she would demand total silence and full attention from her sister and assert herself. Alas, she feared that day lay a long way off.

She walked along the corridor from her bedroom and down the stairs to the dining-room where Olivia Julianne was still agitating over the final minute details of the dinner, moving around the table to smooth a wrinkle that did not exist or to move a fork a fraction of a fraction of an inch and then return it to its original position. Erin shook her head and smiled … Olivia Julianne was, after all, merely being Olivia Julianne.

A maid, who had been dispatched to the front door for the purpose, hurried excitedly back to report the arrival of the guests. Olivia Julianne glanced at herself in a mirror, fingered her hair into place and went to greet the line of carriages that were approaching up the driveway. Erin waited in the hallway.

She watched as the guests climbed from the carriages. There were six of them and with the exception of Brent Masterson all were middle-aged and all dressed in conventional evening wear that presented her with the thought that a line of penguins was waddling its way up the steps to the house. Brent was dressed in a traditional evening suit but it was at least fashionable and he looked quite relaxed – and handsome.

Orell led the procession and kissed his wife tenderly. He saw Erin at the door and smiled warmly at her. As each of the men arrived Erin was introduced and acknowledged with a series of limp handshakes and thin smiles.

Brent, bringing up the rear, took her hand and kissed it.

"My dear Miss Dubois," he said, "I am delighted to see you again," he bent and whispered, "How utterly beguiling you look. I am now assured of a pleasing evening."

The guests were escorted to the dining-room and a maid moved among them offering glasses of sherry. They spoke in groups about business transactions, stocks and bonds and the current financial condition of the South.

Erin was joined by Orell who seemed genuinely pleased that she had come to Natchez to visit her sister. Presently he excused himself and joined three of his guests. She turned to seek a chair in which to hide when she found herself facing Brent.

"I see you are searching for an escape, Miss Dubois," he said, smiling knowingly. "I have come to rescue you. My companions are not the most stimulating of men, all quite excellent in their own way, of course, but not, dare I say it, joyful."

He took her arm and as Olivia Julianne began to direct the others to their places around the table he made certain Erin would be sitting opposite him.

It had to be admitted, Erin thought, that the dinner was a triumph and throughout it when she sneaked a glance across the table she found Brent looking at her. Around her she caught snatches of conversation and from time to time was drawn into it. Her contribution was lively if limited for she saw in it an opportunity to shine for Brent. She offered the charmed company polite small-talk about her recent journey, the proposed length of her stay in Natchez and of the latest news from Northville Landing since several of the men had business interests there.

The dinner concluded after several hours, the sisters left the men to their brandy and cigars and, finally, Erin saw the opportunity of speaking to Olivia Julianne about her visit to Mr McCutcheon and the boatyard.

She and her sister walked together to the garden, where coffee had been set out on a table.

"I have been remiss in not enquiring about your trip to town," Olivia Julianne said, nodding to a maid to pour the tea.

Erin told her what had happened and what she had discovered, all of which Olivia Julianne listened to carefully and with a growing amazement.

"What a simply horrible place this boatyard must have been, my dear," her sister said, accompanying it with a shudder. "But how wonderful that you have received a substantial sum of money. I am truly pleased for you."

And Olivia Julianne was truly pleased for she was wealthy enough not to be envious of her sister.

"You will be able to sell the boatyard and the boat and obtain additional financial security. I have always known you always held father in much greater affection than I ever did and you deserve to reap a benefit from his remarkably great service. What an exciting alteration it will make to your life."

"I am not fully resolved to sell the yard," Erin said.

"I do not understand you. What else could you possibly do with it? I am certain Orell would be able to find you a buyer. There can be no other outcome."

Erin considered her sister's reaction. People – and all of them men – appeared to be able to sell her boatyard and her boat, and she was now firmly of the idea that they were her boatyard and her River Queen, but she was increasingly of the opinion that she should astonish them all by re-opening the yard and restoring the vessel. Indeed, she was adamant that it would be so.

"I know you mean well, Olivia Julianne, but I have determined to see the yard and the River Queen restored to their former glory. My mind is made up and I will not be diverted from the task."

"It is madness, you must in your heart see as much!"

Erin was about to reply when they were joined by Brent and Orell. Olivia Julianne was ushered back to the house to oversee the distribution of the rooms.

"Would you care to walk in the garden, Miss Dubois?" Brent said, holding out his hand to Erin.

"That would be most pleasant, Mr Masterson," she said.

The sun was setting, casting ripples of red across the river. A light, gentle breeze rustled through the leaves and carried the scent from the flowers through the evening.

"I trust you did not find the evening trying," Brent said. "We are all dull businessmen obsessed with the price of everything and lacking in the knowledge of the value of most things. I confess, even I had to make my excuses and seek you out."

"Your timing was perfection itself," Erin said, "I do love my sister but sometimes …"

Brent laughed.

"I know exactly what you mean, sisters can be a trial. I know it at first hand …"

"You have a sister? I did not know it."

"Yes, indeed I do have a sister. Perhaps you saw her at the landing; she came to meet me off the steamer. Her name is Lydia. Alas she is a widow for her husband was killed during the war. I visit her and the children; she has two young girls, as often as I can."

His sister! Erin found her spirits quite lifted by the knowledge that the beautiful lady she had indeed noticed on their arrival was his sister. It was a surprise that it mattered to her.

"It would be most pleasant to meet your sister and the children," Erin said.

They returned to the veranda and sat at the table, watching

the evening darken towards a star swept night. Brent spoke of his plans for the new hotels and she of her life in Northville Landing, though she did not mention the events of the day, largely because she had not fully grasped their significance or what exactly she intended to do about them.

Their conversation was pleasantly inconsequential yet from it Erin selected snatches of information to be stored away for ... for what? She did not, for the moment, want to think why it mattered, only that she felt strangely contented.

"I have a confession to make," Brent said. "I insinuated myself into the company tonight. I have, of course, known Orell and your sister for several years and have often been a guest here in their home, but when I heard Orell arrange for the others to come to dinner I made a point of seeking an invitation."

"That was very forward of you, Mr Masterson," Erin chided him. "Why would you do such a thing?"

"Because I knew you would be here."

She was relieved to know that he would not detect her blush.

They listened in comforting silence to the sounds of the staff clearing up after the dinner and the guests being directed to their rooms. Presently Brent got up and Erin took his offered hand to return inside.

"I must go, but it has been most wonderful seeing you again, Miss Dubois."

"Are you not staying?"

"No, I think I extended my good fortune enough by coming for dinner. I am staying with Lydia and the children. I think you and my sister would enjoy each other's company. I will, with your permission, arrange for you to meet her."

Erin saw him off, watching as he was conveyed from the house and disappeared into the night. She smiled and hugged herself. She walked back into the house hoping to see Olivia Julianne to thank her for such a pleasant evening.

She found her sister and Orell relaxing in the drawing-room. As she entered, Orell stood up and beckoned her to a chair at the crackling log fire.

"My dear Erin," he said, standing at the fireplace so that the smoke from his cigar would not disturb her, "I apologise for not welcoming you properly to Natchez. I am afraid I inflicted the evening on dear Olivia Julianne at short notice, though as always she coped quite magnificently.

"She was telling me of your astonishing day and your good fortune. She also tells me you intend to re-open the Natchez Mississippi Construction Company."

"I would certainly like to but firstly the details of such a move are what I should like to investigate in greater detail. Do you know anything about the company that might assist me in my decision?"

"A little," Orell said. "It was a well considered business until quite recently. I have heard of Mr Riparian but I never met him … he, too, was well considered. But to revive the company and run it successfully would be a major undertaking. Are you seriously considering such a notion?"

"You must discourage her if she is. It is too ridiculous to contemplate, do you not agree?" Olivia Julianne said.

Orell smiled and considered his wife's question.

"It is, my dear, a proposal to be considered carefully … but I do not consider it ridiculous, not ridiculous at all. Indeed, with proper financing and the right management there is no reason why it should not be a success.

"May I ask, Erin, what do you really know of the company?"

Erin told him of her meeting with Mr Frampton, of how he said he could probably get many of the former employees to return, of how highly the company appeared to have been thought of.

"He seems an ideal fellow, this Mr Frampton," Orell said. "I have a proposition for you. Would you permit me to have one of my people meet with your Mr Frampton with the view of seeing around the yard and assessing its viability?"

"I would not object to that," Erin said, "Indeed, I would welcome as much advice as can be obtained. I intended to return to the yard tomorrow and I will tell Mr Frampton to expect such a visit."

"Then it is settled," Orell said. "We shall consider the future of the yard from all possible directions and if it looks viable I might be in a position to attract additional backing."

They sat quietly as the conversation settled in their minds. Presently they rose to retire for the night. As they walked from the drawing-room, Erin could detect Olivia Julianne muttering "madness, utter madness" under her breath and saw Orell place a comforting arm around his wife's shoulder. He kissed her cheek.

"Madness, my dear, has often built great empires."

Chapter 8

ERIN AWOKE EARLY THE FOLLOWING morning. The maids were already up and about and brought her breakfast. A busy, perhaps even life changing, day lay ahead and she was anxious to get it started. She washed and dressed and, looking at herself in the mirror, realised that the blue dress with the flowers that her sister had dismissed as unsuitable for the dinner party was even less suitable for her proposed exploration of the boatyard. She would need to find a store providing more comfortable attire.

She had arranged before retiring for the night that a buggy be provided, the landau she deemed too ostentatious for her needs. She walked to the stable and found the carriage standing ready. She led one of the horses from a stall and hitched it to the buggy. She led the horse and buggy from the building and drove it down the driveway from the house towards the town and the yard.

On the way she looked for a store. Natchez was coming to life, its citizens scurrying to grasp the opportunities of the new day. She saw the establishment she required and guided the buggy to the sidewalk. She entered and made her more suitable purchase.

As she drove along the riverside path she ran the events of the previous evening through her head. Brent had, again, been attentive and had even suggested she meet Lydia, his sister … what should she read into that?

She put the possible consequences to the back of her mind – to be resurrected for future consideration – and concentrated on Orell's surprisingly positive reaction to her thoughts of reopening the Natchez Mississippi Construction Company. She had always considered her brother-in-law as a stuffed shirt yet he had dismissed Olivia Julianne's objections and even offered to have the yard surveyed and, if the survey indicated a promising future, to find financial support.

Well, Erin told herself, Orell was a businessman, it was in his nature to be always on the lookout for opportunities to turn a cent into several dollars, so if he wished, all things being equal, to help her turn around the fortunes of the yard she would certainly not discourage him. He was, she thought, turning out to be a better man than she had previously conceded.

She had, it surprised her to realise, been in Natchez for a mere two days and so much had happened her head was spinning with the possibilities. Today, she felt, was the first day of the rest of her life.

As she approached the boatyard she saw Gabriel, the caretaker and guardian of her legacy, talking to three men at the open gates. He looked up at the sound of the buggy and smiled, waving her into the yard. He followed her and when she had drawn up at the building they had been in the previous day he assisted her down from the buggy.

"Those men I was talking to," he explained, "worked at the yard."

It was clear to Erin that he was determined to see her revive the company. To which end, she thought, he would be enthused by her report of Orell's offer.

Inside the office, Gabriel offered her a coffee from a pot that bubbled on the black stove. She accepted and sat at the desk to explain how events were moving on. He listened carefully, nodding in agreement as she told him of the proposed visit of Orell's surveyors and, dependent on their assessment, on the potential financial support. When she had finished he instantly judged it a fine outcome, adding that she had become, overnight, a most promising business woman.

"I should like to take a look around the yard, if that would be suitable," she said.

"Of course, Miss Dubois, I will show you around," Gabriel said. "Though …"

"Is there a problem?"

"Well, your dress, miss … it could get ruined, the yard isn't exactly the cleanest of places."

"Oh," Erin said. "I quite forgot. I did bring more suitable clothes. Is there anywhere I can change?"

"Yes," he said. "The small room behind the desk." He got up. "You get ready and I'll meet you outside."

When Erin emerged at the front door of the office she offered the waiting Gabriel a strange sight. He looked her over, shook his head and smiled.

She was now wearing baggy black wool trousers that she had tucked into dark canvas boots. She was dressed in a red checked shirt and she had tied her hair and piled it beneath a straw hat.

"Will this do?" she asked, and all Gabriel could do was nod before directing her towards a cluster of timber sheds and workshops at the far end of the yard.

The buildings, he explained as they entered and began to walk around, were the design, carpentry and manufacturing shops where the workforce made the interior fixtures and fittings for their customers' paddle-steamer gaming rooms, restaurants and living accommodation. He added that they had been the finest interiors to be seen the length and breadth of the Mississippi.

Long wooden benches were lined in rows inside the drawing office and scraps of paper lay on the floor. The machinery appeared to Erin to be broken and rusting, though Gabriel assured her it could easily be cleaned, fixed and restored to full working order.

The buildings were clearly in need of major restoration for she could see gaping holes in the roofs and cracked and gaping windows.

Birds wheeled and squawked above her head and a sweet, sickening smell of decay assaulted her senses. Gabriel, anxious to maintain a positive feeling, continued to assure her that all could be returned to its former glory with the minimum of delay.

Erin was not as confident and feared the outcome of the proposed survey by Orell's investigators. Perhaps it was, after all, just an unrealistic dream to have the company back in business. Perhaps she should, as she had so frequently been advised, concede defeat, sell and return to her life as a school ma'am.

"Oh Gabriel," she sighed. "I know you mean well but everything is in such a derelict condition. It would require a great deal of money, which I simply do not feel I can spend to put it right."

They went outside and stood looking at the River Queen. She was moored alongside a wooden jetty that ran at the side of the river bank. She bumped and scraped at the jetty as vessels passed on the river and sent waves lapping around her hull.

"And," Erin said, looking at the vessel's frayed and twisted ropes and cables, boarded-up windows and the cabin doors swinging gently in the wind rising from the river, "I have not even taken that into consideration. Would she even float?"

"Of course she would, she floats even now. The old lady is, I grant you, in need of beautification but she is as sound as when she was the Queen of the river."

"She does not look it, Gabriel."

"Well, Miss Dubois, she is … and when I get the men back to the yard I absolutely guarantee you they'll have her working."

"I wish I could muster such confidence and enthusiasm, but I am thoroughly disheartened."

Erin did not wish to curb Gabriel's clear desire to encourage her. She turned from the vessel and asked if he could show her any plans of it and explain, in as few daunting technical details as he could, why and how the River Queen might be restored. They returned to the office and while he collected an armful of large rolled designs and plans she cleared the desk to accommodate them.

As Gabriel rolled out the documents she could see just how magnificent the steamer had been in her prime for several of them were in colour, now faded but still wonderful to behold.

Gabriel sat down and together they poured over the drawings until he began to explain what she was looking at.

The River Queen had been built in Pittsburgh towards the end of the war, though she had not been put into service on the river until late 1865 when Mr Riparian obtained her after acquiring the Natchez Mississippi Construction Company. She had plied the river between Vicksburg, Natchez, Northville Landing and New Orleans though the company had been unable to establish a regular schedule against more established competitors.

The vessel was 200ft by 46ft and had a 5ft 2ins draft. The 17.5 ton paddlewheel was 24ft wide with an 18ft diameter and had a displacement of 860 tons. She was driven by Rees steam engines that were almost 30 years old but, Gabriel stressed, still in working order ... give or take.

"What of her crew? And how many passengers could she carry?" Erin asked.

"She had a crew of 50 and offered accommodation for 1,000. And, as you can see from the plans, she was a sight to behold. Her restaurant was the talk of the river, not just for its decorations but for its food. And the gaming room was the draw for every colourful character – and rogue and cad – in the South.

"The cabins were equally as grand as the restaurant; Mr Riparian demanded only the best ... the best cotton and linen sheets, the best drapes, the best of everything. Don't judge the old lady by how she looks now, just look at what she was like and think how she could look again."

"You must not lie to me, Gabriel," Erin said and gave him her most serious look. "Do you truly think the River Queen could be brought back to life?"

Gabriel gave the question some thought then looked across the desk into Erin's eyes.

"Yes, Miss Dubois, she most certainly could. Won't be easy, and that's the truth, but I know she could."

Erin weighed his reply and glanced once more at the plans spread before her. She so dearly wanted to see the River Queen back on the river, but she knew how difficult such a task would be. She liked Gabriel, was bolstered by his desire, did not want to abandon him or the men who had worked in the yard ... and she made up her mind.

"Then I shall do all in my power to make it happen, Gabriel. We can only pray that Mr Thynne and his financial associates decide to support our efforts."

She still had not seen around the River Queen and there was, she decided, no better time than now. Gabriel said he would conduct an inspection with her but warned that the vessel was not in the best of condition.

At the foot of the gangplank he took his rag from his belt, spat on his hands and wiped them, holding one out for her.

"Step carefully, ma'am," Gabriel warned, "the old lady has forgotten how to greet visitors."

He assisted Erin up the gangplank, a narrow and rickety affair that shook dangerously as she picked her way up it, threatening to tip her into the river.

The deck, when they reached it, was broken and creaked underfoot from the rotting boards. It was, like the yard buildings, discouraging.

They came to a door, half open, and Gabriel pushed it wide enough for them to enter. It was the restaurant, and it was in a poor condition. The wood panelled walls were water stained, tables and chairs were stacked in the corners and mildewed, torn velvet drapes blew listlessly at boarded and broken windows. Erin could, however, see the remains of what had once been magnificent paintings clinging to memories of a better past: street scenes of Paris, London flower-sellers, snow-capped mountains reflected in green-blue lakes.

"You must understand, Miss Dubois, that the war was not kind to the River Queen."

As Gabriel was exploring the restaurant kitchen, Erin walked back out to the deck and moved along the row of cabins. Suddenly from inside one she heard a noise. Probably a bird unable to escape, she thought. To be on the safe side she looked around her and found a metal pipe. As quietly as it would allow, she eased the door open and crept inside, gradually adjusting her eyes to the gloom.

To her surprise she saw a figure stretched out on a bunk. The figure was sleeping so she moved forward and poked it, stepping back to await developments. The figure turned suddenly and she saw the gun pointed at her. She screamed as the figure rolled from the bunk. It was, she saw, a man, so she screamed again and heard Gabriel running along the deck.

"Damn it, lady," the man said, putting the gun back into his belt, "stop screeching like that and calm down, I mean you no harm."

Gabriel burst through the door and the man reached for his gun. Erin held up a hand to stop Gabriel.

"It is fine, Gabriel," she said. "He looks more dangerous than I suspect him to be."

She looked the man over; indeed he looked unlike anything she had set eyes on before. He was, she guessed, in his late twenties. He had a look of exhaustion about him as he stood silently before her. His clothes were torn and dirty, his boots ripped and scuffed. His hair, long and greasy, hung around his shoulders and he had a black beard that hid a face that appeared not to have experienced the luxury of a shave or a wash for several months.

Erin raised the pipe by way of warning.

"Who are you, sir, and what are you doing on my boat?"

"Your boat, is it? Now that's not something I'd go around crowing about."

She stepped towards him, mustering as much menace as she could.

"I asked who you were," she said, narrowing her eyes for effect.

The man bowed in a clearly mocking manner that infuriated her. She took another step forward.

"I am, ma'am, Matthew Luke Morgan, late Captain of Cavalry in the lamented former Army of the Confederacy. I was just passing through Natchez and found myself unable to pay for a room in a hotel – indeed, I find myself unable to pay for anything at the moment. I came across this …," he looked around in disbelief, "… your boat and shipped aboard."

Erin saw now that his grubby jacket and trousers were grey,

the trousers with a butter-yellow stripe. On the bunk she saw a grey slouch hat. She put the pipe down and surveyed him again. Beneath the grime she fancied there lurked a rather handsome young man. She now established his accent, his drawl, to be pure South.

"You look dreadful," she said. "And if you do not wish to be hounded down and shot by our Yankee guests I suggest you find something less conspicuous than a Rebel uniform. And," she added wafting her hand, "a shave, a haircut and a bath would not go amiss."

Gabriel had watched the drama in silence. He had no idea anyone had been living on the River Queen.

"Have you had any vittles of late?" he asked.

The man shook his head.

"Can't rightfully recall when I last did."

"Then, Mr ....," Erin began but could not remember his name.

"Matthew Luke Morgan."

"Doubtless your mother was also a devout reader of the Bible," she said.

The man looked puzzled so she waved her hand in dismissal.

"Then, Mr Matthew Luke Morgan, come with us and we might be able to find you something to eat. Might we do that, Gabriel?"

"It's your boat, Miss Dubois," Gabriel said and led them from the boat back to the office.

"It really is your boat, ma'am?" Matthew Luke Morgan said. "I'll be damned."

"You will be more than damned, sir, if you continue using that language," Erin scolded him.

"I apologise. I am a tad more civilised than you might suppose. But I would have figured you for a school ma'am ... a pretty tough one at that."

Erin smiled.

"How very clever of you."

While Matthew, whom he suggested they call him, ate the food Gabriel had brought for himself, Erin asked her foreman to join her outside. They walked a few paces from the office.

"That was quite a surprise," Erin said, "What do you make of our mysterious lodger?"

"Couldn't rightly say, Miss Dubois," Gabriel replied. "I figure he's what he says he is, we get a lot of lost souls wandering through, coming from God knows where and going to God knows where. I guess it's always that way after a war, lost souls."

"I am considering asking him what his intentions might be, what he plans to do … I am considering asking him if he would care to stay. The way I see it, Gabriel, is that you could be a busy man in the coming weeks trying to get your men to return to the yard and Mr Morgan could be useful in looking after the yard and the boat. We needn't actually pay him much but we could offer him board on the River Queen. He does seem to have quite settled in already."

Gabriel hesitated. He had no real objection to Erin's plan; it indicated that in spite of the dilapidated condition of both the boatyard and the boat she had made up her mind to stay. It was something he wished to encourage.

"I'm not against the suggestion, ma'am," he said, "but let us find out a little more about him."

Erin agreed and they returned to the office. Erin took it upon herself to start the questions.

"Where have you come from, Mr Morgan?"

He smiled.

"Figured you would get around to that," he said, "I was with the gallant General Edmund Kirby Smith in the Trans-Mississippi Department, the last Reb army in the field. We got to figuring we couldn't get through the Yankee lines to do much to continue the fight so we surrendered at Galveston, Texas – with myself much relieved to be in the company - and started heading home."

"Where is your home?" Gabriel asked.

"Don't rightly know if I still have a home anywhere. But if you need any place named it would be Alexandria. I guess I was heading in that general direction, and then again in no particular direction."

"As I explained, Mr Morgan," Erin said, "I do own that boat, such as it is, and I also own this boatyard, such as it is. Mr Frampton here, he is my general manager and we are planning to re-open the yard. Nothing has been completely agreed, you understand, but that is my intention.

"Would you consider staying here as a sort of caretaker looking after the yard? You could live on the boat … I could not offer you any – well, much – money but at least you would have somewhere to stay."

"Well, Miss Dubois, that is mighty generous of you," Matthew said and gave it some thought. "I guess it's a fine offer. I've had no others, truth be told. So, yes … I figure I'll stay. You own the boat and the yard … I'll be dam …"

Erin hid a smile and squinted disapprovingly at him. She extended her hand and they shook.

"Now, Mr Morgan, for pity sake please go find yourself a shave and a bath!"

She opened her purse and handed him some money.

"And much as I revere the uniform and what it stood for, do find some clothing that will not lead to you being shot at. You may owe me the amount from your wages."

Chapter 9

THE INVITATION WAS DELIVERED BY a rider on an appropriately romantic white horse, at least the maid who received it from the rider declared it to be so. She carried it on a silver platter along the hallway and knocked gently on the door until she heard the Mistress bid her enter. She conveyed the yellow envelope across the polished, dark-stained floor and, with a curtsey, presented it to Olivia Julianne.

Erin's sister had been expecting the envelope for several days but, of course, she now merely placed it on the table beside where she sat reading and treated it as of no significant consequence. In truth, though it was not something she would admit, she had been beset with the notion that it might not come at all. It had, of course, been a notion of such nonsense that she was embarrassed to have even considered it.

If the Delafield's were holding a ball, as they did every year, and if it was universally considered to be THE social event of Natchez's many such occasions, as it most certainly was, then of course Olivia Julianne and Orell Windom Hamelin Thynne III would be invited to attend. It was preposterous to think otherwise.

She waited until the maid had departed and eagerly sliced a paper-knife through the top of the envelope and withdrew the white card with its embossed Delafield crest – ostentatiously depicting two unicorns on either side of a shield, quartered to depict a sailing ship, a smoking factory chimney, an oak tree and a bale of tobacco (which all had contributed to the Delafield fortune), topped by an eagle with spread wings – to read the finely drawn copperplate words.

In short, if rather overly done, Senator Frederick Albert Delafield and Mrs Margaret Catherine Elizabeth Delafield requested the company of Orell and Olivia Julianne for a ball – indeed, for a Grand Ball – to be held five days from the date of delivery of the invitation at Willowford Grove, commencing at 7.30pm.

At the bottom of the invitation, in what appeared to be a passing after thought, Mrs Delafield had written: "I would be delighted if you brought your sister, if she cares to join you."

Her sister, to Olivia Julianne's continued displeasure, was these days more inclined to don her ridiculous and most unladylike trousers, shirt and hat and wander around her disgusting and downright filthy boatyard than contemplate the delights of a ball.

That same evening, Erin, who had truthfully forgotten all about the ball, received a visitor along with her own invitation. She was sitting at the desk in the library when a maid entered and informed her a gentleman was awaiting her pleasure at the front door.

"Then we must surely see who this gentleman is," Erin told the maid. "Please direct him to me."

Not knowing who it might be, Erin returned to the papers on the desk while she waited for the gentleman to be announced. He indicated to the maid that she should say nothing and leave and when she had he couched quietly. Erin looked up and saw that it was Brent. She smiled and got up to greet him, beckoning him into the room. He came to her and from behind his back produced a posy of red, yellow, white and purple flowers. She thanked him for the kind thought, sniffed the sweet scents and invited him to take one of the chairs beside the fire.

"I have come, Miss Dubois, to honour the promise I made to ask you to accompany me to the ball at the Delafield home," Brent said.

"The ball ... oh the ball," Erin said. "I would be greatly honoured to receive your kind invitation and delighted to accept it."

"Then I shall be the most envied of men at it," he said.

Thus began another of Olivia Julianne's hurricanes of preparation for the Grand Ball, preparations which she insisted Erin give her full, her absolutely full, attention to rather than to her boatyard. This, she emphasised on more than one occasion, was quite the most important social event in Natchez, to which only "those who mattered" were invited and she, Erin, should show it the respect and attention it deserved.

"You are, after all, going as the guest of Mr Masterson so you must be perfection itself," she said.

Erin had no intention of doing otherwise, of course, since the boatyard had, she privately admitted, been causing her some grief, largely because while Orell had, as promised, sent his men to look over the yard and the River Queen he had not yet reported their observations and recommendations. The delay was driving her to distraction so the coming ball would be a welcome diversion.

Brent had arranged for him to bring a carriage to collect her prior to the ball and bring her to his sister Lydia's house from where they would all travel on to Willowford Grove.

Olivia Julianne and Erin were driven into Natchez in the landau, it being an ideal vehicle for the shopping they intended to do. Olivia Julianne knew the most perfect seamstress who also owned the most perfect dress shop and the sisters made their way to it. They passed St Mary Basilica on South Union Street and arrived at the most perfect dress shop on Franklin Street where Madam Gabrielle, a small and excited French woman, threw herself upon Olivia Julianne with a warm embrace.

Some time previously, Olivia Julianne had arranged for Madam Gabrielle to make her a dress and she was sure the seamstress could find one suitable for Erin, perhaps one that had been ordered for another occasion but not collected.

"You are going to the Delafield ball, I simply knew you would come to see me," she cried, excitedly, and steered Olivia Julianne to the rear of the shop. Erin, who had not been embraced, fell in behind.

Madam Gabrielle, who in truth was not French, which all of her clients already knew, but originally from Chicago, swished open two red velvet curtains to expose what she called her "special treasures" … several rows of dresses stretched even further into the rear of the shop.

"And this," she cried in triumph, "is the dress I have designed and made for you."

Both Olivia Julianne and Erin were rendered speechless at its beauty for it was a confection of shimmering cream silk, trimmed in delicate blue lace.

"This is my sister, Erin Dubois," Olivia Julianne explained, having quite forgotten Erin in her excitement. "We require a suitable dress for her as well."

Madam Gabrielle looked carefully at Erin.

"Ah, you have been invited to the ball?" she said in a tone that was heavy with incredulity.

She was, however, certain that something could be discovered among the treasures.

The sisters spent the next several hours trying on dress after dress, all of them that greatly appealed to Erin were instantly dismissed by Olivia Julianne while Madam Gabrielle lent her disapproving support with a shake of her head and a curl of her lips … nothing Erin liked would do, simply not do. Olivia Julianne urged her sister to concentrate on the task and take it seriously. Madam Gabrielle nodded in agreement.

Finally, by which time Erin had considered fleeing screaming from the shop, a dress of green silk, trimmed with white lace, emerged from the last row and was greeted with enthusiasm by Olivia Julianne. Even Madam Gabriel nodded and smiled.

"I shall let it out sufficiently to fit you," she told Erin as she pulled and fluffed and fussed at the dress. "I will have it ready for you tomorrow."

Erin thanked her – let it out to fit her was not quite what she wished to hear – and while Olivia Julianne continued to search for a dress for herself she walked to the front of the shop and stepped into the street to calm herself.

Late in the afternoon the sisters concluded an exhausting

expedition and were driven home, surrounded by new shoes, hats, capes, purses, gloves, shifts and corsets. In her room, Erin closed the drapes and lay on her bed, her temples throbbing.

After dinner that evening Gabriel came from the boatyard to see her. A maid showed him to the library where, once again, Erin was studying a pile of documents. Gabriel had come to say that her brother-in-law's representatives had visited the yard and inspected the River Queen on two occasions and had assured him they would report favourably to Mr Thynne. The news greatly heartened Erin who had still not heard from Orell.

"And what of Mr Morgan?" she wished to know.

"Quite the fellow is your Mr Morgan," Gabriel revealed. "Keeps himself mostly to himself, deep as a pit he is, Miss Dubois. But a couple of nights ago he heard a noise and discovered several unsavoury ruffians bent on mischief had got on board the old lady … set about them single-handed and threw them into the river, and then went back to sleep."

"Gracious me," Erin said. "He is a strange character, but I am happy to have him on our side."

"Amen to that, ma'am, amen to that," Gabriel said and added some more information about him. "He's even started to clean up the boat. I found him sorting through the tables and chairs in the restaurant, what he reckoned were worth keeping and what wasn't. And now he's started to scrub the floor … seems he likes to keep himself gainfully occupied."

When Gabriel had departed, Erin sought out Orell, who was strolling in the garden.

She asked, since she had not recently had the opportunity to do so, if there was any news he could provide regarding the yard.

"I understand your impatience, Erin," he said. "But, yes, I have just this morning received the survey from my people and while there is still much to do I feel confident that I will soon be able to deliver encouraging news. Tomorrow I will be meeting at the bank with several potential backers."

Erin was, indeed, encouraged. She had also considered her own financial situation and concluded that she was now wealthy enough to at least pay for the restoration of the yard. She would not, of course, reject any additional investment Orell might be able to attract.

She retired for the night in a mood of optimism and found herself dreaming of Captain Matthew Luke Morgan.

While the hurricane abated for two days it returned in full strength on the day of the Delafield ball, beginning as mild flurries of activity and building, during the afternoon, to full force fury as Olivia Julianne and Erin prepared themselves.

As far as Erin was concerned the preparation seemed simple enough. She would bathe, she would dress, one of the maids would assist with her hair, she would await the carriage Brent had said would call for her, she would be conveyed to his sister's house, they would all journey on to Willowford Grove, she would dance, she would return home after a pleasant evening.

Olivia Julianne, on the other hand, approached the event in the manner of a military operation, full of planning and tactics and manoeuvres.

She quickly had several maids reduced to tears and several others to foaming frustration. And she then decided that Erin should not be permitted to step from her room before an inspection had been conducted.

Naturally, several aspects regarding Erin's appearance would not do, simply would not do.

Orell, well aware of his wife's ability to introduce carnage to the most ordinary of circumstances, remained in his dressing-room and judged himself quite acceptable. He retired to the sanctuary of the library where he poured himself a stiff whiskey and relaxed to await Olivia Julianne. He remained in bafflement over the female of the species.

At 6pm, as arranged, a carriage drove up to the house and Brent announced to a maid who came to the door that he had come to collect Miss Dubois. Erin, attempting with no great degree of success to remain calm, thanked the maid and was assisted onto the carriage by Brent. They drove from the house with a still warm breeze fingering lightly through her hair and he looked at her and thought her the most beautiful creature he had ever set eyes on.

On reaching the home of his sister, Lydia was waiting to greet them. Erin was helped down and Brent led her to Lydia who held out her hands and gently embraced her, directing her inside.

They sat in the drawing-room as two dear friends who had known one another for years. Lydia was even more beautiful than Erin remembered from her first brief sight when they had disembarked from the trip from Northville Landing.

She was in her thirties, slender and charming, her hair cascaded around her shoulders in ringlets and she wore a burgundy velvet dress.

"I am so delighted to finally meet you, Miss Dubois," Lydia said. "Brent has spoken so constantly about you since I met him at the jetty."

"I am flattered; I did not expect him to remember me. And you must please call me Erin."

They sat and talked until two little girls stormed into the room, wide-eyed with excited curiosity about their visitor. They were followed by Brent, who had gone to fetch them.

"Girls, please do calm down," Lydia said. "You are not re-enacting Picket's Charge. Now come here and if you can remain still for a few seconds I shall introduce you."

Erin waited while Charlotte – *"I am nine-years-old and I love horses"* – and Mary – *"And I am six and I can sing and dance"* – were brought forward to shake her hand.

"I am Erin, and I too love horses, Charlotte, but Mary, I am not very good at singing and dancing so perhaps you might teach me." Mary squealed in delight at the idea and threw herself into Erin's arms.

"Gently," Lydia said and rolled her eyes at her daughter's enthusiasm. "You must not smother Miss Dubois or crease her fine dress. Now, say goodnight and go with Uncle Brent."

The girls said their farewells, Mary stealing a kiss, and Brent took them off to the nursery to be handed over to their governess.

"You must forgive them, I fear Mary is six going on fifty-six. Charlotte is showing signs of becoming a little lady, but I think Mary is beyond hope," Lydia said.

"They are both absolutely perfect," Erin said, "Believe me, Lydia, I am a school teacher and I know all about little girls. You can be proud of them both."

"Brent tells me you are the sister of Olivia Thynne."

"Yes," Erin said, "We see each other so seldom but I had some business here in Natchez so it gave me the opportunity of a visit."

"Your sister is a remarkable woman," Lydia said. For Erin it was a statement that might well be interpreted in several ways, not all of them complimentary. She smiled and awaited further enlightenment.

"She is, as you probably already know, a very important member of Natchez society, one of its leading lights. But she has also been responsible for many acts of kindness and charity to our least fortunate citizens. I hold Olivia in great esteem."

Before Erin, somewhat surprised to learn of her sister's good deeds and now, as with Orell, forced to think of her in a more charitable manner, could frame an answer, Brent returned from seeing the girls settled and suggested they make their way to the Delafield ball.

As he led Erin and Lydia from the house to the waiting carriage, Lydia slipped her arm through Erin's.

"My brother is much taken with you, Erin ... very much so," she said. "I hope we will see a great deal more of you and become firm friends."

Chapter 10

WILLOWFORD GROVE, THE HOME OF Senator and Mrs Delafield, was a magnificent estate of some several thousand acres – not even the Senator could have arrived at a precise number – that ran to and for many miles along the banks of the Mississippi.

Like several other such estates in Natchez, Willowford Grove had largely escaped the worst the war had visited upon so much of the South. It had prospered greatly and the Delafield's had been able to restore the house to its pre-war magnificence. It had also allowed its master to become a man of influence and importance in Washington.

The house was an imposing mansion of gleaming white. Pillars stood on either side of a large oak double door and a balcony ran the length of the front. Lanterns twinkled and swayed in the warm air and the welcoming yellow glow of lamps beamed from the rooms.

Brent, Lydia and Erin were driven through Natchez and eventually arrived at the gates of the winding driveway that led to the house. They drove along an avenue of gently creaking, swaying willows, the path lit by brightly coloured lanterns. The house, when they finally came to it, greeted them with the sound of an orchestra drifting from what was an already crowded ballroom.

Across the portal above the wide front door had been strung

banners of red, white and blue and waiting to greet the guests as they stepped from the increasingly long line of arriving carriages and escort them to the ballroom were several liveried footmen.

Maids took the gentlemen's hats and canes, the ladies capes and cloaks and another footman escorted them along a corridor to the ballroom. It too was a delight of lanterns and banners and guests either swirling in the dance or chatting in groups. Maids moved around the room with trays of drinks: champagne, wine, orange and freshly squeezed lemonade.

At the far end of the mirrored room a small orchestra sat on a platform and performed non-stop.

Erin stood beside Brent and took it all in: the colour, the warmth, the chatter, the music, the dancers, the beautiful dresses of the ladies.

"You are, as I thought you would be, the most beautiful creature in the room," Brent whispered in her ear and she did her best to hide a blush.

Lydia, upon appearing in the room, had been instantly whisked away by several friends and was now joining in a dance, accompanied by a handsome young man in the uniform of the Union Army.

"How times have changed," Erin whispered to herself.

"Oh Miss Dubois, is it not positively enchanting?"

Erin turned and saw Amelia Sinclair coming through the dancers towards her. She reached out and embraced the excited young girl.

"Amelia, I am so happy to see you again," Erin held her at arms' length to look at her dress. "You look so lovely, you are now truly a beautiful young woman and I am so proud of you."

Amelia, who could not stand still for her feet were tapping to the sound of the music, wore a dress of pink silk and her hair had been arranged in curls and twists that bounced and shimmered around her shoulders.

"And how many hearts have you captured?" Erin asked.

"None yet, Miss Dubois, but I have only just arrived and have already collected several requests for dances. Indeed, my card is quite filling up. I have been asked twice by a young lieutenant to join him in a five-step waltz ... I do not think papa will be too pleased to see me dancing with a Yankee but I consider it as more of a kindness for the young gentleman is from Philadelphia and feeling quite lonely."

Erin laughed.

"Then you must certainly show the young gentleman all that is best about Southern kindness and hospitality, it will be a truly noble act. The Yankees might have captured the South but I think it is time you gained our revenge and captured as many of them as your card allows."

Amelia hugged Erin and went in search of her young gentleman.

Lydia returned and snatched her from Brent to introduce her to some friends. Brent watched Erin and his sister move around the room and went to join Colonel Sinclair and a group of men who had seated themselves conspiratorially at a table in the corner.

"Colonel Sinclair, gentlemen," Brent said and the colonel indicated an empty seat and he sat down.

"I was expecting you, we have some business to discuss," Colonel Sinclair said, reaching to Brent to pour him a brandy from a decanter.

"So, Masterson, do tell us who the beautiful lady accompanying you and your sister is?" one of the men asked.

The colonel answered.

"She is Miss Erin Dubois, from Northville Landing, the sister of Mrs Olivia Julianne Thynne."

"Ah," the man said, "the sister of the formidable Mrs Thynne ... and quite a lovely addition to our company."

"A fine filly, indeed," another man said.

"And one I think Masterson has cut from the herd for himself. Is that not so, Brent?" another asked.

"Gentlemen, gentlemen," the colonel said. "We have more pressing matters to attend to. Quinion has just come from Sutton County with disturbing news." He looked across the table at a man who had remained silent. "Perhaps you would tell the others what you have learned."

Quinion looked around the table.

"The Curiston Plantation, you might have heard of it, has just been taken over by a Yankee carpetbagger. Henry Curiston and his family have been removed, and removed with some force, by a rabble, and rendered destitute. I have reason to believe that the interlopers have similar designs on at least two other properties and the Sutton Mill."

The men considered the news in silence and then Colonel Sinclair slapped a hand on the table.

"Then we must discourage the ruffians from such intentions. It cannot be allowed. We know what we have to do."

The men nodded in angry agreement.

Brent rose.

"And now gentlemen, if you will excuse me I have another pressing matter to discuss with the charming Miss Dubois."

He found her in conversation with Senator Delafield and his wife, along with Olivia Julianne and Windom. He joined them, standing beside Erin who had just finished dancing with a friend of Lydia.

"If you have not been signed up for all the dances, Miss Dubois, I would be honoured if you would join me in a polka-mazurka," he said.

"I do believe, Mr Masterson, that I can accommodate you for at least one quick dance," Erin said with a teasing smile.

As Brent took her arm to lead Erin onto the ballroom floor he whispered to Olivia Julianne that she might have a word with Mr Quinion and Colonel Sinclair.

For the rest of the evening Brent monopolised Erin, a happy entrapment to which she raised no objections. All thoughts of the boatyard and the River Queen and the finance required to restore their fortunes were swept away as she and Brent danced, breaking but briefly to refresh themselves with a cool lemonade or to exchange greetings with other guests.

From time to time they would encounter an excited Amelia as she whirled past in the company of another of her young gentlemen.

Brent eventually guided Erin from the room to the solitude of the garden. They found a seat under a willow and sat listening to the music and the laughter. The evening air was still warm and heavy with the scent of flowers. Beyond the trees they could see the full, white moon reflected in the ripples of the river.

"What a perfectly beautiful evening," Erin said.

"Made more so by your presence," Brent said and took her hand in his. He lifted it to his lips and kissed it … and as she moved closer to him he held her face and kissed her on the lips, feeling her soften against him. He sat with Erin embraced in his arms and they listened in blissful contentment to the gentle sounds of the evening.

"Forgive me, but I have wanted to do that since I first saw you," he said.

"I think I might manage such a forgiveness," Erin whispered.

Presently they walked back to the house where the dancing had stopped and the guests were moving from the ballroom to the dining room. They joined Lydia and a business associate of Brent and were in turn joined by a flushed Amelia and a shy, beaming young lieutenant.

"You do appear to be enjoying yourself, Amelia," Erin whispered.

"Oh yes, Miss Dubois," Amelia said. "I will never forget my first grown up ball." She turned away to hide a blush. "And … and … he kissed me!"

Erin smiled.

"I would not worry about it, dear Amelia … there seems to be a lot of it going around."

As Erin moved along the long table to select food for her plate she was joined by Orell who asked if she might join him. He indicated two empty chairs by the open windows and she followed him.

"I have good news," he said. "The people I sent to look over the boatyard and the vessel, the River Queen I believe it is called, have reported favourably on the prospects of both. It will, you understand, require much hard work and will not be achieved quickly but if you are still of a mind to restore the yard and the boat, and again I must stress that it will not be easy, then I can most certainly obtain additional finances for the venture."

"Oh Orell," Erin said, squeezing his hand. "I am utterly of a determined mind to do so, and I am most grateful to you. I suspect, though, that Olivia Julianne will raise objections to your helping me."

"That will be my concern," her brother-in-law assured her. "I will deal with any objections Olivia Julianne might raise. You might not know your dear sister as well as you imagine."

Erin was certainly coming to the conclusion that it might be so for she was swiftly discovering that Olivia Julianne was more complex and intriguing than she had ever thought possible. She did not yet know why or how, she knew only that it was so.

She thanked Orell again and went to join Brent and Lydia.

The ball ended in the small hours of the following morning and Brent, Lydia and Erin were driven back to Lydia's house. While she looked in on her sleeping girls a maid brought Brent and Erin coffee in the drawing-room. They relaxed and when Lydia presently joined them they discussed the charm and the enjoyment of the evening.

As Brent drove Erin to her sister's house she slipped her arm through his and he kissed her on the cheek.

"It was a truly magical evening," she said.

"I hope the magic has no end," he said and squeezed her hand.

She thought for a moment and then told him the nature of her business in Natchez. She told him about being left in the will of Mr Riparian the boatyard and the River Queen and of her intention to re-open the former and restore the latter. She told him of Orell's financial assistance.

Brent listened in silence, intrigued that Erin should have so much courage to consider undertaking such a task. As Orell had done during their meeting at the ball, he emphasised the monumental scale of the task facing her, the fact that she had no business experience, no knowledge of running a boatyard let alone a paddle-steamer.

But even as he voiced his reservations he knew she had made up her mind.

"My immediate concern is to return to Northville Landing

as quickly as possible," Erin explained. "I must speak with my friend, Jessie, and we must decide what to do about our home."

"I have business to attend to here in Natchez that cannot be avoided," Brent said. "But if you could delay your journey for a week I would happily accompany you."

Erin hugged him.

"I really must go as soon as I can, you must understand. I have a duty to see that the children are correctly catered for at the school and I owe Jessie for she is an important part of my life," she looked into Brent's eyes, "I will miss you, more than you could know, and I do not want to lose you … but my mind is made up. I will book passage later today and return as quickly as circumstances allow."

He kissed her.

"I do not want to lose you," he said. "And I do understand. You are, my dearest Erin, quite the most remarkable creature I have ever known."

At Olivia Julianne's house he helped Erin from the carriage and embraced her. He watched her enter the house and returned to the carriage.

A most interesting lady, he thought. As he returned to his sister's house he had much on his mind.

Chapter 11

THINGS TO DO ... THINGS to do. Erin sat in the garden of her sister's house with a sheet of paper, folded in half, placed on a book on her lap and with a small pot of ink and a pen on a table beside her seat. She had written 'Things to Do' at the top of the sheet but though a hundred such pending tasks jostled through her head for attention, she could not decide which one to begin with.

She reviewed, as a spur to inspiration, the events of the past week she had spent in Natchez and swiftly came to the conclusion that they had been so numerous – even so astonishingly unbelievable – that recalling them in detail would merely distract her even further. She dipped the pen in the pot, brought it to the sheet and began to list the 'Things to Do'.

    1:    Visit the boatyard and tell Gabriel what has happened regarding the promised finance.

    2:    Encourage Gabriel to attract the men, or as many of them as he could, to return.

    3:    Book passage to Northville Landing.

    4:    Tell Jessie what has happened.

    5:    Sell house in Northville, or not?

    6:    Meet Board of Education about finding a new teacher.

    7:    See a bank/lawyer about boatyard account.

    8:    Buy a home in Natchez, or not?

She reviewed the list and felt there were several more items that needed adding, but she could not think what they might be. She was, anyway, satisfied that she had covered the most important tasks facing her.

To her amusement she found that she had added several doodles to the page, including a drawing of a battered hat and a large heart with an arrow piercing it. She had made no other reference concerning her growing relationship with Brent since she felt none was needed.

Whatever was to unfold between them would be faced when the time was right, or not?

She asked Olivia Julianne if she might have the use of a buggy and one was prepared. She drove to the boatyard to outline the developments to Gabriel.

On arrival at the yard, Erin changed from her dress into what she now considered her 'proper' attire of trousers and boots and as Gabriel and she walked through the yard she told him about the favourable report provided to her brother-in-law and about his promise to bring additional finance to the venture.

Gabriel was greatly encouraged by what she told him. Indeed, his faith in it becoming so had been so positive that he had persuaded several of the yard's former employees to return. Erin was introduced to them and thoroughly approved of Gabriel's progress.

"You might care to take a look around the old lady, ma'am," Gabriel said when they came to the River Queen.

Erin was, naturally, most anxious to see the vessel again. Gabriel was called away to see some other returning workmen so she walked up the gangway and along the deck to the gaming room.

She was pleasantly surprised to see its transformation. As she walked around the room, now with its tables and chairs placed neatly at the far wall, the floor swept and washed, the formerly stained and cracked windows cleaned and replaced, the drapes removed, she did not notice the man watching her from the doorway.

When she did, she did not recognise him.

"Yes?" she said, "May I help you?"

"Well, Miss Dubois," the man said, smiling, "You might remember me for a start."

"Gracious me," Erin said, "I truly did not recognise you, Mr Morgan."

He was clean shaven and though his hair remained long it was washed and he had tucked it behind his ears. He wore a new blue shirt, brown woollen trousers tucked into the tops of new, workmanlike boots and around his neck he had tied a yellow bandana. A Navy Colt, she noticed, was tucked in his belt.

How very different he looked, she thought, from their initial meeting. His eyes, she also thought, had a disconcerting twinkle as though they could see things undetectable to others. His smile was warm yet knowing. He walked into the room and removed his slouch hat.

"I thought you were another ruffian come on an evil deed," Erin said. "Why, you are almost a dandified gentleman."

"Now, ma'am, I have been called many things but seldom a gentleman. I trust you approve of how I have been repaying your hospitality?"

"Indeed I do. I am most impressed. Gabriel tells me you have been working steadfastly around the River Queen and you have even put to flight several intruders. I am also impressed by that."

He raised his battered Confederate hat.

"Oh dear," Erin said. "You have not, I see, quite managed to complete your transformation."

He lifted his hat and held it out to examine it.

"Well, ma'am, this is not merely an old hat, it has been my constant companion and comfort for several years. It has served me well as a canteen, I have used it as a wash basin, I have shaved from it and been kept dry and warm beneath it. It has even suffered the indignity of a Yankee bullet through it," he poked a finger through a hole in the crown, "So it would, you must allow, be most ungrateful of me to cast aside such an old friend. I am more faithful than that."

Erin laughed.

"A most eloquent defence of a hat, Mr Morgan. I certainly would not now advocate you dispose of it. Indeed, I quite like it."

"Thank you kindly, we both appreciate that. Now, might I show you what else I have done around the River Queen?"

Erin followed him along the deck and was not surprised to see that he had done an equally excellent job of cleaning the dining room. Matthew Luke Morgan, with his constant beguiling smile and twinkling eyes, was turning out to be a most valuable addition to the yard's growing work force. And, she conceded, a handsome one.

"Have you formulated any plans regarding the immediate future?" Erin asked, as casually as she could manage.

Matthew gave it some thought, bringing a flush to her cheeks with that infuriating smile.

"Well, ma'am," he said, "I kind of figured on sticking around on account of having no particular place to go. Looks like things could be mighty interesting around here."

Erin turned from that steady, penetrating gaze.

"You may certainly stay, if you wish," she said, pretending indifference. "I suppose we could find useful chores for you to do."

On her way back to her sister's house, Erin stopped at the riverboat office and booked passage back to Northville Landing on the Friday run. She had been asked by Colonel Sinclair, on his being told of her return home, if she would accompany his daughter who was also going back to Northville Landing.

Erin purchased two tickets and a cabin to be shared by herself and Amelia. The colonel had, he explained, important business to conduct and wished for Amelia to be chaperoned away from Natchez.

Erin was as pleased at this development as was Amelia for she feared she would have suffered from an anti-climax travelling on her own. She feared having too much time on her hands to fret and ponder the events of the past week. The diversion of the young and lively Miss Sinclair presented a most welcome alternative.

On her return to Olivia Julianne's house Orell was waiting to speak to her, escorting her to the library.

"My dear Erin," he said, producing a large legal document and placing it on his desk, "I have finalised my proposals for the additional financing of the boatyard, it is all laid out in this agreement. I would suggest you take it with you when you return home and have a lawyer of your own choosing go through it. I trust you will find everything to your satisfaction."

He slid the document across the table and Erin thanked him. She excused herself and ran to her room to examine the agreement more fully.

She lay on the bed and read each paragraph carefully. She did not fully understand everything but when she got back to Northville Landing she would seek the advice of Mr Abernethy, the lawyer whose letter had launched her on such a great adventure.

She was, however, not displeased at what she did understand for Orell had been more than fair and generous in his proposals.

Erin would own 60% of the Natchez Mississippi Construction Company, Thynne would hold 20% of the shares and 20% would be distributed among the financial backers, which her brother-in-law would handle. Erin was to be, as the majority holder, in charge of the day-to-day operations of the company though Orell would make himself available to offer advice. It seemed an ideal arrangement.

Erin planned to go to the boatyard the following day to speak to Gabriel and urge him, now that the finances were guaranteed, to continue recruiting the workforce and to begin preparing the machinery and workshops for use. It would also provide her with another opportunity of seeing the disconcerting and intriguing Mr Morgan.

On reaching Northville Landing, she was met by Jessie and she delivered Amelia into the care of her father's housekeeper. The drive along the riverfront to her home was conducted in an excitement of conversation about what had happened in Natchez. Jessie listened to Erin's tale but could not yet manage to stop its flow with any of the many questions she had.

Safely installed in her home, Erin took the legal documents from her valise and she and Jessie sat at a table on the veranda to go through them in detail.

The outcome, reached after several hours of intense debate to which the wise and level-headed Jessie contributed greatly, was that Erin would keep the Northville Landing house which Jessie would live in. Erin would, now that she could afford to, seek a house in Natchez.

She did not bring it up that afternoon but Erin had been forming the idea of opening an office in Northville Landing for when – not if, but when – the River Queen was restored and ready for business. And she planned to have Jessie run the office for her sudden good fortune, if such it ultimately became, also belonged to her dear friend and companion.

Though she had scanned the proposal given her by Windom, several times, and could detect no faults in it, Erin knew it required the input of a lawyer. She arranged to visit Mr Abernethy and have him guide her.

Early the following morning she sat in lawyer Abernethy's office watching him read the agreement. He made notes on a pad of yellow paper and from time to time glanced up to look at her. Erin was fraught with anxiety as she waited for his verdict. What if he found all manner of hidden problems? What if he still held to his opinion that she, as a mere woman, would be completely out of her depth in attempting to run a boatyard and restore a Mississippi paddle-steamer? Even more concerning: what if he was right?

Finally, after what seemed to Erin an eternity, Mr Abernethy made a final entry on his pad, set the agreement on the desk and looked at her. He smiled.

"My dear Miss Dubois," he said, "I had absolutely no idea of what would follow our initial meeting. What my colleague in Natchez told you is quite remarkable, astonishing even, and it has quite wonderfully changed your life."

"Has it, Mr Abernethy?" Erin said.

"Indeed it has," he said, lifting the document once again from the table. "Your brother-in-law has been most agreeable in his proposals and generous in finding the additional finance you will require. What you propose to do will not be easy, but I suspect you realize that and will not be turned from it.

"You will be in charge of the entire venture and on your shoulders will rest its success ... or failure. But I have a feeling it will be the former and I would certainly recommend you sign the agreement for I can detect no legal or moral impediment to it. It is an excellent document, a fair and honest one, and one you may sign without concern."

Erin had a strong desire to hurl herself across the lawyer's desk and embrace him but she curbed it and simply smiled and thanked him and assured him that he was now the legal guardian of the Natchez Mississippi Construction Company.

As she shook Mr Abernethy's hand and was escorted to the street where Jessie awaited her with the buggy, Erin had the strong feeling that this was the first day of the rest of her life, and she was determined to grasp it fully.

Chapter 12

A PALE, WATERY MORNING SUN was fighting to claw its way into a new day against a mist drifting from the river. Wrapped against the lingering cold of the night, Olivia Julianne, a hand covering the horse's nose to keep it quiet, led the buggy down the driveway and climbed aboard only upon reaching the road. She flicked the reins and turned to the riverside road on her mission.

It was well into the afternoon when she crossed into Sutton County, having stopped briefly to visit with friends and warm herself with a hot, late breakfast. She knew where she was going for on many occasions she had been a guest of the Curiston family in their fine mansion. Only it was no longer their mansion since they had been cheated out of it by Yankee interlopers, the despised carpetbaggers.

The Curistons, she had learned from her friends, were now living in poverty in a log cabin some way out of Sutton City and she had also been given directions to it.

Many families such as the Curistons had lost their homes to the Northerners who had swarmed like a plague into the defeated Confederacy, cheating and thieving their way to the possession of homes, businesses and land of those no longer able to sustain ownership.

Olivia Julianne reached the cabin, a miserable and broken

property, and knocked on the door, listening to the anxious sounds within. Presently the door was eased open and she saw the ashen face of Mrs Lucy Curiston.

"Why, Mrs Thynne," Mrs Curiston said and opened the door fully to beckon her inside.

The cabin was a cramped, two-room building furnished sparely with several chairs set around a table. A fire crackled and sparked in the stone grate and smoke billowed from it into the room. On the table Olivia Julianne saw four tin plates and a pot of now cold meal mash.

Olivia Julianne embraced Mrs Curiston who, she noticed, had clearly been crying. The two Curiston children – Helen and Jeffrey – on hearing the arrival of a visitor came from the bedroom.

"I have come to help you, dear Lucy," Olivia Julianne said, reaching out to draw the children to her to embrace. "You must gather together all your belongings and in the evening some people, friends of mine, will come and collect you and bring you to Natchez."

Mrs Curiston listened in disbelieving silence.

"Where is your husband, Lucy?"

Mrs Curiston gathered herself. "John has gone into town in search of work, as he has each morning since we … since …"

"Since your home was stolen from you," Olivia Julianne said. "And your injustice will be avenged quite soon. In the meantime you must send for John, Jeffrey could go and seek his father, and be ready to move. You cannot live in such awful circumstances a moment longer than it is necessary."

"But where will we live? We have not the means to obtain a better home."

"That has been taken care of," Olivia Julianne assured her. "It will not be as grand as the home you have lost but it will be a home of warmth and comfort," she turned to Jeffrey, "Now, young man, you must hurry along and tell your papa to return as quickly as he can."

"How can we ever thank you?" Mrs Curiston asked.

"By living happily as a good family should. There is no other thanks required," Olivia Julianne said.

As Jeffrey looked for his coat and while his mother's attention was distracted, Olivia Julianne took a roll of Dollars from her purse and slipped it under one of the plates.

"Now, Lucy, I have some people to speak to and I must hurry. This evening, then ... I will see you in Natchez."

She travelled along the main street – in truth, the only street – of Sutton City and stopped at a stone, two-storey building. A sign across the front revealed it to be the Quinion Printing Company. She tied the horse to a post and pushed open the door. Desmond Quinion, the man who had brought news of the plight of the Curistons to the Delafield ball, greeted her and showed her to an office at the rear of the building.

"I have brought news of the house in Natchez for the Curistons," Olivia Julianne said, "And this is a letter Colonel Sinclair asked me to deliver into your hands."

Quinion took the sealed letter and read it. He nodded.

"That is excellent," he said. "Please inform the colonel and the others that we will be ready for their arrival. Tell him we will be some twenty strong."

As he showed Olivia Julianne from the office he thanked her for helping the Curiston family.

Three days following Olivia Julianne's visit to Sutton City several groups of men made their way from Natchez by various means to distract attention from the curious and turned towards Sutton City.

Over the course of several hours they gathered at the printing shop where they were joined by the men Quinion had promised, the total numbering some thirty-five.

"The house is occupied by a man called Thomas Smith, though I doubt that is his real name. He has around twenty-five men protecting the property, mostly drunken ne'er-do-wells gathered from the County's saloons and gaming houses. I have a spy placed among them and I am informed that they have stolen, wrecked or sold most of the valuables and have reduced what was once a house of culture and refinement to a pitiful state," Quinion reported to the men. "One other thing: Smith is not the main man, I am told he is too addled with drink and too stupid to be in charge of the thing. I believe the carpetbaggers to be under the direction of a more powerful man, or group of men."

"And we are here to right a terrible wrong," Colonel Sinclair said. "It is our duty to protect our own people and rid the South of such a calamity. Since Mrs Thynne returned to Natchez I have worked out what I believe will be a successful strategy. If you will gather round I will outline our actions."

He spread a map across the desk and the men pushed forward to look at it. It was a map of the area of Sutton County that contained the Curiston Plantation and the roads and lanes leading to and surrounding it. The colonel quietly outlined what they were about to undertake and each group that had been given a specific task made notes and broke to discuss it between themselves.

"Gentlemen," Colonel Sinclair said after a few minutes, "we will rest for an hour and prepare ourselves. I plan to move out at midnight."

Quinion distributed a tot of whiskey to each of the men and waited for the colonel to propose a toast to the venture.

"Gentlemen, we are about to embark on a dangerous task, but a task that has, alas, become increasingly necessary in these unhappy times. I give you the United Veterans League for Southern Renewal," he raised his glass and they saluted him.

As the grandfather clock in the office of the printing shop chimed 11.30pm the men blackened their faces with ash and soot and donned black, hooded robes. They checked their weapons and, again in small groups, exited the building at the rear and trotted off to where they would meet up for the rest of their journey.

They rode silently, a line of horsemen silhouetted against a white, pale moon, as they approached the Curiston mansion. To minimise the sound of the trotting animals the men rode in two lines along the grass verges of the stone driveway and then split into two parties to ride around the house and encircle it. Quinion led one of the lines and the colonel the other, both clear on what they were to do.

The colonel and two of his men dismounted and crept towards the front of the house. From inside they heard the laughter and drunken cursing of the interlopers and detected several female voices. Colonel Sinclair indicated to one of his men that he should move from hiding to one of the windows, the better to report what was happening inside and how many were in the room.

Presently the man returned and joined the colonel.

"I counted twelve men, they all looked in a sorry state of inebriation, and saw four women, three white and one mulatto, all in a state of undress and just as drunk as the men. The room is in a sorry state, sir, broken and torn furniture."

At the rear of the house, Quinion saw two men, armed with rifles and lounging idly at a half-open kitchen door, passing a bottle of whiskey between them.

He directed a man to join him and together they crept from the cover of the bushes. The drinkers were taken by surprise and the swiftness of the attack. Quinion throttled one of the men with a length of rope and his companion struck the other with a rock. They dragged the men back into the garden and Quinion took a knife from his belt and sliced its blade across their throats. He wiped the blood from the blade on the dewed grass and waved his men forward.

Colonel Sinclair and another of the robed men crept to the front door and knocked on it, listening to the footsteps coming towards them. The door opened and a man, his arm around the shoulder of a naked woman, stepped out to the porch. The colonel moved from the shadows at the side of the door and struck the man's head with his gun. The man groaned and vomited and fell down the steps to lie on the grass. The woman filled her lungs for a scream but the robed man grabbed her, placed a hand over her roughed lips and carried her to the bushes.

"Best get moving," he told the woman. "And don't go raising no alarms. Now get."

"You bastard," the woman snarled. "I got no clothes; let me go get something to wear. I swear I won't tell."

The man glared at her and she spat at him before running off along the driveway.

Colonel Sinclair raised his arm and several of his men took up position at the windows, the rest joining him at the door. He counted to three and nodded.

At the rear of the house Quinion and his men waited for the signal, lined along the wall ready to move inside.

The colonel eased open the front door and stepped inside. He heard the noise from the room just along the hallway to his left and turned to wave the rest of his men to follow him. He told two men to wait in the hallway in case there was anyone upstairs in the bedrooms and peered into the room.

Groups of the carpetbaggers were scattered around the room, drinking and kissing and fondling the women. He watched as one man smashed the glass in a bookcase and grab a handful of volumes to throw onto the fire. Another finished off a bottle of brandy and, laughing, hurled it through the window.

One of the colonel's men pointed to a man seated in a big red leather chair by the fire, smoking a cigar.

"That's the man calls himself Thomas Smith, Colonel," he said.

"I want him alive," Colonel Sinclair said. "If Quinion is correct and he is taking orders I want to find out from whom. The others are riff-raff … it does not matter what happens to them. Go get the men ready, they all know what to do."

When the man had travelled the line waiting and nodded their readiness, the colonel kicked open the door, stepped inside and shot the man who had thrown the books onto the fire. His men followed, firing and yelling.

In the hallway, the two men watched as a man, dressed only in Long Johns, staggered from a bedroom to the staircase. One of the men waited for him to come half-way down the stairs and shot him. The man clutched his throat and blood spurted through his fingers. He stumbled, reached vainly for the banister and tumbled down to the hallway.

Quinion and his men heard the shooting and rushed through the back door.

The fight, conducted in loud confusion and screaming from the terrified women, lasted for some twenty minutes and concluded with the surviving trespassers surrendering and begging not to be shot.

Smith had made a futile attempt to escape the fight but was

caught as he frantically tried to open the windows leading to the garden and freedom. He was dragged to face the colonel and Quinion while his companions and the women were pushed outside.

Quinion grabbed Smith by the throat.

"Who ordered you to evict the Curistons?" he demanded, slapping Smith's face.

"I don't know his name, honest to God mister. I never met him," Smith snivelled.

"That is most unfortunate, Mr Smith," Colonel Sinclair said. "For if you cannot tell us what we wish to know you are of no significant use to us, are you? Indeed, you are of no further use to anyone."

"Swear to God, mister, I don't know any names. I only know the man who hired me and the boys is a Northerner ... we didn't mean no harm, honest to God."

"One last chance," Quinion said, pushing his Colt under Smith's chin. "You give us his name and just maybe you'll get to walk out of here instead of being carried out."

"Damnation, I'd tell you if I knew."

Quinion shook his head in disappointment ... and fired his gun.

The colonel ordered his men to search the house thoroughly in case any of Smith's men were hiding out and when this was done with no stragglers found he told several of his men to get the wounded to a doctor. He told his men to leave the bodies where they lay, as a warning to others.

"We are finished here," Colonel Sinclair said. "Let us go." He turned to a companion. "Are we all here?"

The man reported no major injuries save some flesh wounds and the colonel ordered them all outside to where the women and the surviving carpetbaggers had been gathered.

Quinion walked to the group.

"You all have until dawn to get the hell out of Sutton County ... and if any of your miserable faces are seen this side of the Potomac ever again you'll be strung up."

He fired into the air and the group scattered in panic into the trees and along the driveway.

The party returned to Natchez in the small, inconspicuous groups they had come in while Colonel Sinclair went to satisfy himself that the Curiston family had been conveyed safely to their new home.

Chapter 13

THE MAN AT NO TIME made contact with Gabriel or any of the workmen, save for a vague nod of the head in passing. He carried several sheets of paper folded in half and made notes as he walked around the boatyard and along the jetty to look up at the River Queen. He did this for two days and then vanished from sight.

Matthew had viewed the stranger with suspicion from the deck of the riverboat and conveyed his suspicion with a look that seemed to intimidate the man for he made no attempt to board.

"That man," Matthew asked when he had the opportunity to speak with Gabriel. "Who was he?"

Gabriel shrugged his shoulders.

"Damned if I know," he said. "Figured he was connected with the money men, maybe one of Thynne's associates. He kept out of my way so I wasn't complaining. I got enough work to do getting the place manned and ready for when Miss Dubois returns."

"And the sooner she does the better," Matthew said. "Until then I suggest you detail six of your toughest men to patrol the yard, armed with rifles and accompanied by several hungry mutts. And if I were you I would post a notice on the gate warning any visitor you don't recognize instantly that he better report to the office before you set the dogs on him."

Gabriel mulled the thought in his head and nodded.

"Guess we could do that very thing."

"It would put an end to strangers roaming about making copious notes," Matthew said. "I'm not partial to strangers making notes about the River Queen."

He had quite taken to living on board the riverboat, to working relentlessly on making it shipshape. Miss Dubois had already expressed her gratitude and, to his surprise, he found himself thinking about her. He was, of course, well aware of his indebtedness to Erin for providing a roof over his head and money in his pocket, given the sort of accommodation he had had to endure in the service of the Army of the Confederacy, a bivouac if he was lucky though more often than not a sheet of torn canvas tied between two blasted stumps in a waterlogged field, if he was lucky enough.

Indeed, he thought of the River Queen as his personal project ... but increasingly he thought of Miss Erin Dubois.

Brent accompanied Colonel Sinclair to Northville Landing on the Delta Pride for he was anxious to see Erin. News of the raid on the Curiston home had spread throughout the Sutton County area and had been reported in the Natchez Weekly Courier, though with no discernible sympathy for the carpetbagger victims.

As they sat in the riverboat's saloon Brent referred to the raid but merely received a vague reply concerning the "difficult times we live in" from the colonel. He chose not to press the matter.

"You are, you say, going to Northville Landing to see Miss Dubois," Colonel Sinclair said. "Do I detect an interest in the lady?"

"We have, I confess, developed a warm friendship," Brent said. "I spoke yesterday with Mrs Thynne who informed me her sister was preparing to return to Natchez. As you say, we do indeed live in difficult times and I would not have Miss Dubois travel on her own. I have some business to conduct in Northville Landing and will offer my assistance should the lady wish it."

"Oh, I think she will most assuredly wish it."

Having considered the advice of lawyer Abernethy concerning the proposals regarding the restoration and financing of the Natchez Mississippi Construction Company, Erin telegraphed her brother-in-law with a positive response. She would, she informed him, sign the contract and return as quickly as she could to Natchez.

Orell's prompt reply contained the heartening news that one of the backers he had attracted to the venture was anxious to discuss the building of several barges for his trading company.

Early in the morning following his arrival in Northville Landing, Brent rode to Erin's house and was ushered inside by Jessie who asked him to wait in the drawing-room while she went to find Miss Dubois. She hurried off and found Erin sitting in the garden.

"You have a gentleman caller," Jessie said, a wide and knowing smile lighting up her face. "A handsome gentleman caller he is too."

"Well gracious me," Erin said, "a handsome gentleman caller you say. We must not keep such a paragon waiting, then. Please bring the gentleman to me. Did this caller provide a name?"

"Yes, he said he was a Mr Brent Masterson, a friend of yours."

While Jessie went to fetch him, Erin composed herself. Even in the midst of her activities since returning to Northville Landing Brent had been increasingly in her thoughts, and he was now come to call upon her. It was, in every sense, a moment to be cherished.

He stood at the open windows looking at her and when she turned to greet him he walked from the house and took her hands in his, lifting them to his lips.

"My dear Erin," he said, still holding her hands, "I hope I have not come calling at an inopportune moment."

"Not at all," Erin said and still holding his hand she led him to the chairs on the porch.

"I have missed you," he said. "I had business here in town and your sister said you were to return shortly to Natchez … if you have no objection, I should be honoured if you would allow me to escort you."

It would, she said, be an excellent arrangement for she did indeed plan to take the Delta Pride when it returned from New Orleans.

From the house, Jessie watched the little drama. She knew already about Mr Masterson for since she had returned from Natchez Erin had spoken of him, often and with some passion. He was, she allowed, quite the most handsome of men and he seemed, even on such a brief sighting, to care a great deal about her friend. She would, still, reserve a concluding judgement on the gentleman for Jessie was by nature a cautious soul.

She went to the couple to ask if they cared for some refreshment and Erin suggested a jar of lemonade would be ideal for the morning sun was glowing from a cloudless, purple sky.

Brent stayed until the early afternoon, walking with Erin to look at the river busy with boats and barges, and departed to attend to business matters. He promised to return in the evening to join Erin for dinner.

Erin watched as he rode from the house and turned towards the town. When she was certain she could no longer see him she returned to the garden but though she held several pages of important documents her thoughts were elsewhere.

Three days later Erin had completed her business with lawyer Abernethy and discussed her plans for the immediate future with Jessie, including the proposed setting up of a booking office in town for when the River Queen was ready for service. They also talked about the retention of her home which Jessie would continue to live in and maintain.

She and Brent boarded the Delta Pride and returned to Natchez.

Olivia Julianne, who was still not won over to the idea of her sister running the boatyard or attempting to restore the River Queen, was nevertheless happy to have Erin back in Natchez. She even joined Erin, with surprising enthusiasm, in looking for a house; Olivia Julianne knew the best locations, the right people and had, though few people realised it, purchased several houses herself.

Several days after launching their search the sisters found exactly what they were looking for and Erin made the necessary financial arrangements to secure ownership.

It had once belonged to a family Olivia Julianne knew well before the war. The family had lost two sons at the siege of Vicksburg and had moved to Charleston. It was a white painted, timber-framed house that had four spacious bedrooms and though Erin initially considered it too large she could not help herself taking to its faded charm and particularly to the large plot of land it sat in. And anyway, she could afford it and was further assured by Olivia Julianne that with proper restoration it would increase in value and would become one of the "great houses" of Natchez.

Olivia Julianne, to Erin's amusement, was beside herself with the anticipation of furnishing and decorating the house. Erin was, though she would never have confessed it, quite content to turn her sister loose on the task – while retaining a semblance of control over how far she would allow the work to go – since she had other, pressing matters to attend to regarding the yard.

And, of course, regarding her growing relationship with Brent. Since their return to Natchez he had been a constant visitor, had escorted her twice to the theatre and on several riverside drives and picnics.

So much so that their families and friends now considered them as handsome a couple as they could ever hope to see, a couple clearly destined to …

To what?

Erin was sure, or as sure as she could be, that Brent cared for her. She was equally sure, or as sure as she could be, that she returned such feelings. Yet neither had actually said so, not in so many words, and she was often troubled by doubts over where they were going. If Brent cared for her, did he love her? If she cared for him, did she love him?

She was uncertain, and of that she was sure. And she wondered why she was uncertain for he was kindness and consideration itself, he was handsome and wealthy and thought highly of by those who knew him and she had never felt quite the same about any of her previous suitors.

It was anyway, she concluded, a distraction she did not need. She was driving the buggy to the yard and that was distraction enough. She needed to obtain a detailed report from Gabriel on the work still necessary to bring the place into full operation and that should be her main occupation.

As she steered the buggy to the front gate she found it was locked and guarded by a large man with a rifle and a dog that eyed her with suspicion. She got down and approached the gate.

"Yes, ma'am," the man said. "Are you lost?"

"No, I am most certainly not lost."

"Beg your pardon, ma'am, but who are you?"

"Would you be kind enough to open the gate and let me in?"

"Now then, Charlie, no need to keep the lady waiting."

Erin saw that it was Matthew.

Charlie still seemed reluctant.

"This is Miss Dubois and she is the owner of the yard," Matthew said and walked forward to unlock the chain securing the gate.

"I was beginning to have doubts about it being my yard," Erin said. "And I am surprised to see you are still here."

She somehow always considered him a will-o-the-whisp given the manner of his arrival in her life.

"Nowhere better to go," Matthew said. "And I still have work to do on the lady …." He smiled his infuriating smile. "On behalf of Charlie and Rex, that's the dog by the way, I apologise. We had a snooper recently and had to discourage curious visitors. I guess Gabriel can fill in the details."

He tipped his hat – that infuriating old gray hat – and pulled open the gate, bowing elaborately as she passed through.

Gabriel was sitting at a desk in the office when she entered. He stood to greet her.

"Good to have you back, Miss Dubois … you got a look, a look that says you 'aint in an easy mood."

"Well I had to obtain permission to come into my own yard from that Mr Morgan who has a devilish way of annoying a person."

Gabriel offered her a cup of coffee and she sat down.

"That's as maybe," he said, "but he's sure been useful to have around and a stranger was about the place couple of weeks ago making notes. Matthew didn't much care for him."

"I suppose he threw him in the river, it seems the sort of thing he would do."

"Nope," Gabriel said, "but we decided to look to our security arrangements. Sorry if it threw you out of kilter, ma'am."

"No, not at all. I will speak to Mr Thynne about the matter for I imagine your curious stranger was merely one of his men. What has been done regarding your workmen?"

Gabriel explained that he had managed to sign up almost all of the men who had worked in the yard for Mr Riparian and they had been set the task of restoring the machinery, repairing the workshops and generally making ready the yard. They had even commenced preparations for the construction of the barges ordered by one of the financial backers.

He further told her that her brother-in-law had visited the yard and explained that the money to pay the men and to cover the work had been deposited in the First Trust Bank of Natchez and as foreman he had been given the authority to control such payments, weekly statements being forwarded to Orell pending her arrival back in Natchez.

"Goodness," said Erin. "Then we may safely say that the Natchez Mississippi Construction Company is truly in business. I am very proud of what you have achieved, Gabriel."

"Might I show you around the yard, ma'am?"

They walked from the office and Gabriel escorted her from one workshop to another, introducing her to the men. They walked along the jetty to where the River Queen remained moored.

"And what of Mr Morgan?" Erin asked as she looked up at the vessel. "Has he been gainfully occupied?"

"Indeed he has. Tread carefully and follow me and you will see for yourself."

Gabriel held out his hand and together they walked up the gangplank and along the deck to a narrow staircase leading down into the boilers and engine room.

Lamps and candles cast islands of yellow light through the darkness and Erin stood halfway down the staircase while her eyes adjusted.

She finally saw Matthew. He was standing in a pool of evil-smelling black oil, stripped to the waist and smeared in grease and dirt. He was hammering at a large pipe, the clang-clang-clang bouncing off the walls of the vessel.

A gang of equally dirty, sweating men busied themselves with removing and replacing parts of the engines and boilers.

"I think he's determined to get the River Queen back on the river, he never stops hammering and banging," Gabriel said.

Erin watched Matthew, who had not noticed her presence, and smiled. He was wearing his slouch hat.

"Does he never take that infuriating hat off?" she asked.

Erin continued her tour of the yard and returned home towards the late evening to be met by an excited Olivia Julianne who was waiting for her at the front door with a piece of notepaper in her hand.

"Erin," her sister called and raced to meet her. "We have been invited by Brent's sister Lydia to attend a dinner party in her home tomorrow evening. Is that not excellent news?"

"Well it is certainly pleasant news for Lydia is a perfectly pleasant person. Is the dinner in honour of some important event?"

"I do not know of any particular event, though I suspect there might well be an important announcement during its course. But tomorrow you must forsake going to your awful boatyard and we will visit my dressmaker and find you a new dress ... you never have a suitable dress to call your own and the lack must be put right."

Erin smiled thinly and cringed inwardly.

At heart she was still a school ma'am, albeit now a wealthy, business owning one, and searching for suitable dresses never ever appeared on her list of vital things to do.

"How positively delightful," she said with a degree of forced enthusiasm she prayed would satisfy Olivia Julianne.

As they sat at dinner, having been joined by Orell, Erin asked who else would be attending Lydia's dinner and found that her companions would be Lydia, of course, Brent, of course, and Olivia Julianne and Orell.

"A small, intimate gathering," Olivia Julianne said quite

unnecessarily. "But the most important thing is that your dear beau will be there."

"My beau," Erin said. "Who might that be, pray tell?"

Olivia Julianne flicked her napkin as though shooing away an irritating moth. "I think we are all aware of who that is. Now, finish your dinner and we will plan tomorrow's expedition into town."

They were driven the following evening to Lydia's home. During the day Olivia Julianne had, indeed, found a most suitable dress for Erin, who realized from the outset that she had no personal contribution to make in its selection. She was, happily, not discontented with it for it was a concoction of white silk trimmed at the sleeves and hem with a line of green. She conceded that she felt quite presentable in it.

Lydia's young daughters, Charlotte and Mary, were standing with their mother as the carriage approached the house and when they recognised Erin they danced and waved in delight. When the carriage came to a halt the girls raced to embrace Erin as she stepped down to the driveway. They took her by the hands and led her into the house, chattering excitedly, to where Brent was supervising the selection of wines for the meal. He turned on hearing the commotion and held out his hand to Erin.

"I apologise for not meeting you, my dear, we were having a problem getting the logs to catch fire."

"They seem to have surrendered to your expertise," Erin said, pointing to the flames now flickering brightly around the logs, "so you are forgiven."

Brent, still holding her hands in his, stepped back to look at her. "You look beautiful," he said and raised her right hand to his lips. Charlotte and Mary nudged one another and giggled.

Lydia took Erin's arm and seated her, Olivia Julianne and Orell in the circle of chairs around the fire. A maid offered the ladies sherry while Brent, raising a decanter in Orell's direction, poured two glasses of whiskey.

"Your brother was very kind to escort me back to Natchez on the Delta Pride," Erin said to Lydia. "I appreciated his thoughtfulness."

"He is a thoughtful man and would not countenance your travelling alone," Lydia said. "Now please relax while I see how dinner is progressing."

She arose and as she reached the door the girls burst into the room and threw themselves on Erin, who hugged them.

"Girls, girls," Lydia said and rolled her eyes, "You must not smother Miss Dubois. Indeed, it is time you were getting ready for bed."

"Oh mama," Mary pleaded. "Might we not stay up a little longer?"

"No, you may not for you have school tomorrow so off you go."

"May Miss Dubois read us a bedtime story, mama?" asked Charlotte.

"Miss Dubois is here as our guest, not as your nursemaid."

Erin stood and placed an arm around each of the girls, steering them towards the door.

"It would give me great pleasure to read you a story," she said and ushered the girls up the staircase to their room.

When the girls had donned their nightdresses and Erin had tucked them in she sat on the bed.

"I will not read you a story," she said and the girls protested in disappointment. "But you will tell me a story instead, starting with you Charlotte and then you Mary will continue it."

She listened with a smile as the girls invented fairies and elves, forest creatures and a good witch in an elaborate adventure. And she waited until their eyes drooped and, clutching a small ragdoll each, they fell fast asleep.

She kissed them on the cheek and rose gently to leave. At the bedroom door Brent stood watching her and waiting to escort her to dinner. As they walked along the corridor to the stairs he stopped Erin, pulled her to him and kissed her.

"The girls adore you, you must see it," he said. "You certainly have a way with children."

She clung to him, uncertain of what to say, what to do, only to hold him. He kissed her again and, taking her arm in his, led her down the stairs.

As they approached the drawing-room door Erin took a deep breath and as best she could composed herself.

"Will you walk with me in the garden after dinner?" Brent whispered and Erin nodded, her heart racing.

Chapter 14

COLONEL SINCLAIR CHECKED THE TIME on his pocket watch as the gloom of evening crept into his office. It was 6.56pm. He had been working at his desk for most of the day and suddenly remembered he had arranged to collect Amelia at her dancing class just along the street from where he had his office.

He opened a desk drawer and from it took a key. Collecting the papers in front of him he rose and locked them in a large safe. He tucked the key into his waistcoat pocket and patted it. He looked around the room, turned down the lamps and walked to the street.

Northville Landing was concluding another day's business, its citizens walking or driving to their homes. As he made his way to Miss Virginia Sweeney's Dance Academy to meet Amelia he greeted several friends and business associates.

Since experiencing the excitement of her first ball, Amelia had become obsessed with learning all the latest dances for she had determined to attend as many such balls as she could and vowed that no lack of knowledge or ability would reduce her to a frustrated wallflower … if a handsome young gentleman sought her hand in the dance she would be able to perform it with elegance and confidence. Miss Virginia Sweeney was greatly accommodating her in her quest.

Colonel Sinclair walked into the Academy and stood at the

back of the room listening to the tinkling piano and watching Miss Sweeney, clutching a long staff which she tapped on the hardwood floor to the beat of the music.

"Girls, girls," Miss Sweeney kept ordering. "To the wall, centre, turn, to the wall."

The colonel smiled as he caught his daughter's eye.

Miss Sweeney nodded curtly at the pianist and the music stopped. She walked around the girls – all girls – now standing in pairs.

"Excellent, quite excellent," she said, while still adjusting the pairs into better positions. "I am delighted at your progress. Now, you may go and collect your things … and the next class is at 5.30pm on Friday."

Amelia rushed to hug her father.

"You are a most accomplished and beautiful dancer, my dear," the colonel said and placed an arm around her shoulders.

"Might we hold a ball soon, papa? It would be so pleasant to have a ball."

The colonel smiled. There had not been a ball, nor a dinner party, at his home since the death three years past of his wife, Amelia's mother. Perhaps, he conceded, it was time laughter and colour were restored to the house.

He and Amelia walked along the boardwalk. The number of people had thinned out considerably as father and daughter approached the livery stable to collect their landau.

Neither saw the figure standing in the shadows of a narrow alleyway between the bank and a general store, not until the figure stepped from the dark and stood in front of them. The figure wore a scarf wound around his mouth and a hat with its brim pulled down to cover the eyes.

The figure stepped forward and plunged a long knife into the colonel's ribs, twisting it several times. The colonel staggered forward, clutching his stomach, and stumbled from the boardwalk into the street as his attacker turned and ran back along the alleyway.

Amelia screamed and kneeled to cradle her father's head. Blood stained her dress and she placed her hands over the wound in a vain attempt to stop the pumping blood, oozing through her fingers. Her continued scream brought people to her.

They carried the colonel across the road to a doctor, Amelia clutching his hand, but there was nothing to be done that would save him. The doctor gave Amelia a sedative and his wife helped her to a bedroom.

Jessie, who came across the commotion while leaving the general store, conveyed news of the death of Colonel Sinclair by telegraph to Erin in Natchez. It was further covered several days later by the Natchez newspapers since he had been prominent in local business circles as well as a highly regarded hero during the war. The main point of the dispatches was that he had been slain by an unknown hand for reasons that were equally obscured.

Erin, on reading Jessie's telegraph, subsequently sought details regarding the situation of Amelia and discovered that the girl had been left a considerable sum of money as well as the Sinclair home but would be alone in the house save for a housekeeper.

She gave the matter some thought and, after consulting Jessie, Erin arrived at a decision. She had always held Amelia in great affection for she had taught her and watched her grow into a charming and beautiful young woman. Therefore, she would ask Amelia to come live with her in the Natchez house, which was certainly large enough, and would do so as soon as she could return to Northville Landing.

Erin, still greatly upset at the colonel's tragic and mysterious death, had placed her intentions before Olivia Julianne and had been supported enthusiastically by her sister, who promised to do all she could to make Amelia welcome. Furthermore, since Jessie was to remain in Northville Landing, eventually to run an office on behalf of the Natchez Mississippi Construction Company and for the service Erin planned for the River Queen, Olivia Julianne sought the services of a small staff for the new house.

There was, though, something far more pressing for Olivia Julianne to consider: what had Brent said to her sister when they had walked in the garden on the evening of the dinner at Lydia's?

Erin had been annoyingly tight-lipped over the events that so consumed Olivia Julianne and she was determined to satisfy her curiosity. She sat with Erin in the drawing-room, idly fingering the unread pages of a book.

"He asked you to marry him, did he not?" Olivia Julianne said, the direct approach being, she felt, the best.

Erin, who was clearly taking a teasing delight in her sister's anxiety, merely smiled, attempted to convey the silliness of such a thought and returned to her needlework.

But Olivia Julianne was not to be diverted.

"Lydia told me herself that Brent was determined to ask you to be his bride," she said. "So I think you should tell me if he did or not."

Erin put down her sewing and smiled.

"My darling sister," she said. "If you think it sufficiently of interest and if it will calm your vapours then I can tell you that Brent did, indeed, say he would be the happiest man in the world, indeed I distinctly recall he said in the entire universe, if I consented to become his wife."

Olivia Julianne screeched in delight and embraced Erin.

"And of course you said yes," she said.

"I said I would give his kind and tender proposal a considerable amount of thought and present him with an answer as swiftly as I can."

"How could you toy with his affections in such a thoughtless manner," Olivia Julianne said. "You really are a mystery. He is as fine a gentleman as you would find – you are, indeed, fortunate to have found him – and you would be foolish to reject him."

"I did not say I have rejected him, nor that I intend to reject him," Erin protested. "I merely said I would give the idea some thought. I do not think it will cause him any untoward harm to be kept waiting. I will, therefore, keep him waiting …"

"And then what will you say?"

"And then I will quite possibly say I am flattered and would be extremely happy to become Mrs Brent Masterson."

Olivia Julianne screeched again and again embraced Erin.

"Impossible," she muttered. "You are impossible!"

There was another matter that constantly occupied Olivia

Julianne's thoughts, that of her sister's involvement in the boatyard. It was a matter she could never be reconciled with and here was an opportunity to put it to rest.

"When you are married," she said, "where will you and dear Brent live?"

"I have absolutely no idea, Olivia. I believe he mentioned several hotels so we might live in one of them. I have two homes of my own. I have given it so little thought, I confess."

"But now, of course, you will have to give up this ridiculous obsession you have developed with your boatyard."

Erin wondered how long it would take her sister to stray down her well-worn path and was determined to have the matter settled once and for all. She once more set aside her needlework and glared at Olivia Julianne.

"Why," she began, "would I wish to give up my company? It is certainly not a ridiculous obsession, indeed it is a most worthwhile venture with an extremely promising future. So much so, indeed, that your own husband and several of his business friends have invested in it, one has even presented us with a contract to build him barges.

"All of that being the case, Olivia, why would you think such a thing?"

"But you will be marrying one of the wealthiest men in the South ... and, besides, it is not ladylike, most decidedly not ladylike. A lady should not be working in a boatyard."

"A boatyard she owns. A boatyard in which this particular lady has provided employment for some thirty men who would otherwise not have two cents to rattle in their pockets. I may be, as people have been too prone to reminding me, a mere woman but we are living in the 19th century and not the dark ages and a woman, mere notwithstanding, may follow whatever path she chooses ... and that is an end to any further discussion on the matter."

Olivia Julianne huffed her displeasure and returned to flicking angrily through her book. She would, she decided, let the matter drop for the moment. Perhaps, she considered, she would broach the subject with Brent. Working in a filthy boatyard with thirty ruffians, the very idea! Brent would surely not stand for it.

Erin had, of course, spoken the truth for the Natchez Mississippi Construction Company was thriving. The workshops were busy and advertising placed in newspapers in all of the large centres along the river was attracting attention and, even better, orders.

Erin, though, wished to devote her full attention to restoring the River Queen and to seeing it ply its trade along the Mississippi. She had plans for the paddle-steamer ... and she found herself smiling at the thought of discussing them with Gabriel and Matthew, the infuriating Mr Morgan.

Chapter 15

IT WAS, ERIN TOLD GABRIEL as they walked through the rooms and cabins of the River Queen, to be the finest, most lavish, most talked about vessel on the river, she would have it no other way. It would provide the best service between Natchez, New Orleans and all points between and beyond. People would book passage on board her even if they had nowhere in particular to go, simply for the privilege of telling their friends they had been on board.

It would serve passengers the best food and drink on the finest linen and with the finest china plates and silver cutlery, it would pamper them in the most comfortable cabins available on the Mississippi with the softest sheets and it would entertain them with the best singers, dancers and musicians that could be found. Crystal chandeliers would hang from the ceiling to charm and dazzle the travellers.

Though she did not express it in such an indelicate manner, it would also relieve the passengers of their money in such a luxurious gaming-room that they would return for more financial humiliation and love every minute of it.

"But, ma'am," Gabriel said cautiously, "have we the finance to provide all that you wish?"

"We have," Erin assured him, "and if we run out of it we

will find more. It is up to you and your men to see that the River Queen is restored to glory and on the river as swiftly as possible."

They returned to the office where Erin handed Gabriel several rolled drawings and plans of how she wished the vessel to look. It was, Gabriel thought as he unrolled the papers and studied them, a mammoth undertaking.

"Can it be achieved? Can you and the men do it?" Erin asked.

"Guess we can, Miss Dubois, guess we can."

"That is all I need to hear, the rest is in your hands."

She had searched for Matthew during her tour of inspection for Erin wished to thank him once again for the work he had contributed to cleaning up the boat. She had not, however, seen him.

"Has Mr Morgan finally deserted us?" she asked coyly, as though the answer would be of little consequence to her.

"Not at all, ma'am," Gabriel said. "I reckon he is below still working at the boilers and engine. He sure is putting in an effort. He and the men have caulked the old lady and she's as watertight as she's ever been. Why do you ask?"

Erin shrugged, as indifferently as she could.

"Gracious me, no reason whatsoever. Judging by the manner of his coming I always suspect his going will be equally suspicious. Other than that, I have no particular reason to give Mr Morgan a moment's consideration."

She busied herself with the idle flicking of papers around the desk and Gabriel smiled to himself.

"Didn't think you had," he muttered under his breath.

Erin took a shawl from the back of a chair and, draping it around her shoulders, walked across the yard to speak to the men in the carpentry workshop. Gabriel gathered some of the rolls, tucked them under his arm and walked across the yard towards the river where the barges were being built.

Presently Erin returned across the yard to the office and when she entered she was surprised to see Matthew standing at the desk examining the remaining plans for the River Queen. She gasped at seeing him. He glanced up and tipped his hat.

"Mr Morgan, I am surprised to see you and surprised and relieved to see you have not drawn a gun on me. What are you doing?" Erin asked.

"Ma'am, always a delight," Matthew said. "I came looking for Gabriel to tell him we have finished work on the boilers but we need some new pipes, I can't find any old ones good enough to salvage."

"I see you have found the plans for the River Queen," Erin said, moving to his side. "I am sorry to tell you we will soon be invading your adopted home. What do you make of the plans?"

Matthew flicked through the documents.

"Guess I will just have to find somewhere else to live, ma'am. But I think you have done the old lady proud, she will be a truly fine Queen. Why, I might even sign on as a deck-hand when she's on the river, with your permission of course."

"I do not think you have ever sought anyone's permission to do anything, Mr Morgan, but you may sign on as anything you like."

"Well, that is surely generous of you, Miss Dubois ... means I can get to New Orleans and have some adventures there."

"I expect you will," Erin said. "Doubtless some adventures with ladies of ill repute. I expect you have many such friends."

Matthew smiled ... that infuriating smile. Erin, realising what she had just suggested, was discomforted by her lack of decorum.

"One thing, ma'am," he said, simply returning to the plans. "You going to paint the Queen in blue and white?"

"I have not fully decided. Have you any objections to such an idea?"

"It's your boat, ma'am, but I never counted blue as my favourite colour."

He bowed and put his hat on. At the door he turned and smiled ... and walked off across the yard.

Erin sat down and slapped her hands on the desk.

"Oh!" she fumed. "That infuriating man!"

She had, however, a more pleasant task awaiting her in the afternoon, for when she had returned to her sister's house to work in peace and quiet on some papers and contracts she found Brent sitting in the garden with Olivia Julianne.

Erin stood at the door of the library overlooking the garden. She had the feeling that Olivia Julianne was pressing Brent for a progress report on his proposal and knew that she was required to provide him with an answer, of one sort or another.

He was, she thought, running the pros and cons through her mind, quite the most handsome and attentive of men, he was wealthy and well considered by his friends and associates, he was in all respects a catch. Erin could find no prominent reasons to reject his proposal.

She pushed open the door and walked from the house to the garden. Olivia Julianne saw her and rose and was joined by Brent who had followed her gaze. He moved towards Erin and kissed her hand.

Olivia Julianne, sensing that an important moment had arrived, excused herself on the pretext of going to order a jug of fresh lemonade. Brent sat beside Erin on the wooden seat and held her hand.

"My dearest Brent," she said after a moment's thought, "I have given your proposal a great deal of thought …"

"And?"

She took his face in her hands.

"And I would be happy, very happy indeed, to become your wife."

Brent drew her to him and kissed her passionately. From the house Olivia Julianne watched and offered up a silent, heartfelt prayer.

The happy couple walked arm in arm to the house to deliver, officially, the tidings to Olivia Julianne who embraced them both and who, Erin could detect with alarm, was already planning every aspect of the wedding. Erin knew there would be no gainsaying her sister in the task.

Brent decided they needed some privacy and arranged for cook to prepare them a basket of food and drink and shortly after he drove his bride-to-be to the house she had purchased and which Olivia Julianne was overseeing, with enthusiasm, the refurbishment of. In truth, Erin had been too occupied by the affairs of the boatyard to take much of an interest on her house and was anxious to see what progress had been made.

Quite a great deal, as it turned out. On their arrival Erin was surprised to see several rooms had been painted, drapes put up, carpets spread around polished wooden floors, paintings hung and comfortable furniture placed eloquently about. Even the garden had been attended to, the grass trimmed, seats and a large table positioned in the shade of a tree, flowers planted … Olivia Julianne had certainly worked wonders.

She and Brent stood side by side in the garden and watched the late afternoon sun drift gently through small, fluffy white clouds. Above them birds sang and chased one another through the leaves.

"What a perfectly wonderful day," Erin said.

Brent smiled and reaching out drew her into his arms and kissed her.

They ate the food and toasted their future with a bottle of Orell's finest wine that cook, being informed of the occasion, had tucked into the basket. It was, indeed, a perfectly wonderful day.

Presently Brent took Erin's hand.

"I must, alas, leave you for a short time," he said, and sensing Erin's concern quickly assured her. "I have important business to attend to at one of my hotels, the one in Lynchburg, and I cannot avoid it. But I will return as quickly as I can … and I want us to be wed without delay. I love you very much, my dearest Erin."

They spent the rest of the day exploring the house and walking in the garden until, reluctantly, they returned to Olivia Julianne's house and Brent departed to tell his sister, Lydia, of Erin's acceptance and their coming wedding.

Erin stood in the driveway and watched him leave. She returned to the library and sat in a pool of candle light to sift through the day's events. She loved Brent – yes, she did indeed love Brent, who could doubt it? – and she thought of all the wonderful years to come with him by her side. Of course she loved him.

She occupied the days awaiting Brent's departure by contacting the lawyer Abernethy in Northville Landing regarding the arrangements for Amelia, who was still mourning the death of her father, to join her in Natchez. She was certain Amelia would look upon the move as a new beginning, and planned to have Jessie bring her to Natchez.

In addition, as she had anticipated, she found herself taken under the wing of her sister regarding the eventual wedding. It had been a bloodless surrender for she was also busy with the boatyard and the work of restoring the River Queen.

Brent, for his part, attended to his duties as a husband-to-be with diligence for he spent all of his albeit limited time with Erin, introducing her by way of dinner parties, picnics and social gatherings to friends and business associates. The bulk of his time was, necessarily, occupied with preparations for his return North.

A week after Erin had accepted his proposal she accompanied Brent to the Natchez landing to see him board the paddle-steamer Sunset Glory on the long journey to Lynchburg that would take him through Memphis and Louisville with a stagecoach journey from Kentucky into Virginia.

Erin went with him to his cabin, not only to see him settled in but to see as much of the vessel as time would allow for she was constantly eager to look at and whenever practical copy the best of what she saw.

The mournful blast of the whistle echoed into the cabin signalling the steamer's departure and Brent held her close to kiss her and, when she had pulled free, to brush his thumb across her cheeks to stem the tears.

"I shall miss you every second of every day, my darling," he said. "But I will conclude my business as swiftly as I can and return in no time."

She watched as the Sunset Glory churned slowly from the landing, sway gently in the middle of the river and pick up power to begin its journey. When the vessel had gone she walked to the buggy and drove to the boatyard.

In his cabin, Brent worked at the writing-desk on papers and listened to the steady throb of the vessel's engines and the slap-slap-slap of the paddles as they rolled through the water. He checked the time on his pocket watch and went to the door to find a steward and order a hot bath before dinner.

It would be a long journey and he hated having to make it on his own. He wished he could have brought Erin but she was busy. He missed her already.

He bathed and dressed and as he heard a clock somewhere on board strike seven he left the cabin and walked along the deck to the saloon and the restaurant. He hoped he might meet someone he knew to help alleviate the feeling he loathed of being alone when so much was happening around him in the dining rooms and the gaming room.

A group of businessmen, or so he guessed them to be since they were routinely rotund and discussing stock prices and potential deals, was clustered at the bar and he gently elbowed his way through and asked for a brandy.

He took it and turned to look around the room, scanning the tables for somewhere to sit until he went in to dinner. The room was full and every table was occupied.

A couple sat together at one of the tables set in the far right-hand corner alongside a window. The couple, he guessed, were married for neither had uttered a word since he first saw them. He and Erin would never grow so distant, never run out of things to say to and entertain one another with. The man sat facing the room, his companion sat with her back to the bar, as if she wished no part of it.

Presently the man looked up and said something to the woman. The man raised a hand in Brent's direction and indicated an empty chair at the table. The woman turned to look at him.

She was beautiful, in the manner men considered a true Southern Belle should be. Her auburn-red hair was tied into a tail by a red silk scarf and around her shoulders she had a lace shawl clipped at her breasts with a silver, butterfly-shaped pin. She was pale-skinned but her cheeks glowed and her full lips glistened with scarlet paint. She smiled across the room, fluttering a feather fan in invitation.

Brent bowed, turned to ask the barman to have a waiter bring drinks to the couple and walked to join them.

At the table he introduced himself and thanked them for their kindness in asking him to join them. The man shook his hand and said he was Mr Arthur Gordon Blackburn and his companion was Helen Blackburn, his wife.

"My husband thought you might care for company," the woman said. "It can be most distressing sitting alone. You are most welcome, Mr Masterson."

The drinks arrived and Brent looked across the table at Mrs Blackburn. She was, he guessed from her accent, a Kentuckian and shortly she confirmed she was a native of Lexington. Her husband, she added, was also from Kentucky.

"Are you travelling far, Mr Masterson?" Helen asked.

"Yes, ma'am, a fair distance, eventually to Lynchburg in Virginia. And you two?"

"To Louisville," Mr Blackburn said. "I have a ranch just beyond the city where I breed thoroughbreds. You must allow that the finest horses come from Kentucky."

Brent laughed and raised his glass.

"I must, indeed, sir. To Kentucky horses … and its beautiful women," he said and smiled as a flush came to the cheeks of Mrs Blackburn.

"You are travelling on business?" she asked.

"I am, ma'am. I own a hotel in Lynchburg and I am also to meet some associates when I get there."

"A hotel, how very interesting. Is it a large hotel?" she asked.

"A substantial one, to be sure. It is, if I may say so, quite the best such establishment in Lynchburg … though I may be a tad biased in the matter."

"I am sure you are merely being truthful. I should like to judge it for myself one day."

Arthur raised a hand to attract the barman and circled it around their drinks. Helen put her hand over her glass and shook her head asking her husband to wait until they went in to dinner.

"I feel like another drink, my dear," he said coldly and repeated the signal.

When the drinks arrived he downed his brandy with just a

single gulp and called, rather too loudly for several people looked up, for more.

"No, my dear," Helen said and patted her husband's hand. "Please do not drink any more."

He shook off her hand and glared at her.

"I will decide when to drink and when to stop ... and I have decided to drink."

Brent watched the unfolding drama in embarrassed silence, not so much for himself as for the beautiful Mrs Blackburn. He figured the best solution to an awkward situation would be to go to the restaurant and eat. He rose and suggested a meal might be in order. He did not care for the company of Mr Blackburn, but his wife was another matter altogether.

The Blackburns, somewhat to his surprise, rose and agreed to accompany him to the restaurant. Helen took her husband's arm to steady his faltering steps.

They took a table near the door and as isolated from the other diners as Brent could find. He had a feeling that Mr Blackburn had not yet decided to stop drinking and feared more embarrassment for himself and Mrs Blackburn. He wished he had not accepted their invitation to join them but now that he had he felt a responsibility for the lady.

He was correct in his foreboding; Arthur ordered a bottle of wine and proceeded to consume it. The meal, when it came, was merely picked at as Mr Blackburn became increasingly inebriated and his wife increasingly humiliated. And finally Brent realised they could no longer remain at the table. He stood and looked at Helen.

"I think it would be best if we leave," he said. "May I help your husband back to your cabin?"

"That would be most kind of you, Mr Masterson. I am quite embarrassed," she said.

Together, Brent and Helen assisted her husband from his seat and steered him as quietly as they could from the restaurant to the cabin. Inside, Brent flopped Arthur onto the bed, pulled off his shoes and drew a cover over him. Helen watched in dejected silence, dabbing at her eyes with a silk handkerchief.

"I am so sorry, Mr Masterson, I cannot think of how to cover my humiliation."

"Please do not trouble yourself, Mrs Blackburn," Brent said. "There is no need for you to apologise for the actions of your husband." He moved towards the door. "Now I suggest you put the matter out of your mind and retire. Perhaps we can meet in the morning for breakfast, when your husband has recovered."

She followed him to the door and as he stepped out to the deck she touched his arm and smiled her thanks.

Brent walked to his cabin and considered the events of the evening. A beautiful woman with a drunk for a husband made for a tragic combination, one that Mrs Blackburn did not deserve. He removed his jacket and shirt and poured cold water into the basin on the dressing-table at the side of his bed, splashing it on his face. Water dribbled from his chin and trickled down his chest. As he reached for a towel there was a knock on the cabin door.

Holding the towel in his hand he eased open the door. Mrs Blackburn stood in the shadows, a bottle of wine and two glasses in her hands.

"Mrs Blackburn," Brent said, startled. "Has anything happened?"

She slipped past him and stood in the centre of the cabin, holding up the wine.

"I think something has indeed happened, Mr Masterson," she said with a smile.

Brent looked at her and thought how beautiful she was. She was wearing a silk nightdress and her hair tumbled around her shoulders. She held out a hand and he stepped towards her, taking her in his arms and kissing her.

He lifted her in his arms and carried her to his bed.

Chapter 16

GABRIEL CARRIED A BUNDLE OF plans in his arms and walked up the gangplank of the River Queen in search of Matthew. He found him, dirty, sweating and stripped to the waist, sawing timber beams on a workbench in the gaming room, or what was to become the gaming room, for it had been stripped back to the bulkhead.

Several men were hammering the beams into place.

Matthew, looking up and seeing Gabriel, wiped his face with a cloth and put down the saw. He pointed to a stove on which stood a bubbling pot of coffee and Gabriel poured two cups.

Matthew joined him and they walked from the room to the deck, drinking the coffee and leaning over the rail to watch the activity below in the yard. Gabriel rolled a cigarette and coughed his way through it.

"Sure come a long way, eh Gabe," Matthew said. He finished the coffee and shook the bean dregs over the side. "You've worked wonders on the place."

Gabriel looked in satisfaction across the yard, at the noisy workshops and the smoking, clanging forges, and nodded.

"We all did, Matthew, we all did. I know Miss Dubois is mighty grateful for what we all managed." He turned to look at the River Queen. "And what you done to get the old girl shipshape."

"She's sure going to look good when she's finished, the pride of the river."

"The Queen of the river, eh?"

Matthew pushed himself from the rail and stretched to ease his back.

"No rest for the wicked," he said, "I'll get back to my sawing."

As they walked back to the gaming room, Gabriel stole a nervous glance at Matthew.

"You heard about Miss Dubois?" he asked.

Matthew stopped and looked at him.

"No," he said. "What about Miss Dubois?"

"Guessed you hadn't. She's gone and got herself spoken for … she's getting married."

Matthew stopped and leaned against the wall of a cabin.

"When? Who to?"

"Soon as possible, I guess," Gabriel said. "He goes by the name of Brent Masterson, from up North but he's well connected around here. Hear he's wealthy, owns a couple of hotels. His sister lives here in Natchez … don't know much else, just figured you would like to know."

"Good luck to her, she's a fine lady," Matthew said. "I hope this Mr Masterson appreciates her. Anyway, makes no never mind to me so I best get back to work."

Gabriel watched his young friend return to the gaming room.

"No never mind, now why don't I believe you?"

Matthew stood at a window and looked through the cracked and broken glass down to the brown, dirty river slowly lapping at the hull of the steamer and swirling in small, angry whirlpools. A gnarled trunk of a tree, its branches poking from the water like desperate, grasping fingers, floated past … going nowhere in particular.

He banged a fist into the wall and turned. He grabbed his jacket and hat and walked down the gangplank and across the yard. From a line of snorting, restless horses he selected one and rode towards Natchez. He was going to get drunk.

The brittle sounds of a piano being played badly mingled with the mirthless laughter from a brightly lit street of saloons, gaming houses and bordellos. He selected one and, dismounting, tethered his horse to the hitching rail. He glanced up at the sign – *Broken Promise Saloon* – and pushed his way through a group of unsteady men and painted women.

He did not look around him when he entered for it mattered nothing to him what the place was like, only that it had a bar and served strong, memory sapping drink. He ordered a whiskey and poured it down his throat. He ordered another one.

"Well, lookee here, we got ourselves a Johnny Reb!"

Matthew looked up and turned from his drink. A Yankee sergeant was standing in front of him so he turned back to the bar and pointed to his empty glass. The barman poured him another.

The sergeant had now been joined by three other men in blue uniforms.

"Guess Johnny Reb don't care much for us," the sergeant said. "Guess he forgot we whipped their asses and ..."

The barman, watching the soldiers, leaned over and asked the sergeant not to cause any trouble.

"You a Reb too?" one of the soldiers asked.

"Just a barman who don't want any trouble."

The soldier grabbed a bottle from the bar and swung it at the barman who staggered back against the rows of bottles and glasses, scattering them around his head, blood pouring from his wound.

Matthew turned and faced the sergeant and his men.

"Why don't you ease up, sergeant, just drink up and leave."

"You hear that, boys?" the sergeant said. "Johnny Reb is ordering us to leave." He stepped forward and grabbed Matthew by the throat. "We don't take orders from a gray belly."

Matthew felt the grip tighten around his throat and gathered his strength. He struck the sergeant on the temple and followed it with a punch on the chin as the grip loosened and his attacker sagged to the floor.

As the three soldiers moved in to attack a shot scattered the watching drinkers, gamblers and saloon girls. A young lieutenant stood at the door with several soldiers, surveying the scene: the sergeant still unconscious on the sawdust covered floor; the barman holding a blood stained cloth to his head; the broken bottles and glasses and Matthew coughing and spluttering air into his throat.

"Take him," the lieutenant said to two of his men and they stepped forward to grab Matthew.

One of the saloon girls moved from the crowd.

"You got it wrong, mister," she said. "It was the sergeant started it, 'aint that so?" She looked around her and found support.

"If you say so, ma'am," the lieutenant said. "But I'll have to take this man till we sort it out officially. Anyway, guess he'll be safer in a barrack cell than in here."

He backed slowly towards the door and marched Matthew to a waiting US Army covered wagon.

"If what the lady said is true," he told Matthew as he helped him into the back of the wagon, "you'll be free before dawn. Just keep your mouth shut."

At the yard the following morning, Gabriel was told of Matthew's absence. He had not known that Matthew had left work the previous afternoon to go into Natchez and had expected to find him either sleeping in his cabin or working on the River Queen.

It suddenly came to him that their conversation and his news regarding Miss Dubois might have something to do with it but in the meantime he organised a thorough search of the vessel and the workshops. It was to no avail for it seemed as if Matthew had gone.

Gabriel considered Matthew's departure as a great loss, not simply because he had been an excellent worker but because he liked him, a great deal. He had increasingly come to realise that Matthew held Erin in more than a passing friendship's regard and there had been times when he suspected she felt the same, for all her muttering about how infuriating he could be. Her approaching marriage notwithstanding, Gabriel stuck firmly to his assessment.

And that being the case, he was not looking forward to telling her that Matthew had finally gone, in the silence of the night and just as mysteriously as he had appeared. He took out his watch and flipped open the silver lid. It was just off 8am, the time Erin usually arrived at the yard, so he decided to walk to the gate to meet her and tell her Matthew had moved on. He wasn't looking forward to it.

He sat on a rock just outside the yard fence and waited. Presently he saw the buggy and rose to meet her.

"Miss Dubois," Gabriel said when she pulled to a halt alongside him. "Seems Mr Morgan has lit out."

"What do you mean, Gabriel?" Erin asked.

"He's gone. Seems he left in the middle of the night. Thought I'd come to tell you. Look, it's none of my business, ma'am, but I guess we both knew it was bound to happen one day … guess the war made men like Matthew, no place left for them to call home so they lay over for a spell and then get kinda restless for somewheres else. I liked him, truth to tell, he was a good man … but seems his time came to move on."

Erin considered what Gabriel had to say and then she climbed back onto the buggy pointing for his to join her.

"I liked him too, but if he's gone there is nothing more to be said."

They stopped at the office and went inside. Gabriel handed her a cup of coffee and Erin sat at the desk to look at some papers. The sound of a horse galloping through the yard and the hurried thud of boots running to the door interrupted their thoughts.

"Gabe! Gabe!" a man called and burst into the office. He saw Erin and removed his hat. "Beg pardon, Miss Dubois, but it's about Matthew Morgan …"

"What about Ma … Mr Morgan?" Erin said.

"He's got himself arrested by the army. They're holding him in the post in town."

"Slow down, Charlie," Gabriel said. "Why has he been arrested, do you know?"

"Just what I picked up in town; 'pears he was in a fight in some saloon with a couple of soldier boys and, like I say, got himself taken to the stockade."

Erin hid a relieved smile with a stern glare. She rose and headed for the door, turning to Gabriel.

"Then we better go get him out. You coming, Gabriel?"

"Sure am, Miss Dubois."

As they climbed into the buggy and Erin flicked the reins, Gabriel heard her muttering.

"He really is the most infuriating of men."

They reached the army post and went inside, demanding to know where the office was. A soldier directed them to a stone building, the windows of which had thick bars.

Inside, a soldier was sitting with his legs stretched up to a table. He was reading a periodical and glanced up from it when Erin rapped on the counter.

"My name is Miss Erin Dubois," she said, as forcefully as she could. "I am here to see about a man you have incarcerated … his name is Matthew Morgan."

The soldier put his periodical on the table and swung his legs to the floor. He walked slowly to the counter.

"Mr Morgan, you say," he said, turning a ledger in a circle to check the names in it. "Yep, ma'am, we took him in last night … he struck a sergeant, hell of a fight it was. What do you want with Morgan?"

"I want him released and back at work," Erin said.

"Can't do that, ma'am, can't just let him go 'till he does his time. Regulations."

"My good man," Erin said but Gabriel, who had been quite enjoying watching her in full flight, touched her arm and nodded towards the open door of a room to their left. A young lieutenant was looking at her. He came forward and tipped his hat.

"Miss Dubois," he said. "You will not recall me but we met at the Delafield Ball, I had the pleasure of dancing with your friend, Miss Amelia Sinclair. I am Lieutenant Desmond Parker and I was the one who brought Mr Morgan in last night."

"I am pleased to meet you again, Lieutenant Parker. And now will you kindly be the one who lets Mr Morgan out?"

"He's in a deal of trouble," the soldier said to the lieutenant, "He struck a sergeant …"

The lieutenant waved aside the soldier's protest.

"From what I hear, Trooper, it appears the sergeant struck the first blow and Mr Morgan was merely defending himself, and therefore he is free to return to work. Please go and fetch him."

They waited for the arrival of a chastened Matthew, still showing signs of his throttling, and Erin offered him a cold, angry stare. She and Gabriel, accompanied by the lieutenant, escorted Matthew to the buggy.

"If you will accept some advice, Mr Morgan," Lieutenant Parker said. "I would buy myself a new hat if I were you. A gray hat with a Reb cavalry badge acts like a dangerous signal to drunken Yankees, would you not agree?"

As the lieutenant assisted Erin into her seat he cleared his throat.

"Might I ask, Miss Dubois, how Miss Amelia is doing? I heard of the sad death of her father ... I was just wondering ..."

"Miss Amelia is as well as can be expected," Erin said. "Indeed, she will shortly be coming to Natchez where I have offered her a home. I am sure meeting you again would be a great comfort. When she has settled in might you be able to join us for dinner?"

The lieutenant smiled.

"That is very kind of you, ma'am. I would certainly be honoured to join you ... and Miss Amelia." He tipped his hat and Gabriel steered the buggy from the post.

It did not take Erin long to glare at Matthew and treat him to a stern lecture about being a disgrace, about being an aimless drifter who knew nothing about responsibilities, about bringing ridicule upon the Natchez Mississippi Construction Company ... about being the single cause of the fall of mankind.

"And," she said, ending her speech, "I told you that infuriating hat would be the end of you."

"Guess you did, ma'am," Matthew said and exchanged a wink with Gabriel.

While the episode had been of a trivial nature and Matthew had been the innocent – indeed, the injured – party its aftermath was to be momentous. Having returned to his work on the River Queen he kept returning to the events of the previous days, mulling them over in his head.

He allowed that he deserved the lecture Erin had given him,

at the time had even considered it amusing, but he came to the conclusion that what she said contained more than a passing element of truth. Since the war he had become an aimless drifter and he conceded that he accepted no responsibility for the direction his life was taking. He concluded that he ought to do something about it.

He had kept himself to himself in the days following his return to work, spending time in his cabin on the River Queen formulating a plan and finally he resolved to alter the course of his life, in whatever manner fate presented.

Late one night, with a pale crescent moon hanging low in a misty sky, he packed his belongings, what little there was of them, in a saddle-bag and sat at the table beside his bunk to write a letter in the yellow light of a flickering candle.

He read it when he had finished and folded it, placing it on the pillow. He put on his jacket and hat – and smiled at the agitation it had so often caused Erin – and checked to see that the yard was empty. He walked down the gangplank to the horses, slung the saddle-bag over one and led it towards the gate, his hand covering the horse's nose. He continued walking the animal along the road until he was sure he would not be heard, mounted it and trotted into the night.

He had no idea where he was going or of what lay ahead. The pieces, he felt, would fall into place.

Chapter 17

THE MEN WAITING FOR HIM on his arrival in Lynchburg indicated clearly by their expressions of gloom and despondency that the coming discussion would not be of a cheerful nature. It had been a tiring journey from Natchez, though one not without its compensations, and Brent was not encouraged by what he saw.

His hotel was not as full as he would have wished, and the instructions he had left prior to travelling to Louisiana and Mississippi regarding refurbishment and re-decoration had not been carried out, indeed scarcely begun. As he walked through the lobby and as he inspected the dining-room and several of the bedrooms, he realised the hotel was failing, and failing badly.

The two men, both accountants looking after his financial interests and, more importantly, those of his investors, did not relish the approaching conversation.

Brent adopted a cheerful look, though he did not feel cheerful, and asked if they would care for a drink or coffee. They declined and as Brent sat down at his office desk the men produced several ledgers and bundles of bills, mostly unpaid, and spread them out in front of him. They had the appearance of undertakers about to discuss the burial of the dead, which in a way they were.

"We have," one of the men began, tapping a thin finger on an open ledger, "gone into your affairs, Mr Masterson, several times over, and the prospects for success are not encouraging. Indeed, for several months your establishment has been progressing at a considerable loss. The books indicate as much quite clearly."

"But the James River Hotel is the finest in Lynchburg," Brent protested.

The other man shook his head and indicated the bills.

"Alas, that is not the case, sir," he said. "It might have been a fine hotel at one time but even you must concede that it has become, shall we say, tired, of late. There are at least two other hotels in Lynchburg that are more successful, shall we say less tired, and are attracting a greater number of satisfied customers."

"Then we shall endeavour to put matters on a steady course," Brent said, "I have been, as you know, south on business and am confident of gaining control of a magnificent hotel in New Orleans …"

The first man coughed and brushed the news aside with a slight movement of his hand.

The second man took up the threads of the discussion.

"Alas, shall we say, that appears no longer to be a viable option. Several of your backers have, indeed, indicated they are no longer confident enough to continue their support. Three of your previously most enthusiastic investors have been contacted by a competitor and are willing to switch their allegiance … a regrettable turn of events, I agree, but one which can hardly garner them any disapproval. They simply do not see the James River Hotel being rescued, nor do they see a fruitful outcome of an investment in another hotel in New Orleans."

"Indeed, anywhere," the first man added.

Brent sat in silence staring at the ledgers and bills. The men rose, nodded silently at him and hurried from his office.

Just like that, he thought angrily, just like that: two tight-lipped, thin-faced vultures with armfuls of ledgers and bills come to pick over the bones of his business and having done so depart like ghosts.

"Damnation!" he yelled and swept a hand across his desk, scattering the ledgers, bills, ink-stand and most of everything else onto the floor. When he had calmed somewhat he poured himself a whiskey and threw it back in one choking gulp, then poured another. He stood at the window and glared out at the street below, busy with carriages and people whose lives had not suddenly been wrecked.

He refilled his glass and returned to the desk. He did not bother to pick up the papers from the floor for he was well aware of the message they conveyed ... his hotel had failed and the promised investors had melted like snow in a searing sunshine. He collected his tumbling thoughts and considered his options.

He was about to marry Erin Dubois in Natchez. She owned a thriving boatyard and a magnificent paddle-steamer ... and he would soon become her loving, and extremely supportive, husband.

He rose and walked to get a drink from the silver tray on the sideboard. He raised it in a salute to his better prospects and drank it.

Erin, who had occupied the days of Brent's absence with the swiftly progressing restoration of the River Queen, sat in solitude on a bench in the bow of the vessel and watched the sun slide towards evening.

She still could not understand why Matthew had left and remembered how angry she was that he had when Gabriel told her of his departure.

As she was deep in thought she did not notice Gabriel approach along the deck.

"Miss Dubois," he said on reaching her, "the men have finished on the barges and are heading home, is there anything else needs doing?"

Erin looked up and shook her head. As Gabriel turned away to oversee the close of the day's business she asked him to join her.

"Why do you think Matthew left so suddenly?" she asked when Gabriel had stretched out to lean against the rail. "Was it because of what happened at the army post?"

"It's not for me to say why folk do what they do, ma'am," Gabriel said defensively. "Best just accept it's what they want to do."

"But was he not happy working here?"

"Again, it's not ..."

"... for you to say. Yes, I know that, Gabriel, but I would value your opinion."

He looked at Erin and shrugged his shoulders.

"Men like Matthew, they're restless, they don't stay in one place too long. The war made them like that, I guess, and Matthew just reckoned there was something else, somewhere else, he should be. Maybe he reckoned it was time to move on."

"That really does not give me an answer, Gabriel."

"Guess there isn't an answer, Miss Dubois," Gabriel said. He did not mention that he guessed why Matthew had left.

Erin stood up.

"Well," she said. "He's gone and that is the end of the story. He was a most infuriating man and we will not at all miss him."

She flounced off and Gabriel followed her along the deck, down the gangplank and watched as she climbed onto the buggy and drove from the yard.

"Guess you're right," he said to himself. "We won't miss him at all."

Erin had, anyway, other coming events to keep her from fretting about Matthew, for in two days time Jessie was scheduled to arrive in Natchez with Amelia Sinclair, who had been encouraged to come and live in Erin's home. The house had now been completely refurbished and redecorated under the relentless supervision of Olivia Julianne – and to Erin's complete satisfaction and delight – and a small staff of a housekeeper and a maid had been employed to look after it and Amelia and, if she could pull herself from the boatyard long enough to actually visit it, Erin.

Olivia Julianne had also, with her sister's approval, obtained a coveted place for Amelia in one of Natchez's most prestigious colleges "for the education and advancement of young ladies." It was the sort of college girls were enrolled for at birth so Erin wondered, but was not entirely surprised, at how Olivia Julianne had managed such a feat. She decided it would be prudent not to ask.

The other event occupying her thoughts was, of course, the wedding. Though she and Brent had not arrived at a concrete date, other that it would be soon after he returned from his business in Virginia, Erin was well aware that Olivia Julianne was working steadfastly on plans for the ceremony. Again, Erin felt prudence would best be served if she did not ask questions. She had a feeling that one evening Olivia Julianne would simply tell her not to arrange any meetings for the following day but to turn up at a suitable church.

She was aware that such seeming indifference and disinterest to so important an event in her life might easily be misunderstood by others but she had accepted Brent's proposal; she did love him, did she not? She had no other intention but to marry him and be a faithful and loving wife and when the time came, irrespective of the plans and schemes of Olivia Julianne, it would be a wedding ceremony of her approval and desire.

Until the moment for such a decision arrived she was content to allow her sister to indulge herself. It amused her to accept the situation, for the moment, if for no other reason than it left her free to get on with the business of growing and expanding the boatyard.

Each day she spent at the Natchez Mississippi Construction Company did indeed provide evidence of growth and expansion. Orders were being placed at regular intervals for work on the paddle-steamers of other operators – and even though the River Queen had not yet been finished, she considered herself an operator – and the construction of smaller boats of every shape and size. A suggestion from one of the men had even opened another outlet for a team was now welding iron railings and gates for many of the Natchez mansions. Erin was always open to suggestions for growth and expansion.

Gabriel, following the departure of Matthew, had taken on the additional task of completing work on the River Queen and the vessel was looking quite magnificent, inside and out. He predicted with confidence that the steamer would be ready for full-scale trials within weeks, news which turned Erin's thoughts to opening the office in Northville Landing and a further one in New Orleans. Additional offices would follow in other locations along the river when business demanded them.

Brent had sent her several letters, full of ardent love and promises of their bright future. He missed her greatly and would do all in his power to conclude his business and return within the month to marry her.

Meanwhile, Erin had Jessie and the delightful Amelia comfortably installed in the house and the latter introduced to the Natchez College for the Education and Advancement of Young Ladies where she instantly made several new friends.

And, as she promised, Erin sought out Lieutenant Desmond Parker and invited him to join her, Jessie, Olivia Julianne, Orell – and, of course, Amelia – for dinner. She smiled conspiratorially when, after the meal, she saw the young couple walk in the garden.

In Lynchburg, Brent walked down the steep street leading from the Court House to the river. He checked the signs of a row of drinking and gaming establishments, each more dilapidated than the other, and came eventually to the one he required. He pushed open the door and was met by a sickening smell of sweat and spilled drink and the sound of mirthless laughter, a tuneless piano and anger.

At the bar he asked where he might find a Jack Milton and when the barman had given him a suitably suspicious scrutiny he was directed to a door at the side of the bar. Brent walked between the gaming tables, dismissed the clinging attention of a saloon girl who swore at the slight and knocked on the door. It was eased open and an unshaven face squinted between the crack. He was ushered inside where two other men were seated around a table laden with bottles of whiskey.

Brent pulled out a chair and sat at the table. He looked at each of the men.

"A damn disaster, eh?" he said. "The Sutton County business lost us – lost me – a lot of money, and the Curiston place …"

"And lost us Smith and a handful of good men," one of the men said.

"Smith was a damn drunken fool, he deserved what he got. And you …" Brent looked at the men in disgust. "… all scampering back like whipped dogs."

"We got rid of Sinclair, didn't we?"

"And didn't get back the Curiston place," Brent said. "But there is another opportunity, maybe not to get the Curiston place but to get something more valuable."

"I 'aint going back there," one of the men said. "You was well away from what happened, but we was in the middle of it … they had a damn army coming at us. And I damn well 'aint going back to get myself strung up from a tree."

Brent reached across the table and pointed a gun at the man's forehead.

"You'll go back if I say you'll go back. This new job will be a lot easier, so you'll go back and make it happen. I have a plan and you'll carry it out when I say so."

Brent stood up and threw a handful of bills on the table.

"Just be ready when I send word," he said and left.

Chapter 18

ERIN, WRAPPED IN A WARM coat with a fur hat on her head and a muff shielding her tingling fingers from the chill, stood watching the paddle-steamer edge its way to the landing. A gusting wind was whipping the water into angry waves and spray drifted up to the crowd around her.

Brent was finally returning from his business trip in Virginia and had telegraphed her with a message full of love and happiness. Erin had been occupied with the completion of the River Queen's restoration – and with keeping a cautious eye on Olivia Julianne's enthusiastic schemes for the coming wedding – and was longing to hold him once again in her arms.

She felt complete and at peace with the world. Brent was coming home.

Jessie, who had taken shelter in the booking office, came to join Erin to get another look at the man who had managed to capture her friend's heart, something she had long considered a task of impossible dimensions. She watched him as he eased his way through the other passengers on the deck. She allowed that he was as handsome as when she first saw him.

The steamer swayed and creaked to the landing and the waiting crowd pushed forward to see their friends or relations who were now lined along the decks preparing to disembark. Erin, too, scanned the rows of passengers and finally she saw Brent and fluttered a handkerchief at him. He smiled, blew her a sly kiss and made his way to the gangway.

"There he is, Jessie," Erin said, clutching the arm of her friend. "Is he not quite the most handsome of men?"

Jessie watched him as he eased his way through the other passengers. He was, she allowed, certainly handsome but she had a feeling that he knew it and with this knowledge came a seam of vanity, albeit a vanity cloaked in an easy charm.

"Quite," Jessie said and as Brent reached the bottom of the gangway she moved back into the office to allow Erin her moment of privacy. Brent, on reaching his bride-to-be, embraced her tenderly and kissed her cheek. Together, arm in arm, they walked to meet Jessie.

"Oh Brent," Erin said as the three made their way to Erin's carriage, which her sister had insisted they use instead of the usual buggy. "I am so happy to have you back. Was your business concluded successfully?"

The driver put Brent's luggage in the carriage and assisted Erin inside.

"Yes, my dear," Brent said. "Everything is well, indeed thriving, but I cannot fully describe how awful it was to be absent from your side; so very lonely. I trust your own ventures are prospering."

"Indeed they are," Erin said. "The River Queen is almost finished and is quite the most beautiful boat on the river. And there are moments when I find we are so overwhelmed by orders that my head will explode ... the yard is a hub of frantic activity ..."

"Well, my dearest, you must not become obsessed completely with your little venture, I do expect to occupy most of your time now that we have reunited," Brent said, in a manner that Jessie, sitting silently behind them in the carriage, considered ... well, less than pleasing.

He asked to be taken to the home of his sister, Lydia, so that he might unpack and freshen up after the journey, and when they got there Erin walked to the house to see him inside and to pay her respects to Lydia and the girls.

Jessie watched as Erin entered and shortly after returned to the carriage.

"We must hurry home," Erin said, settling back with a rug tucked around her knees. "Brent will be joining us for dinner. Is he not quite the most charming of men, dear Jessie?"

"Quite," Jessie said.

It was 7pm sharp when Brent rode from his sister's house to Erin's, a fine house that he had not until then had the opportunity of seeing competed.

Lamps and candles flickered bright and cheerful in the front rooms as he dismounted and tied his horse to a hitching post at the foot of the stone steps that led up to the wide porch and red maple door.

He removed his hat and stroked a hand through his hair. He knocked and heard footsteps coming towards him. The door opened and Jessie, with a yellow apron tied around her waist, beckoned him into a hallway.

"Miss Jessie," he said and handed her his hat.

She led him to the drawing room where Erin was seated with Amelia Sinclair.

Erin rose and held out her hand which he took and kissed. He looked at Amelia and to her he reached out both hands, taking hers.

"My dear Miss Sinclair," he said. "I was so very distraught to learn of the death of your father. If there is anything I do to help ease your sorrow you have merely to ask."

"That is very kind of you, Mr Masterson. I know how highly my father thought of you."

"And I of him," Brent said.

Jessie stood at the drawing room door and waited until the greetings and commiserations had been concluded. She wiped her hands on the apron.

"Miss Dubois," she said presently. "Dinner will be ready shortly. I will call you." She turned and walked to the kitchen where she had been preparing the meal from the moment she and Erin had returned. As she began stirring a bubbling pot of soup she looked up and saw Erin standing by the stove.

"Jessie," Erin said. "You know Olivia Julianne has provided us with a cook and a maid for the evening, will you please come and join us?"

"I would rather see to the dinner," Jessie said. "This is an evening for you and Mr Masterson so I will remain here. Do not worry, Miss Erin, I will be perfectly contented …"

"Jessie, you know you mean more to me than a cook or a maid or a cleaner. Have we not been friends for many years?"

"We have, and we will remain so," Jessie said. "But tonight I must decline your request. Now, do go back to Mr Masterson or the soup will not be worth serving."

Erin looked at her friend and smiled and walked back to the drawing room.

Brent was deep in conversation with Amelia and as she entered Erin heard him ask the girl if the law had any information regarding the death of her father. When Amelia shook her head, he nodded.

When dinner had been concluded and the maid had taken the dishes off to the kitchen. Amelia excused herself and retired to her room, discreetly leaving Erin and Brent alone. Together, they walked to the garden where Brent lit a cigar.

"I missed you terribly," he said as they stood watching the moon in a cloudless, purpling sky. He took her in his arms and kissed her. "And I do not wish us to delay our marriage. May we announce a date, my dearest Erin?"

The moment had arrived, Erin thought, the moment she had long wished for.

"I do love you," she said. "Do let us announce a date."

They returned to the house and in the library, which Erin used as her private office away from the yard, they consulted a calendar in search of a date, like two commercial businesses arranging a merger.

The following morning Erin visited her sister to inform her that the wedding would take place in four weeks time. Olivia Julianne hugged Erin and immediately had a fit of the vapours … there was so much to do and so little time in which to do it: the invitations, the trousseau, the church, the attendants and bridesmaids, the wedding breakfast. Erin held up her hands to stop the flow.

"My dear Olivia Julianne, do calm yourself, it is merely a marriage ceremony. I do suspect you have already considered all of the necessary arrangements so let us sit down together and go through them ... calmly."

Erin, who had previously indulged her sister's flurries of activity concerning the wedding, was now much relieved that she had so energetic an assistant for the trivia did not in any way occupy her thoughts. Had it been left to her she would happily have sneaked off to a small country church and completed the deed with the minimum of anxiety and stress and returned as Mrs Brent Masterson, the deed done and no more to be said of it.

She had, anyway, other things to concentrate on, though the chief of which did have a bearing on the wedding. Work on the River Queen was almost complete and Gabriel had assured her one further week would see the steamer ready for duty. Erin wished to travel to Northville Landing on board as her honeymoon, indeed they might even go as far as New Orleans. It would be her gift to Brent.

Gabriel, at the request of Erin, had already gathered a potential crew and had persuaded the last Captain of the River Queen to return. Erin had supervised the decoration and furnishing of the cabins, restaurant and gaming room and the selection of cooks and waiters and maids, all of it was exactly as she had told Gabriel she wished it to be. For much excellent work and advice she had Jessie to thank for her friend showed an easy way with the many black maids and waitresses on board.

The maiden voyage of the 'new' River Queen would be announced in the Natchez newspapers and periodicals and on posters widely distributed and the passengers, even those who did not know of her marriage, would all be part of her new life with Brent.

Brent had business of his own to conduct, in no manner associated with the wedding. He rode from Lydia's house to the telegraph office in Natchez and sent a carefully worded message to Lynchburg requesting Jack Milton and several of his associates to make their way south as quickly as possible; he had need of their services.

With just two weeks to go to the wedding, Captain Victor Charles returned to the wheelhouse of the River Queen and with his new crew and Gabriel and the men who had worked on the vessel steered it from the yard's dock and put it through its paces, running it at full speed up and down the river until he was satisfied.

As the vessel churned back to the yard, Captain Charles took two men to his cabin and brought back two wooden boxes of champagne he had specially ordered from New Orleans. He gathered the entire crew on the deck and toasted their worthy efforts.

"I never imagined I would ever see the River Queen back on the river," he told the celebrating men. "Many a day I passed her as she lay, a virtually forgotten half-ghost from the past, and remembered her in her glory … but here we are and I am proud to congratulate you all. The old lady has been re-born, more beautiful than ever."

Erin, who had allowed the men their moment of triumph, waited at the yard and watched the River Queen arrive. Gabriel and the captain were the first to disembark, walking to her to report the vessel ready for duty.

Erin smiled and thanked them and turned towards the office where she closed the door, sat at her desk … and burst into happy tears. She had come a long way.

With the remaining crew members confirmed and on board the River Queen getting accustomed to the steamer and to their various tasks, Erin now turned her undivided attention to her coming wedding. She conceded that her sister had performed wonders but it was now her turn to make her mark on the preparations.

When one becomes wealthy and successful one passes into the eagerly grasping hands of every newspaper reporter who can put three words in the correct order and who has an imagination that is not merely fertile but a raging inferno of adjectives. One is no longer merely John Smith, one is the dark-haired, bespectacled, stoop shouldered John Smith. Why, the newspaper reporter will argue, use one word when he can enlist the services of three, four or five?

Thus, to her enormous amusement, Erin was lavishly described in the Natchez and Northville Landing publications when they reported on her engagement as 'the renowned Mississippi beauty' and 'the lovely flower of the South', none of which she considered herself to be.

Olivia Julianne, on the other hand, was delighted and not at all flattered since she accepted it as simply the unvarnished truth to be referred to as 'the Queen of Mississippi society'. She certainly considered herself as such.

For his part, Brent was somewhat disappointed to be described merely as 'handsome' and 'charming'. He was all that but he felt they might have also added 'successful' and 'distinguished' and 'respected' and 'influential'.

Vanity, Jessie thought to herself on reading the reports and on hearing the reactions to them, all is vanity.

And if such superlatives flowed and gushed over the announcement of the wedding, Erin did not dare think what would be written about the wedding itself. That small country church appealed even more to her.

It is an absolute requirement of a wedding morning that it is beset by panic and confusion, frayed nerves and simmering tempers and so it was in Olivia Julianne's home on the big day. Erin, who had decided to float serenely above such an unseemly commotion, was grateful that Jessie was on hand to maintain calm, largely by agreeing with everything Olivia Julianne demanded and then doing things her own way.

Lydia arrived to deliver her two young daughters, Charlotte and Mary, and on seeing the panic and confusion departed as quickly as she could, excusing herself on the grounds that she had to attend to the flowers at the altar.

Charlotte and Mary were to be flower girls whose task was to walk before the bride and scatter from small baskets red and white rose petals in her path.

Amelia was to be the bridesmaid, accompanying Olivia Julianne as matron-of-honour while Brent had selected as his groomsman a business associate Erin confessed she had never heard of nor ever set eyes upon.

As the guests began arriving for the ceremony it seemed that the entire population of Natchez and a large section of citizenry from Northville Landing had been invited. Gabriel and Captain and Mrs Victor Charles, he splendid in a new company uniform, were there, as were twelve of the workmen and their wives and-or sweethearts, chosen by ballot by their colleagues.

Olivia Julianne had, on learning of their attendance, failed to hide her displeasure at "such grubby and unkempt persons" mingling with proper folk but was placated by Erin who assured her sister that they would be clean of dirt and grime, would be dressed in appropriate manner and would not disgrace the occasion.

"As long," Olivia Julianne said in an attempt to issue the last word, "as they do and as long as they sit at the back of the church."

"They are my men and they will sit wherever they choose," Erin said, and that was the last word.

Outside, on the driveway, stood a coach with four white, plumed horses and inside Erin had the finishing touches applied to her dress of white silk and lace. It had a fitted bodice, a small waist and a full skirt that hung over hoops and petticoats. The veil was of fine gauze attached to a coronet of orange blossoms. She wore short white gloves and carried a handkerchief embroidered with the initials of her maiden name. On her feet were delicate flat shoes decorated with ribbons at the instep.

The task completed, she was led to a mirror where she examined the results of Olivia Julianne and her dressmaker's efforts … she conceded that she had been well served by all concerned.

"Oh, Miss Dubois," Amelia, standing at her side, said, "you look beautiful … and so happy."

"Yes," Erin said, "I do declare I look quite presentable. But I have one important request of all of you." She looked from her sister, to Amelia, to Jessie and to Charlotte and Mary. "I do not want to see a single tear or hear a single sniffle. Now, let us be off to the church."

Chapter 19

HAVING HAD THE BANNS OF Matrimony posted in Our Blessed Lady the Virgin Mary Catholic Church it was to this recently dedicated church that the carriage bore Erin and her party. This was where Orell and Olivia Julianne worshipped and so much influence did the latter exert that the ceremony was conducted by Bishop William Henry Elder, the cleric who had been thrown in jail by the Yankees for refusing to hold prayers for the President of the United States.

As Erin proceeded to the altar to become Mrs Brent Masterson she glanced around at the packed pews. Natchez and Adams County contained more millionaires than anywhere else in the United States and, to her sister's satisfaction and pride, every one of them appeared to have accepted the invitation. Such was her influence.

The ceremony concluded with the minimum of tears and sniffling and the couple returned to Olivia Julianne's home for a Grand Ball. Erin noted that it could not have been other than a Grand Ball. Still, she allowed, it was her big day and she owed much of its success to her sister. And she always did enjoy a ball, even a quite ordinary one.

And while the festivities were at their zenith and while attention was, for a moment, diverted from them, Erin and Brent made their escape and drove to Erin's house to spend their first night of marriage.

Two days later life returned to as normal a pattern as it could for Brent rose early in the morning and departed on business matters while Erin prepared to drive to the yard for the final work to be completed on the River Queen.

Immediately following the wedding, Jessie had been dispatched back to Northville Landing with instructions to set up a booking office and berthing rights and to employ whatever assistance she felt would be required. Such a task provided Jessie with the opportunity of returning to sanity and of being useful.

Bookings for the maiden voyage of the River Queen were overwhelming, as both Gabriel and Captain Charles had predicted, for the vessel was as grand as Erin had planned.

She and Brent were to join the other passengers and, it had been decided, travel on to New Orleans. Brent had readily agreed to this since he, being successful and wealthy, had important business in the city.

It seemed, when the day of departure arrived, that the entire population of Natchez had turned out to witness the event, accompanied by a band that played vigorously and loudly, even through the speeches until Erin sent several of the men to request a moment's silence during which the words could be heard.

The River Queen was covered in brightly coloured banners and flags, the crowd lined along the landing and the banks of the river waving more flags and fluttered handkerchiefs ... and as soon as it judged the speeches had taken up enough time the band struck up once more and anyone who still felt they had something important to say simply folded their notes, pocketed them and went in search of liquid refreshment.

Captain Charles stood in the wheelhouse and regularly consulted his pocket watch for he determined that his vessel would leave right on the appointed second. Gabriel watched the excited activity from the top deck and then made his way below to be ready for the captain's signal to start the great stern paddles churning and bubbling to life.

Brent had watched events from the edge of the group of

worthies clustered around his wife and turned and walked to the cabin Erin had selected for them. He had, he felt, been completely sidelined and it displeased him greatly. He opened the door and looked for a waitress, telling her to bring him a bottle of brandy. When the bottle was delivered he sat in the cabin and emptied it.

Some time later Erin returned to the cabin.

"Well, my dear," he said, "I am delighted to have your company, I wondered if you had forgotten already that I was your husband."

Erin was somewhat shocked at Brent's condition and attempted to placate him for she had certainly not considered her behaviour during the launch ceremony as demeaning towards him.

"My dearest," she said calmly, going to him to put her arms around him, "I thought you were happy to see such support and enthusiasm for what I and the men have done to the River Queen. You know I love you and would never consider in any way slighting you."

"Other than ignoring me and having me moved to the fringes of your great moment," Brent said.

"Such was not my intention," Erin said, feeling that she was in an argument that had no satisfactory conclusion and unable to control its direction.

"Then we must resolve the matter," he said. "You are my wife now, Erin, and as such I expect, indeed I have the right to demand, that you conduct yourself as a wife should. When we return to Natchez I want you to reduce your time at the yard and devote yourself to our marriage."

Erin realised it was not the time to confront her husband on such an expectation. She reached to kiss him but he brushed her aside and walked unsteadily to the cabin door.

"While you reconsider your position, my dear," he said, "I shall be at the gaming tables."

Erin stared in disbelief as he left the cabin and in the ominous silence she wept.

Brent stood at the bar of the gaming room and looked around at the crowded tables. The River Queen was now moving sedately down the river towards Northville Landing and the passengers were enjoying its magnificent services and interior splendour. He resented it that his wife had made it all such a splendid reality.

He saw an empty chair at one of the tables and moved towards it. Five men were playing cards and he asked if he might join in. He clicked his fingers for a waiter.

"Bring me a bottle of your finest champagne, and mark it down to my wife, Mrs Brent Masterson, your employer."

Brent lost heavily at the table and drank equally heavily until the first traces of dawn lightened the night sky. He scribbled several IOU's to cover his debts and made his way back to the cabin with the assistance of one of his fellow players and a waiter.

When he awoke towards noon he found Erin had gone. His head ached and he felt sick. He shaved, washed and sloshed cold water around his mouth. He dressed and went in search of his wife.

Erin was standing with Captain Charles and two of the passengers just along the deck. Brent took a deep breath and joined them.

"Darling," Erin said, not wishing to further upset him or indicate to her companions what had happened. "You have met Captain Charles, and this is Major Grassman and his wife Caroline. They are on their way to New Orleans."

Brent shook the major's hand and kissed that of Mrs Grassman.

"This is a beautiful vessel, Mr Masterson," the Major said. "You must be very proud of your wife's achievement in restoring it to such glory."

Brent placed his arm around Erin's waist and said he was very proud indeed. They continued their conversation for several more minutes and when they parted he gently steered Erin back to their cabin.

"I am so terribly sorry, my dearest, for my behaviour last night," Brent said. "It is not the manner in which I normally act and I beg your forgiveness. It will not happen again."

Erin kissed him and assured him once again of his importance in her life.

"I have a suggestion that will surely help us both, but you

in particular, my dearest," Brent said. "I know how hard you have worked for the success of the yard and the River Queen and, as your husband; I know I must be of more assistance and support. I wish to join you in running the company and help remove unnecessary stress from you. With my help you will have more time to do the things your success provides for."

"That is a splendid idea," Erin said cautiously.

Peace, Erin felt, had been restored, even if she did not fully understand why it had broken down in the first place. But the unhappy events receded as the voyage continued. Brent made love to her as often as decorum permitted and he was gentle and tender.

Each evening, Erin and Brent dined in the restaurant and entertained in the lounge, listening to the orchestra and laughing at and applauding the minstrel troupe. They danced and listened to the wonderful litany of praise for having provided such a triumph as the River Queen.

When they reached Northville Landing, Erin was impressed at what Jessie had done. There was a wooden booking office bearing the name of the Natchez Mississippi Construction Company and beneath it a board proclaiming the building to be the Ticket Office for the River Queen's regular service between Natchez and New Orleans. Space for a detailed timetable had been added and inside there was a comfortable series of waiting rooms for First Class passengers and Ladies.

Jessie, well aware of prevailing social conditions, had hired a former pupil of Erin's to be the office manager. The appointment allowed her to concentrate on maintaining the house Erin had kept in the town.

The River Queen stayed in Northville Landing for three hours, long enough to board the passengers and to replenish the food and drink, and at 8pm in the evening it moved from the jetty and turned south towards New Orleans.

Erin and Brent had discussed travelling to the vessel's ultimate destination and since it was the maiden voyage Brent thought Erin should go. She agreed for several reasons: she did wish to be on board the steamer she and her men had so lovingly restored and to be on board for the entire trip; she had never been in New Orleans, which was another excellent reason for remaining on board; she hoped the time spent with her husband would compensate for the unfortunate start of their journey.

Brent had his own reasons for wanting to be in New Orleans.

Erin would have been content to remain on board the River Queen when it reached New Orleans but Brent, determined to distract her from the vessel, presented her with the argument that they should rather take a room in one of the city's fine hotels and allow the crew to prepare for the return journey to Natchez. It was, after all, their honeymoon and nothing could possibly be too good for his bride.

The hotel he chose was in the French Quarter just along from the Cathedral-Basilica of Saint Louis, King of France. The cathedral was set between the Cabildo, the old City Hall and just recently turned into the Louisiana Supreme Court – Louisiana having just been admitted to the Union – and the Presbytere. It sat alongside Jackson Square, named after Andrew Jackson whose likeness sat on a horse.

Since Brent had several business associates in New Orleans, he and Erin found a regular supply of invitations to dinner waiting for them each morning. And Brent had further arranged for the wife of a close friend to meet with Erin and escort her on numerous sightseeing and shopping expeditions, which he hoped would take her mind off the River Queen.

Erin fell instantly in love with New Orleans, judging it to be even more beguiling and charming than Natchez. She could not, of course, divorce her thoughts entirely from the Natchez Mississippi Construction Company or the service she wished the River Queen to provide so on her shopping trips she looked for a building that would serve as an office.

She did not mention this to Brent, not for the moment at least.

It was as well Erin had been provided with a companion for she scarcely saw Brent from early morning till late evening, he being involved in constant business meetings. He would return exhausted and irritated to the hotel full of assurances that he was prospering, that he hated having to spend so much time from her, that he loved her and that what he was doing was for their future.

Chapter 20

AN EARLY MORNING SUN WAS climbing from the blue-red remains of dawn, rising from a hill far off to his left. Matthew Morgan guided his horse through the trees along a narrow, rutted path that began to slope down to where the forest was thinning out to a ridge of cracked and broken boulders, a carpet of stones and blowing, swirling dust.

He had no clear idea of where he was, though by a vague reckoning based on little more than a feeling he figured he had crossed over into the New Mexico Territory, though maybe he was still in Texas. It did not matter one way or the other, he was simply moving … from somewhere to somewhere else.

Since leaving Natchez several months ago, how many he could not with accuracy recall, he had been moving. He had taken a steamboat up the Mississippi and had ended up working on it, for the simple reason that since he had worked so hard on helping restore the River Queen he might as well see how such a boat actually operated. When he thought about the River Queen, which he tried not to do, he wondered if Gabriel and Erin had completed the task and got the old lady into service.

When working the river no longer attracted him – too many discomforting thoughts and memories crowded around him – he picked up whatever work he could find in countless dusty, one-horse towns, earning enough money to take him to the next dusty, one-horse town, and the next, and the next, and the next.

As he trotted through the trees he tried to recall the name of the last town but it would not come to him … it was just another dusty, one-horse town.

He eased his hat from his head and wiped the grime and sweat from his face with a dirty bandana, smiling at how much anxiety the hat had caused Erin. He brushed his cheek with his hand and felt the fingers rub through the growth. He longed for a shave and a bath, clothes that did not smell, a sit-down steak dinner with a silver knife and fork, a china plate set on a fresh linen tablecloth … maybe even a pretty woman to sit across from him.

At first he did not accept what he had heard, the sharp crack of gunfire coming from below the crest of the hill. When he did realise it he spurred the horse forward and rode to a copse of trees clinging to the edge of the forest. He dismounted, took the Sharps Carbine from his saddle and crouched to peer down to a flat plain that was covered in dry, brown scrub and bushes. The sun was in his eyes so he took off his hat and shaded his eyes from the glare.

Below him to his right he saw a stagecoach, drawn by six horses, racing desperately along a rough, straight road. Following the coach but still some distance from it he counted four masked men. A man was bent as low as he could be in the front of the stage, yelling at the horses and flicking a whip at their flanks. Beside the driver there appeared to be another man, slumped forward.

Matthew lay and watched the drama unfold below him. From where he was there was little he could do to assist. The chasing men were catching up on the stagecoach and Matthew could detect random shots being fired from inside the vehicle, to no purpose he could see, for the four men with scarves tied around their faces were not being deterred from the pursuit.

One of the men drew ahead of the others and Matthew watched as he pulled a rifle and fired at the nearest leading horse. The animal staggered and its front legs buckled as it fell, dragging its companion to one side, sliding and tumbling in a shower of stones and dust.

The driver fought to keep the stagecoach upright as it tilted to one side with the other horses thrashing in panic. The coach slithered sideways, its wheels bouncing back to the road, and skidded to a halt with the driver and the slumped man Matthew figured was – or had been – the guard thrown from their seats.

The four men circled the now immobile stage and Matthew heard them yelling for the passengers to get out. He saw two men open the door and jump to the ground and then he saw a young girl still cowering inside. One of the attackers got off his horse, reached inside and dragged the girl from the coach by her hair and slapped her in the face. She fell and lay at his feet.

With the frightened passengers standing with their arms raised one of the robbers climbed to the top of the stage and began throwing bags to the ground. Another was at the back of the coach pulling at a locked strongbox.

"Damnation!" Matthew said and picked up his carbine. He waited to see what would happen next and when he saw the man at the strongbox point a gun at the still prone girl he mounted his horse and slithered down the hill. He took aim and fired. The man spun around and fell as the bullet struck him in the chest. His startled companions stood in shocked surprise looking around to see from where the shot had come.

Matthew took aim again and shot the man on top of the coach, who tumbled to the ground.

"Where the hell they coming from?" the man who had brought down the coach's horse yelled as he crawled under the vehicle.

The two passengers ran to the side of the coach away from the shooting, leaving the girl.

Matthew waited and when he saw the man who had struck the girl try to reach his horse he aimed, fired and brought him down. The man hiding under the coach wriggled free and threw himself onto his horse. Matthew watched as he wheeled around and galloped off.

Matthew reached the bottom of the hill and rode to the stagecoach. The two passengers were now kneeling over the girl, wiping her dust-covered face with a cloth.

"How is she?" Matthew shouted when he got to the coach.

"She's fine, just shook up a little," one of the men said. "Sure owe you a deal of thanks, mister …"

Matthew waved the thanks aside and went to tend to the driver and guard.

"He's dead; they shot him back a spell," the driver said. He was sitting with his back against a rock, holding his shoulder.

Matthew helped him into the coach and told the passengers to join him. He lifted the body of the guard in his arms and carried it to the door of the coach, lifting it up to the passengers.

The girl told him her name was Edith McMaster and she was travelling to Albuquerque to stay with her aunt. One of the other passengers was a travelling salesman and the other a businessman.

Matthew told them to settle down and tied his horse to the back of the stage. He cut the dead lead horse from its traces. He was about to climb onto the coach when he realised he did not know where he was or where the stage had been going.

He called down from the seat and the driver struggled from inside to join him.

"If you can drive, mister, I'll tell you where to go," the driver said.

"Guess I can," Matthew said and flicked the reins to get the five horses moving.

"Levington," the driver said, pointing ahead. "We're the Santa Barnardo-Levington stage; where we're going is five miles ahead, just head for them hills. And thanks, we owe you."

They rode in silence for some fifteen minutes until Matthew heard the driver groan and curse.

"Easy," Matthew said. "What happened, did you get shot?"

"Naw," the driver said. "Just got my shoulder smashed when I fell from the stage. Hurts like hell." He looked at Matthew and saw his gray hat. "Never thought I'd be happy to see a Reb … we owe you, mister."

"Name's Matthew, Matthew Morgan … you?"

"Henry Telford."

"Where are we?"

"What?" Henry said.

"Where are we? Texas or ..."

"New Mexico," Henry said. "Where the hell you been, mister?"

"Nowhere special," Matthew said. "Just kind of passing through."

"Damn, you sure can pick your moments."

"Sure can."

"You heading in any special direction?" Henry asked.

"Nope," Matthew said after some consideration. "Just passing through. Why, got something in mind?"

"Yeah, sure have. That strongbox them fellers was trying to get, it's full of money. So you rescuing it oughta go down big with the bank in Levington, maybe even with the stage line. Maybe they'll push a reward in your direction. If you need any back-up, like, I'd be glad to help."

Matthew gave the idea some thought. He could certainly use some money. He nodded a thank you to Henry and they continued on to Levington.

It was not much of a destination, as Matthew discovered when he brought the stage to a stop outside the depot late that night. Levington was a one-street, one-horse town. It looked like it had only two buildings constructed in more than weathered, cracked timber: the stage depot and, across the street, the First Commercial Bank were red brick buildings. Everything else looked like it had abandoned all hope years back, though there was, to Matthew's surprise since he wondered why anyone would want to stay in the town, a hotel.

When he and Henry had seen to the still shaken passengers and the dead guard and dazed girl had been delivered into the hands of the town's doctor – who also provided dental, undertaking, veterinarian and legal services, apparently – Matthew nodded towards the hotel.

"What's that like?" he asked.

Henry shook his head.

"I've been in better, but it's the only hotel in town so there's no room for complaining. I usually bed down in the back of the depot so I can take tomorrow night's run back to Santa Barnardo. You're welcome to share, guess we owe you a free bed at least. I can send a boy over to the hotel to get us some grub. Coffee's always on the brew inside."

Matthew accepted the offer and further learned he could find a bath house and a shave at the back of the depot. Henry left him to settle in while he made out a report for the company on the hold-up attempt.

Together they carried the strongbox across to the bank and Henry related to the manager how Matthew had saved its contents and would not be offended by any financial gratitude the bank might care to show.

On leaving the bank, Matthew found a general merchandise store and bought two shirts, socks and a pair of trousers before returning to the stagecoach depot for a hot bath and a shave. Feeling many times better, certainly cleaner, than he had in weeks, he and Henry sat around the depot's stove and shared the meal and a bottle of whiskey.

The following morning Henry's plea to the bank paid off. A clerk arrived in the depot and handed Matthew an envelope stuffed with $1,000 bills and a note of appreciation from the bank.

"Where you plan to go?" Henry asked as he and Matthew stood at the door of the depot watching Levington stir itself to what might, with a stretch of the imagination, be called activity.

"Figure I'll head up North," Matthew said. "I hear Santa Fe's a good place. I don't have any set plan, just …"

"…passing through. You got that down to a fine art," Henry said.

Matthew peeled off $100 and gave it to Henry. He walked through the depot to the stables at the rear and saddled his horse, leading it around to the street where Henry stood on the boardwalk. They shook hands, Matthew tipped his hat and trotted along the street … to nowhere in particular.

He rode for over a week, from one nowhere town to the next, stopping just long enough to eat and sleep, if it was available, in a bed. Mostly, though, he slept under the stars and ate whatever he could shoot or trap. He was drifting – just passing through – and it suited him as well as anything else fate threw in his direction. He fought the memories of what he had known in Natchez, but it was always an uneven fight for he could never shake them off completely.

Somewhere, across another desert or over another mountain, he figured his life would find a settled path. Things, he told himself, had a way of working themselves to a passing conclusion.

He crossed the Canadian River with the Sangre de Cristo Mountains rising to his right and on a parched and dusty afternoon he came upon a railway line. He stopped his horse and, shielding his eyes against the sun, rose in his stirrups and squinted first right then left, debating which way to go.

It did not, of course, matter since he had no nowhere in particular he wanted to go. He chose to follow the single line left and early the following morning he saw far ahead a wooden shed standing alongside a platform. It looked completely out of place in the middle of a dry, rutted desert but black smoke curled listlessly from a pipe at the side of the building and he rode towards it with the hope of finding a mouthful of coffee and information regarding a train … going anywhere. Just out from the station there was a paddock with two horses so Matthew figured his mount would get something to eat.

As he trotted to the shed and dismounted, a tall, thin man with a streak of white hair across his otherwise bald head came to the door and looked at him in surprise.

"Howdy," Matthew said, stepping onto the platform.

"Where in hell did you come from?" the man asked.

Matthew threw a thumb over his shoulder towards the desert.

"I'll be damned," the man said, shaking his head. "You want a coffee?"

"Sure do, and if you have any fixins I wouldn't turn them away."

"Sit there," the man said, pointing to a wooden bench. "I'll see what I have."

Matthew walked along the platform and discovered he had arrived at Duncairn Station. He found a barrel of water and a pile of straw in the paddock, scooped some of the water into his hat and took it to his horse before returning to sit on the bench and stretch out his legs. The man brought him a tin mug of black coffee and a tin plate of bacon and beans.

"Duncairn Station," Matthew said, nodding at the sign. "Don't recollect seeing Duncairn."

"There 'aint no Duncairn," the man said. "This is for the Duncairn Ranch, kinda private. Old man Duncairn had it built and sends one of his men to get me to stop the train if he needs to go anywhere. You're lucky I was here, we had a cattle train couple of hours ago and I was getting set to head home."

"Well, at least trains do run," Matthew said.

"Two a day, one each way and maybe the odd freight. You aiming to get anywhere special, mister?"

"Depends on where the trains go," Matthew said. "I have no set plans."

"If you're looking for work, you could ride out to the Duncairn place. They're always looking for hired help."

Matthew shook his head.

"Thanks, but I guess I'll pass ... all I know about cows is they have a leg at each corner. Where do the trains go, must be somewhere big?"

The man considered and pointed to the right.

"Twenty miles thataway is Cherry Creek Wells, but big it 'aint, and ten miles t'other way is Thompson Bend, and that's even smaller. Next train through is going there, oughta be here around 5.30pm ... but don't lay money on it. If you want it to stop let me know quick like so I can wire ahead and warn the driver."

Matthew took out his watch and said he would give it some thought. The meal finished, he went to fetch his blanket roll from his horse and took it to one end of the platform where he used it as a pillow, put his hat over his eyes and fell asleep.

He figured he would rest for a couple of hours and then get the man to stop the train to Thompson Bend and see where he could get to from there.

He awoke at 4.10pm and asked the man to stop the train.

He purchased a ticket for himself and passage for his horse. The total came to $4, the horse cost more than he did.

Like the man said, Matthew would have lost his bet for the train eventually arrived at 6.20pm, hissing and clanking alongside the platform. The conductor stepped from the single carriage to witness the unusual sight of a passenger, with only two legs, actually boarding at Duncairn Station.

The train consisted of an engine and a tender stacked with logs – along the side of which ran the name of the Great New Mexico Western Railroad, which Matthew considered a tall boast for a single line that ran from nowhere to nowhere else – followed by the passenger carriage, a flat cart with slatted and broken sides, a freight car and a caboose.

He led his horse onto the flat cart and tethered it to the side. In the carriage there were only two other passengers so he took a seat at the end, stretched out and fell asleep.

Chapter 21

BRENT SAT AT THE DESK in the library of the home he now shared with Erin, the house she had purchased in Natchez, and worked at the pile of papers scattered across it. He had received news from his accountants in Lynchburg that indicated what he already knew and could not face ... the hotel was draining away what money he had left and their advice, expressed in the most urgent of terms, was for him to accept one of three offers they had garnered from potential purchasers.

Try as he might he could not find an answer to his growing financial dilemma, other than the one he had started formulating during the journey to New Orleans.

It was a solution he knew would need to be supported and proposed with the greatest of care, a solution that required to be cloaked with the best of intentions.

Erin, to Brent's frustration, was still at the boatyard so he went in search of the housekeeper and told her he did not require dinner as he had an important business meeting to attend. He rode for several miles beyond the limits of Natchez, along a narrow track, through a thickening forest and came to a log cabin.

He dismounted and tied his horse to a tree. He lifted off a saddle bag, slung it over his shoulder and walked across the clearing to knock on the cabin door.

The door was eased open and a man peered out at him. Brent did not wait for an invitation to enter but pushed past him and told the man to get "the others". While the man scurried off to do his bidding he went to the fireplace, threw on a log and stood waiting.

"We was wondering when you'd turn up," a voice said and Brent turned towards the door to glare at the four men who had been rounded up.

"It isn't your damn concern when I turn up, or don't turn up," Brent said and, moving to the circle of chairs arranged around the fire, indicated that the men should sit down.

"We been stuck in this damn shack for near two weeks, is all I'm saying. When we gonna get some action?" the man said.

"When I say so. Now, shut up and listen," Brent opened the saddle bag and spread a map on a table. "You'll soon get all the action you need."

The man glanced at his companions and nodded. They leaned forward to look at the map. It was a hand drawn depiction of the river with a more carefully drawn street plan of Northville Landing.

"We goin' there?" the man asked.

"Yes, I want you all on the way soon as I leave," Brent said. "But don't all go in a damn group, go singly and plan to meet up in a week's time."

"Damn glad to get out of here," the man said, "We was warned not to show our faces …"

Brent waved the man to silence and brought a folded paper from the saddle bag.

"How in hell are we expected to get to Northville?" another of the men asked.

"Whatever way you like … take the steamer, ride, run, crawl … just make sure you're all there in a week's time," Brent handed the paper to the first man. "You're in charge. Read this and you'll know what I want doing. Now pack whatever you need and start moving."

Satisfied that Jack Milton and his men knew what they had to do in Northville Landing, Brent returned home. Erin was waiting for him in the drawing room and on hearing the approach of his horse she asked the maid to bring the supper she had instructed the housekeeper to have ready.

Brent was at his most tender and caring when he entered the room, hurrying to embrace her and kiss her before sitting beside her to eat the supper.

He explained that he had been to an important business meeting regarding an intriguing proposition, once more assured her of a happy, loving future and eagerly sought news of her day at the yard.

They sat holding hands and watched the logs spark and crackle in the fireplace as a crescent moon hung low in the night sky. They retired to bed and made love.

The following morning, one of warm sunshine and a cloudless azure sky, they breakfasted on the terrace.

"My dear," Brent said after a moment's silence, "I have been giving some thought to Miss Sinclair. You have been so kind to her and she is growing into a lovely and charming young woman but I believe she would be happy with girls of her own age – you know better than I how they love one another's company – and to this end I have spoken to the college and they have assured me that dear Amelia would prosper further if she were to become a boarder, that she would even be happier with her friends."

Erin listened to him with growing horror.

"But Brent, Amelia has suffered so much in her young life; we cannot contemplate sending her from us. Indeed, my dearest, I could not bear it … I will not consider it. You must understand."

"I do," Brent said. "But my mind is quite made up … it is Amelia I am thinking about, her complete happiness and her future."

He rose from the table, his determination adamant: he wished Amelia to be sent to live at the college. He kissed Erin and said he would be late home from another business meeting.

A week later Jack Milton arrived in Northville Landing on board the Delta Pride and obtained a room in the Jefferson Hotel overlooking the bustling landing and the main street. He signed himself in as a travelling salesman and awaited the arrival of his companions.

One by one and by various methods of transport, the four men arrived and found lodging in several inns around the town. Their instructions had insisted that they in no way were to be seen together or indicate that they were acquainted until Milton brought them together.

Milton walked along the main street until he found a livery stable where he bought a horse. He rode it to the landing and mingled with the crowd awaiting the arrival of the River Queen, which had just started its regular service from Natchez to New Orleans. This he discovered as he stood at the booking office to examine the blackboard with the schedule hand painted on it.

He walked to where bales of cotton and wooden crates awaited to be loaded and sat down to keep an eye on the Natchez Mississippi Construction Company office across from him. He watched the passengers enter to purchase tickets and tradesmen enter to confirm the shipment of their goods, and he made notes.

He had earlier glanced through the window and noted that there was a young man who sat at a roll-top desk – he assumed he was the manager – and a girl who issued tickets and wrote the transactions in a large ledger. Around noon he saw a black woman drive a buggy along the jetty and enter the office. She spoke to both the manager and the girl for some twenty minutes and then drove back towards the town.

Milton put his mind to figuring the best time for what he planned to do. He decided to take a look along the jetty and when he found what he wanted wrote in his notebook. The best time would be when there was plenty of activity along the landing so that five additional bodies would not arouse suspicion.

At one of the other buildings he discovered that a large shipment of freight would be loaded onto a barge at 9pm. He returned to his observation spot for a spell and finally rose and rubbed the stiffness from his back and legs and rode back to the hotel, noting along the way that there was a suitable meeting place in the Dancing Lady Saloon.

He had arranged prior to arriving in Northville Landing a meeting with one of his men. The man was to be at a small square each day at noon and when the time was right Milton would leave instructions for him to pass on to the others. He and the man did not meet face-to-face, it was not necessary.

The following evening Milton entered the Dancing Lady, ordered a bottle of whiskey and took it to a table in the far corner of the saloon. Presently the others entered, saw him, ordered a drink and joined him for a card game.

"We gonna make our move?" one of the men said. "I'm getting addle-brained sitting in that damn room waitin' for some action."

The others nodded in frustrated agreement.

"Yeah, we're going to move ... there'll be plenty of folk working on a shipment of goods so we won't attract much attention," Milton said and poured them each a drink. "You put all the stuff in place?"

"Sure," another of the men said. "It's hidden behind a water tank at the back of the building."

"Then we wait until ...," Milton checked his watch, "... nine, and then you'll get all the action you want. Now, drink up." He threw a whiskey down his throat and pushed back from the table, "Meet me there."

As he anticipated, a gang of workmen was busy loading the wooden crates and bales onto a barge. He crept to the back of the Natchez Mississippi office and peered inside. The girl was still at the counter counting a handful of Dollar bills and putting them into a metal box. To his surprise he saw the front door open and the black woman enter. She and the girl were talking and the black woman moved to a stove on which there was a coffee pot. As the girl continued counting the money the black woman scooped ground beans into the pot and set two cups on the counter.

"Damn it," Milton said.

There was nothing he could, or wished to, do. He had his orders and, anyway, the sooner he got the job done and got the hell out of Northville Landing the better. He knew also that the men would not be willing to stay in hiding for much longer.

The men had now joined him so he decided to go ahead and hang the consequences. He set two of the men to splashing kerosene over the walls of the office and to lay a trail of it around the building. When they did so he told them to get going while he fired up a handful of dry, brittle straw. He waited until the flames burst into full force on the straw and tossed it onto the kerosene.

At first neither the girl nor Jessie realised what was happening and the men working the barge were too busy to see it. Wisps of smoke curled under the door and suddenly it burst into flames. All around the building the fire was starting to rage, out of control, with flames surging up the walls and across the roof.

The girl screamed and Jessie, trying to find an escape through the inferno, turned to help her. At first she could not see the girl through the thick, black smoke but finally she saw her cowering behind the counter.

Outside, the workmen were running with pails of water and clawing at the building.

Jessie grabbed the frightened girl by the hair and dragged her from her hiding place. The girl was burned badly, her clothing charred by timbers falling from the ceiling, but Jessie lifted her in her arms and, choking and spluttering, her eyes stinging and raw, she looked for a way out of the fire.

The workmen were forming a line, passing the pails along it. The fire was now, they realised, beyond control.

Jessie could not find anywhere to get out. Above her she could hear the creaking and splitting timber and suddenly the ceiling exploded around her and came crashing down, a burning beam falling across her legs as she threw herself across the body of the girl. And the building then surrendered to the flames and imploded around them.

The workmen stood helpless, still in a futile line, and watched the tragedy reach its awful conclusion.

The following afternoon they found the charred remains of the girl locked in the embrace of Jessie.

News of the fire did not reach Natchez for several days. It came by telegraph and was delivered to Erin's home. She, with Brent, had been staying with friends but Amelia, who had received the news, was waiting for Erin with the message clutched in her hand and as Erin stepped from the carriage she ran to her and hugged her.

"Gracious," said Erin. "What has brought about such a warm welcome home?"

Amelia was weeping and simply handed the message to Erin who read it in silence ... and with the realisation of what she was reading she screamed.

Brent, who was lifting their bags from the carriage, turned at the noise and saw his wife collapsing into the arms of Amelia. He ran to her and gathered her in his arms to carry her into the house.

"What has happened?" he said to Amelia as he placed Erin in a chair, holding her hands in his.

"It is Miss Jessie," Amelia said as she took the message from Erin and handed it to Brent. "She has been killed in a fire."

"God in Heaven," Brent said. "When? How did it happen?"

He read the message but it merely contained the briefest of details regarding the fire at the booking office and the deaths of the girl and Jessie. There was no information touching upon the apprehension of whoever had been responsible.

He ordered the housekeeper to bring him brandy and smelling salts and to have the maid go instantly to bring back a doctor. He wiped the tears from Erin's cheeks and fingered strands of wet hair from her eyes.

Erin was in shock, choking with grief. Brent held her and got her to sip a small trickle of brandy which she could not keep down for she dribbled it from her trembling lips.

"Oh God," Amelia said. "It is too awful, dear Jessie and that poor girl ..."

Brent looked at her sternly.

"Please try to control yourself, Amelia; Erin needs us all to be strong." He walked to the door and called out, "Where is the doctor, has he been sent for?"

The doctor arrived presently and administered a tincture of laudanum flavoured with cinnamon to calm Erin who had been carried to the bedroom. There was, he said on returning to the others in the drawing room, little more he could do, other than to advise rest and peace until the grief had subsided. In such sad circumstances, he added by way of sympathy, there was little else to do but allow Erin to come to terms with what had occurred.

Amelia, as grief stricken as Erin, said she would sit with Erin and Brent, having seen the doctor depart, thanked her for her kind support.

When the house had returned to a semblance of order and calm, he went to the library to collect his thoughts. He composed a message to be telegraphed to Northville Landing seeking more details about the fire and who had been apprehended for it.

Erin, with Amelia her constant companion, remained in bed for the following day but eventually felt strong enough to sit in the garden and attempt to sip at a light beef tea.

Brent joined her, telling Amelia to rest.

Erin sat silently, trying to understand what had happened, trying to grasp the dreadful thought that her dear Jessie was dead.

"My dear," Brent whispered, reaching to take her unresponsive hand. "I know how you feel but we must discuss what we can do. I think we should journey to Northville Landing to speak with the girl's family and to attend to what business might be necessary. May I make the arrangements?"

Erin nodded.

"Forgive me for raising the matter now," Brent continued. "But what has happened makes it even more imperative that you allow me to assist you in the company, for your own protection. There are clearly competitors who would stop at nothing to destroy you and I will not allow them to succeed. It is my duty as your husband to be with you in the matter."

Erin nodded.

Chapter 22

THE LETTER WAS SITTING ON the office desk when he arrived to begin work. It was addressed to Gabriel Frampton, Esq., Natchez Mississippi Construction Company; Natchez, Miss. and he saw that a date from five weeks previous had been hand-printed in the top left corner.

Gabriel held the envelope at arm's length, as though something ghastly would spring from it and attack him, and stared at it. He was not a man who regularly – indeed ever – received letters, he could not call to mind anyone who would wish to communicate thus with him.

He set the envelope on the desk and smoothed it down with his fingers, wondering what it might contain. He thought that it might have been sent to him by mistake, that it was really intended for Mrs Masterson, who had gone to Northville Landing with her husband in the aftermath of the deaths of the girl and Jessie.

That was probably the case, Gabriel told himself, and he placed the envelope for safekeeping in a ledger. He walked from the office to organise the completion of two new barges and it was not until late in the afternoon that he thought of the letter.

It might, he figured, indeed be for him for if it was intended for Mrs Masterson surely it would have been addressed to her. On the other hand, he thought, if it was incorrectly addressed and contained a big order for more barges or even for a new riverboat she would have wished him to read it and set the men to work. But then again ...

"Damnation!" he said. "It's only a letter!"

One of the men standing beside him looked at Gabriel.

"Once heard tell of a man got himself locked away for doing that," the man said.

"Doing what?"

"Mumbling mush-brained things to himself ... they figured the man was simple-minded and found him a dark, padded room."

"You should be in a minstrel show," Gabriel said. "It's just that I got a letter ..."

"Was it bad news?"

Gabriel shrugged his shoulders and tried not to look as foolish as he felt.

"Dunno," he said. "Haven't opened it. Might not be for me."

"Well, what god damned name was on it?"

"Mine."

"Then," the man said, "you got to figure the letter was meant for you, you're name being on it."

"Guess so," Gabriel said.

"Just a thought, Gabe: go and read the damn letter so we can all rest easy."

Gabriel walked across the yard to the office, sat down at the desk and pulled the envelope from the ledger. He twisted it nervously in his hands and finally tore it open. Inside was a single sheet of paper, written on both sides. He turned it over to see who had sent it and when he read the name he slapped the desk.

"I'll be damned," he said and began to read the letter.

It was from Matthew and it had been written in somewhere called Maguire in the New Mexico Territory. Matthew had written about his wanderings and how he had found himself in New Mexico, adding that by the time Gabriel got the letter he had no idea where he would be, but that he would keep in touch.

Gabriel read the letter again then folded it back into the envelope and tucked it into his trouser pocket.

"I'll be damned," he said again.

Maguire was not worth staying in. It lay, the dry and bleached remains of somewhere that one harboured ambitions, in the Tularosa Valley with the Sacramento Mountains to the east and the San Andreas to the west.

Matthew had ridden west from Levington, which had not been worth staying in either, and to his surprise had come across Maguire, in the middle of nowhere. It lay below him as he crested a hill and he sat in his saddle looking down on the town through his field glasses. There was one street and he counted twelve wooden buildings on one side and nine on the other, and nothing else. He scanned the street and stopped at a two storey building that he saw was a hotel. He spurred his horse and guided it down the hill.

He trotted slowly along the street. Four old timers were seated outside a dilapidated general store. They sat in silence chewing tobacco and squirting the brown juice into the dusty street. As he passed the men they followed his progress and when he reined up in front of the hotel they returned to their silent chewing.

A woman dragged a small girl across the street, glancing suspiciously at Matthew as he tied his horse and removed his saddle bags and roll. She hurried into the store. Sand blew in small tornados along the street of the otherwise empty and listless town.

"God Almighty!" Matthew muttered and entered the hotel.

Inside the lobby a thin Mexican was disturbing the dirt by brushing it without enthusiasm from one side to the other. He stopped on seeing Matthew, leaned on his brush and watched as he approached the hotel desk where a small, rotund clerk was pretending to be busy.

"You got a room?" Matthew asked.

The clerk looked up from his pretend important work on a registration ledger and turned to indicate a numbered board behind him.

"We got nine of them, mister," the clerk pointed to the keys dangling from the board, "Three of them taken so if you've a mind to you can pick one from six. It'll be $5 a night, two more if you want hot water for a wash."

Matthew took seven Dollars from his pocket and slapped them onto the desk, turning the ledger around to scribble his name.

"For $7 I'd have expected the town band to greet me and a couple of redheads to carry me to the room," Matthew said.

"Life is beset with disappointments, mister," the clerk observed dryly and plucked a key from the board. "Room Four, top and two along on the left. You want the hot water?"

"Paid for it … guess I want it."

The room was small but so surprisingly clean that Matthew assumed the Mexican was never allowed upstairs. He threw his saddle bags and roll in a corner and went back downstairs to see to his horse. The clerk directed him to the stable Matthew had already spotted from the hill.

To his further surprise he found on his return to the room that a tin bath had been brought and filled with scalding hot water. He stripped and lay soaking away the aches and the grime of his ride.

He lay naked on the bed and slept. When he awoke it was heading towards evening and he felt hungry. He dressed and asked the clerk where he could eat. The clerk pointed across the street and Matthew walked to the door, passing the Mexican who was still tormenting the dust.

The eating house was clean and the grub passable and cheap and when he had finished and paid he walked up one side of the street, crossed over and walked down the other. A saloon was filling up with people who appeared to come to life only at night, like Maguire was somehow a haunted place. He decided not to go in.

He asked the clerk if there was a stagecoach service out of the town.

"Sure we have," the clerk said. "We 'aint no backwater, why wouldn't we have a stage, mister?"

Matthew held up his hands in defence.

"No insult intended, just asked. So where do I get a ticket?"

The clerk pointed across the street – everything of importance in Maguire seemed to be located across the street – and Matthew followed the directions to the Gregory Overland Passenger and Mail Stagecoach Line. The office was open but there was nobody inside. Matthew called and waited.

He examined the browning, torn notices nailed to the wall:

THE GREGORY STAGECOACH LINE
WELCOME.
BE IT NOTED THAT YOU WILL BE
TRAVELLING THROUGH INDIAN COUNTRY AND
THE COMPANY CANNOT
VOUCHSAFE YOUR SAFETY …
THAT IS IN THE HANDS OF YOUR GOD.

Below this encouraging warning another notice laid out in the strictest of terms what the Gregory Overland Passenger and Mail Stagecoach Line demanded of its customers:

IF FEMALE PASSENGERS ARE TRAVELLING,
NO SMOKING OF CIGARS OR PIPES IS PERMITTED.
CHEWING TOBACCO IS PERMITTED, BUT GENTLEMEN
ARE ASKED TO SPIT WITH THE WIND, NOT AGAINST IT.
SWEARING IS NOT ENCOURAGED IN THE PRESENCE OF
LADIES.

ABSTAINENCE FROM STRONG LIQUOR IS REQUESTED,
BUT IF THERE IS NO DISAGREEMENT SHARING THE
BOTTLE IS ADVISED TO AVOID
THE IMPRESSION OF UNFRIENDLINESS OR
UNNEIGHBOURLINESS.

BUFFALO ROBES ARE PROVIDED FOR ALL PASSENGERS
BUT IF A PASSENGER HOGS HIS SHARE HE WILL BE
ORDERED TO RIDE WITH THE DRIVER.
SNORING IS DISCOURAGED.

FIREARMS MAY BE CARRIED BUT DO NOT SHOOT FOR
THE PLEASURE OF IT OR AT WILD ANIMALS AS IT OFTEN
AGITATES THE HORSES.

IF THE HORSES RUN AMOKE DO NOT LEAP FROM THE MOVING STAGE AS YOU WILL GET HURT, AND WE DON'T STOP FOR STRAGGLERS.

DO NOT DISCUSS SUBJECTS THAT CAN CAUSE ALARM, SUCH AS STAGECOACH ROBBERIES OR INDIAN ATTACKS.

UNCHIVALROUS BEHAVIOUR TOWARDS LADY PASSENGERS WILL RESULT IN BEING REMOVED FROM THE COACH.

THANK YOU FOR YOUR BUSINESS AND ENJOY YOUR JOURNEY.

"God Almighty," Matthew muttered.

"You need help, mister?"

A small, tubby man appeared from the rear of the office.

"Need a ticket and can I hitch my horse to the back end of the stage?" Matthew said.

"See no reason why not," the man said. "When you thinking of travelling? We got the noon tomorrow going south and the night run going north."

"Makes no difference," Matthew said. "Guess I'll go north."

The man wrote the booking on a small bill and handed it over.

"Twenty Dollars. I'll let the horse go free. North run takes three days to Corona and you can get connections through to Lamy and Santa Fe … long trip, mister, but I guess that don't disturb you. Still, I guess I ought to warn you we don't go in for that fancy dan stuff … but you'll get there."

Matthew thanked the man for his unbounded confidence in Mr Gregory's stagecoach service and returned to his hotel room and wrote to Gabriel.

Chapter 23

ERIN VISITED THE GRAVES OF the girl who had worked in the booking office for the River Queen and that of her friend Jessie. She met the girl's family and she sought the services of a sculptor, commissioning him to produce a suitable headstone monument for Jessie.

She and Brent stayed in the Northville Landing house and while he conducted business in the town Erin sat quietly in the garden to grieve and come to terms with the loss of her friend and the tragic death of the girl.

Brent was at his most solicitous. He pampered Erin with tender care and adamantly refused to allow the steady stream of well wishers who came calling to upset her further. He was at her side each day as soon as he returned in the early evening, and though he took it upon himself to look after those business chores that were necessary he did not burden her with tiresome documents he could look after himself.

He made a special trip to the office of the Northville Landing Sheriff to seek information regarding the perpetrators of the fire and indicated severe displeasure on learning that no suspects had been identified and therefore no arrests were imminent. On behalf of the Natchez Mississippi Construction Company he posted a $1,000 reward for information leading to the arrest of those involved. As an afterthought he also posted $1,000 as an inducement for information leading to the arrest of those responsible for the death of Colonel Sinclair, of which there had also been no progress or likelihood of.

Eventually Brent persuaded Erin that no further good would be achieved if they remained in Northville Landing longer than necessary. He cited the crowding in of memories, the thoughtless people who wished to see her and perpetuate her grief, the need for her to be surrounded by her family and friends in Natchez ... and, of course, to be comforted and sustained by his love and devotion.

He would now, he said for he believed it to be even more necessary for her own peace of mind, take over the running of the boatyard, even if only until Erin felt strong enough to resume. It was for the best.

He further did not feel it necessary, for the moment, to burden his grieving wife with the task of selling the house in Northville Landing so he undertook it himself.

On the return journey to Natchez, Brent escorted his wife on short walks along the deck and sat with her in the afternoon sun, the better to discourage unwelcome sympathisers. At night he had their meals brought to the cabin where he served her and made love to her.

They had been unable to make the journey in the River Queen, their own vessel had been delayed by inclement weather in New Orleans, but the crew of their competitor's steamer was kindness itself.

Erin could not shake off the constant feeling of fatigue but supposed it to be a form of delayed reaction to what had happened and assumed it would pass in a short time. In the meantime, she did not object to the attention Brent was paying her, or to the visits of Olivia Julianne and Lydia who, along with Amelia who devoted all of her free time to sitting with her, were permitted by Brent.

Brent took it upon himself to start paying increasingly regular visits to the boatyard where he informed Gabriel that as the husband of Mrs Masterson and mindful of his obligations and rights in that regard he would be charge of the company's affairs.

He asked specifically to be shown the accounts relating to

every aspect of the Natchez Mississippi Construction business and when Gabriel had a clerk take them to the office Brent locked the door and spent the afternoon examining them.

Gabriel was naturally concerned for he had not seen or spoken to Erin since her departure to Northville Landing to pay her respects to Jessie and the girl. He could merely assume that Brent did indeed have the authority to run the company and that Erin had agreed to the arrangement. Still, he thought, the yard was a great success with orders growing for barges and other smaller boats and the service provided by the River Queen was rapidly becoming the talk of the Mississippi … he hoped Mr Masterson would see all of this and allow it to continue with the minimum of interference.

On several occasions, to his disappointment, Gabriel had asked after Mrs Masterson's health and progress towards its complete recovery and had been told by her husband in no uncertain terms that how Mrs Masterson felt was not his concern.

Olivia Julianne was growing concerned at the uncertain state of her sister. Each visit with Erin indicated a worrying lack of progress to full recovery but when she broached the subject with Brent she was reminded that as Erin's husband her welfare and recovery were to be left in his hands.

Brent continued to assume increasing responsibilities for the running of the company and, worryingly for Gabriel, the ordering of timber, iron, steel and other essential materials of which he had no useful knowledge. Furthermore, Gabriel discovered, the goods ordered were of an inferior quality and purchased at a much lesser cost, with no accounting of the financial difference.

Gabriel considered his loyalty lay with Mrs Masterson as well as to the boatyard and the men he had himself brought back to work in it. It was not, he realised, his business to question the actions of Mr Masterson if his wife had agreed to them but he harboured grave doubts that she actually knew what was happening.

Even worse was to strike the yard when Brent ordered Gabriel to dispose of the services of around one dozen of the men. Gabriel argued fiercely against the lay-offs for the men were skilled and much needed to complete the orders on the company books. Brent, however, did not wish to listen, he had made up his mind that the men were costing the company too much money and were to be culled as quickly as possible.

Gabriel now decided to do something to rectify an increasingly disastrous situation. What he decided to do was not, in truth, in his nature for he was a man who was not afraid to let people know where he stood but in this instance he considered his opponent to be a devious and dangerous one who was likely to seek revenge on those who were within range, innocent or not.

Gabriel sat in a cabin on the River Queen, as secret a place as any he could think of, and composed a letter outlining exactly what had recently been happening at the yard. He included documents and figures supporting his allegations and when he had covered three pages he read them and sealed them in an envelope.

That evening, he went to the home of Orell and Olivia Julianne and pushed the envelope under the front door. Orell, having been an enthusiastic supporter of Erin's ambitious plans for the boatyard and the River Queen and having attracted substantial backing for the Natchez Mississippi Construction Company, would be the best person Gabriel could think of to confront Brent and Erin about the situation.

The following morning a maid found the envelope and took it to Orell who was working in the library. He thanked her and sliced the envelope open, removing the pages and studying them with growing concern and anger. He had no idea that Brent had assumed so much authority in the affairs of the company and he was not enamoured with the idea. He knew, having been informed by his wife, that Mrs Masterson was taking the deaths of Jessie and the girl badly, but he had not been aware that his wife's sister appeared to have been removed entirely from the running of her own company.

He resolved to seek out Brent for an explanation for he felt it his duty to the backers he had brought to the venture.

Erin awoke in the arms of Brent who, disturbed by her movement, kissed her and made love to her. She lay in a warm glow of love and watched him as he dressed. He returned to the bed and leaned down to kiss her before leaving to instruct the cook to prepare a breakfast and have it sent up to his wife. The maid brought the tray to Erin but found her dozing. "The Master said you were to keep your strength up, and to eat this," the maid said, placing the breakfast on the bedside table.

Erin stirred and smiled. "I will, just leave it there and I will enjoy it presently," she said and stretched contentedly.

When she awoke fully it was almost one hour later and for the first time since returning to Natchez she did not feel weak or nauseous. She fluffed the pillows behind her head and rang the bedside bell to attract the maid.

"I am so sorry," Erin said when the girl appeared. "I fell asleep again and did not have breakfast. Would you kindly bring me a cup of coffee ... I am determined to return to normal so please also prepare a hot bath."

The maid hurried off to fetch the fresh coffee and to report the good news that Mrs Masterson was quite her old self once more.

Orell was driven to the Masterson home towards the lunchtime and was informed by the housekeeper that Mr Masterson had left some time previously and would almost certainly be at his office.

Orell asked after Mrs Masterson and was told she seemed to be on the mend. On learning that his sister-in-law was not available for the moment, he asked that she be informed of his visit and good wishes.

Brent was working in the small office he kept in Natchez and was surprised when Orell was announced by the doorman. He rose to greet Orell as warmly as he could for he did not care much for the man.

Orell waved aside the offer of a drink and sat across from Brent. He took the envelope from his pocket and removed its contents, spreading them on the desk.

"I usually place no credence on letters sent to me anonymously," he began, pointing to the pages. "But I find this most disturbing. I cannot for the moment claim I know what the letter says to be true and I am willing to dismiss the claims ... but since I have an obligation to Mrs Masterson and the backers of her company, I would like an explanation."

Brent lifted the letter and read it. He felt the blood drain from his face and prayed it would not be noticed. Presently he set the pages down on the desk and dismissed them with a curt wave of his hand.

"Someone is clearly intent on causing trouble," he said. "Certainly I have become more closely involved in the company since my wife suffered her tragic loss ... but as her husband, I have the perfect right to involve myself in her affairs."

"I fully understand that," Orell said, "but is what has been alleged true?"

"Of course it is not true," Brent said. "And I would ask you to leave my office this instant ... and if I hear any more of this business you will find yourself facing my attorneys."

Brent rose and held open the office door. Orell gathered the pages from the desk and left.

Brent spent the rest of the day fuming in anger ... and drinking. Someone had dared confront him publicly regarding his dealings with the yard.

He drove home and alarmed the servants by blundering through the house demanding to see his wife. He found her walking in the garden for it had been the first day in a long time that she felt strong and lively.

Brent crossed the garden and Erin, on seeing him, smiled and walked to greet him. He stood in front of her and glared angrily at her.

"Brent, darling, what on earth has happened?" she asked, reaching to embrace him.

"Your little message to Orell, my dear wife, that is what has happened," he said, flecks of spittle spraying from his twisted mouth. "Your letter complaining ..."

"But Brent, I do not know what you are referring to ... what letter, what complaints?"

"You sent Orell a terrible litany of wrongdoings you lay at my feet ..."

Erin tried to draw him into an embrace but he pushed her away. "And you deny it, you lie about it! Who else could have sent it?"

"I do not know. All I know is that it was not I," Erin protested.

Brent looked at her and dismissed her denial. And he slapped her on the cheeks before turning back to the house, leaving her sobbing on the grass.

Chapter 24

MATTHEW STRETCHED OUT HIS LEGS at the Gregory Overland Passenger and Mail Stagecoach depot and watched his fellow travellers arriving for the night run north to Corona. They were the usual assortment of stagecoach travellers; a couple of men with large carpet bags, Matthew figured them to be commercial travellers; a young girl, off to college or to visit an aunt; a large, formidable lady, with a feathered hat any discerning Indian would envy, accompanied by a small, thin man who, laden with luggage, scurried in her wake – a husband, a hen-pecked husband, and his brook-no-nonsense wife. It did not hold the promise of a scintillating journey.

He gave the group one more look and pulled his hat down over his eyes to wait for the stage to arrive. He guessed the clerk would be correct with his prediction of the vehicle arriving late. The evening drifted towards night and a hot breeze lingering from the day was making Matthew's slumber a welcome pleasure.

At around midnight, the time confirmed by the chiming of a clock from within the office, Matthew was aroused by the sound of the stagecoach rattling along the street and creaking to a stop, the animals snorting and stamping up a cloud of drifting dust.

The clerk had also been correct in his description of the Gregory line being no fancy dan affair for the coach was an old, ramshackle celerity that held out the unsettling prospect of a journey that would rattle the bones and ache the head and limbs. It was, in addition, drawn by four surly looking mules who viewed the surrounding humans with glowering suspicion.

"Get moving, folks," the clerk called, herding the others from the office to the coach. "We're running a mite late and there's a long way to go."

The driver was on top of the coach catching the luggage being thrown to him by the clerk. Matthew led his horse to the rear of the coach and tethered it to the boot. He took his saddle and hefted it up to the driver who tied the luggage down.

Matthew stood aside as the passengers boarded the coach and, as best they could, made themselves comfortable on the hard wooden bench seats.

"You got a guard?" Matthew asked the driver who was now standing with the clerk checking the passenger and mail list.

"Naw," the driver said, aiming a brown jet of tobacco juice into the dust as his feet. "He didn't sober up in time. Why you ask?"

"Figured I could ride on top with you, I can handle a shotgun."

"Glad of the company, mister," the driver said. "Climb aboard, we gotta get going."

If he was – glad of the company – the driver did little to encourage it as they bounced and shook their way out of Maguire. He veered towards the strong, silent type whose only utterances were directed towards the mules by way of a string of colourful swear words and yells and a long whip cracked across their flanks.

Eventually, as if suddenly realising Matthew was sitting in the box beside him, the driver tried his hand at a conversation.

"You're going to Corona, according to the clerk."

"Yep," Matthew said.

"And then?"

And then, indeed, Matthew thought.

"Nothing hard and fast," he said. "Thought I'd head to Santa Fe, maybe cross into the Colorado Territory ... nothing written in stone."

"Fine place Santa Fe," the driver said. "Good looking

women, good food, good drink ... fine place. Colorado I can take or leave ... full of damn mountains."

That, for the moment appeared to be the extent of the conversation and they continued the journey beneath a black, cloudless sky scattered with stars and a big, white moon. It was also cold and Matthew found himself shivering as a biting chill clawed itself through his coat and shirt to squeeze his chest and bones. He pulled his hat down to his ears and tugged his collar up to shield him against the cold.

The driver stooped down and brought a blanket from beneath the box seat. He handed it to Matthew who thanked him and wrapped it around his shoulders. Again the driver stooped and brought up a bottle of whiskey. Matthew slugged down a warming mouthful and handed the bottle back for the driver to drink.

They rode through the night and as the faint promise of dawn washed across the horizon the stagecoach twisted along a dirt path through the Tularosa Valley with the Sacramento Mountains off to the right and the San Andreas to the left.

The driver leaned from the box seat and called down to the passengers, telling them that a short stop would be coming up in an hour's time.

"Tennyson Relay Depot," he said to Matthew. "I change there and take the stage back to Maguire. There's a connection going north tomorrow night and the stage going west leaves this evening. You can get a feed and I'll see if old man Tennyson can give you a bed for the night ... course, if you've a mind to, you can get a refund and start out on your own, it's up to you."

Matthew gave it some thought and figured he would decide after stretching his cramped limbs, getting a hot meal and maybe a bath and a shave. He was not being pressed by time to do anything in particular. He was still of a mind to get to Colorado, more so since meeting a man in a Maguire saloon who had tales of gold nuggets just waiting to be collected from every river, stream and trickle of water ... Colorado seemed the likely place to be.

Trailing a choking cloud of dust that billowed into the coach, they reached the Tennyson depot. There was a stone building with smoke curling from a chimney and a small paddock and stockade where several equally scrawny and mean looking mules listlessly chewed at a pile of dry, yellow straw.

A man was standing at the door of the building and as the coach slewed to a halt he nodded a greeting to the driver and moved to open the door to let the tired, dirty and discomforted passengers alight.

"Got chow and hot coffee inside," he said, flicking a thumb towards the building. "Meal costs $4 and I throw in the coffee. If anybody wants a wash there's a tub back of the building ... it'll be another $2."

The driver nodded towards Matthew and the man shook his hand.

"This young fellow is getting the stage to Corona," the driver said as the three men walked to the building. "If he decides to stay you can find him somewhere to sleep."

The man, who though no names had been exchanged Matthew assumed was Tennyson, said he had one room and Matthew figured he would take it and decide what he wanted to do – take the stage or head out on his own – in the morning. Inside, Matthew was introduced to a striking Indian woman who was married to Tennyson and whose name was Moonflower.

The prospect of a night in a bed lasted all of five minutes for the formidable lady and her put-upon husband made it clear to Mr Tennyson that, being more important than an aimless drifter and knowing Mr Gregory as a lifelong friend, there was no question whatsoever but that the room should be theirs.

Matthew listened in silence to their demand and as graciously as he could doffed his hat and said they were more than welcome to it.

His graciousness was ignored for the formidable lady had made up her mind anyway. Her husband, looking suitably embarrassed, followed her to the room and smiled thinly to Matthew.

The two businessmen and the young girl, Matthew discovered during the meal, were booked on the westbound stage and the formidable lady and her husband on the following day's northbound to Corona, a discovery that helped Matthew make up his mind ... he would travel on alone, and he had a plan to help him do it.

"Guess the lady won't want to join me in a bath," Matthew said. "So I'll indulge myself if that's permitted."

Bathed and shaved, he found a suitable spot in the stable where he gathered several armfuls of straw for as clean and comfortable a bed as could be expected. He had known worse.

When the evening stage left and he was alone with the Tennyson's, Matthew put his idea to the depot boss. He had noticed work that required doing around the place – fences mended or replaced, wood chopped, the stable tidied, the mules fed and watered, a lick of paint or whitewash here and there – so if he did it would Mr Tennyson give him enough provisions and one of the mules to take him to Santa Fe and, maybe, on to Colorado?

Mr Tennyson considered the proposition and reckoned it a worthwhile one. They shook hands on the deal and Matthew worked feverously for three days and earned the provisions and the mule. Mr Tennyson figured since they belonged to the stagecoach line and it would be considered as ample reward for the effort Matthew had made, if anybody even bothered to ask about the transaction.

Matthew loaded the mule and mounted his horse. He thanked Mr Tennyson for the food and rode from the depot, to wherever the fates directed him. A bright, hot sun splashed the landscape in reds and yellows and long shadows snaked across the stony and rutted pathway along the valley. To his right lay the outline of the Sangre de Cristos Mountains and ahead lay a four day ride to Santa Fe.

As Matthew rode through the burning landscape his thoughts turned to Natchez and a riverboat ... and the memory of a beautiful woman he could not shake off.

Chapter 25

IN THE WEEKS FOLLOWING THE incident in the garden, when Brent had struck Erin, he resolved to be the perfect husband, a caring, loving and supportive husband who would be a bulwark against all with which life tested them. He had resolved to provide Erin with the gentle tenderness he felt sure would restore him in her eyes and in this he felt he was succeeding for it seemed abundantly clear to him that she had forgiven him his terrible, violent lapse and had even conceded to his wishes to be more fully involved in the affairs of the Natchez Mississippi Construction Company.

He felt that his arguments concerning his desire for her happiness and peace of mind, and his arguments that now she was a successful and wealthy woman – with a successful and wealthy husband – she should embrace a lifestyle that permitted her to enjoy the fruits of her success and wealth, were now understood and accepted.

Subsequently, Brent and Erin were increasingly seen in the best restaurants in Natchez, at the most glittering of balls and in the homes of the most influential citizens ... a charming couple who were so very much in love.

Brent brought her gifts of the finest imported jewellery, the most fashionable of clothing – also imported – and one morning he even led her into the garden to present her with the most magnificent of Arabian stallions and a new coach. In smaller, though no less important, matters he was not to be found lacking for each morning he awoke Erin with breakfast on a silver tray, decorated by a red rose.

His lovemaking was gentle and passionate and increasingly they spoke of having children.

At the shipyard, Gabriel noted the welcome tranquillity that had come upon Erin, at least he noticed it on the increasingly fewer occasions she came to the yard. For the most part it was now Brent who controlled the progress of the Natchez Mississippi Construction Company which continued to cause Gabriel some concern.

It was understandable, Gabriel conceded, that Brent did not possess the technical knowledge to make decisions regarding the construction or refitting of river craft, yet he continued, often against his advice and the various shop foremen, to make decisions that proved to be detrimental to the company. And Gabriel's raising of the dangers only soured relations between them even further.

Another thing that continued to trouble Gabriel concerned the financial standing of the company. On the few occasions that he was now permitted by Brent to glimpse the books, Gabriel could not quite understand them ... there were never quite the amounts, the profits, he thought there should be. He was certainly no accountant, he allowed, but he was an experienced builder of boats and well aware of what their construction cost and what the profits thereafter should be ... and too often the two figures simply did not reach expectations. It troubled Gabriel deeply.

It would have troubled him tenfold had he been permitted to study the books Brent kept hidden in a private safe secreted in a small room at the rear of the yard office. These were the books holding the secret of Brent's increasingly futile attempts to save his crumbling business interests in the Lynchburg hotel and his chances of rescuing the situation with fresh financial support for the hotel he still planned in New Orleans.

All of this was, he prayed, to be accomplished with the money he had been extracting from the Natchez Mississippi Construction Company.

His argument, if all of this was ever to be exposed, would be, in his own firm estimation, merely the natural order of such matters. He was married to the woman who had brought about the success of the company and had a husband's right to put the money to their mutual benefit. It was his right and that was an end to the matter.

As he sat in the locked office, Brent took from a folder several documents recently arrived in Natchez from Virginia. He knew what news, what troubling news, they contained yet he read them again, in the hope that he had misinterpreted them initially. Of course he had not for the documents were from his accountants in Lynchburg and they contained the most disturbing of news. The hotel had finally failed and his backers and creditors were gathering like hungry wolves around a fallen deer to pick through the carcase. In short, there was no alternative but that the hotel be sold, and sold for a fraction of what he had invested in it.

In addition, the backers in New Orleans had been informed of the situation and were clamouring for a meeting as swiftly as possible, chiefly to convey their displeasure and to withdraw their promised funding.

Brent faced no other choice but to journey to New Orleans and plead his case for their continued confidence and support.

He had also, of course, to maintain the harmonious relationship he had so carefully constructed with Erin, who was unaware of the disaster that embroiled him. He would continue to be her loving Brent and that very evening he would explain that he needed to go to New Orleans from where he would return with quite excellent news.

During dinner Brent told Erin of his plans and asked if she would like to accompany him, knowing that she already had a prior engagement with Lydia and the girls and hoping that she would not consider altering the arrangements. He made much of his disappointment when she reluctantly declined and the following morning he made arrangements to take passage on that evening's voyage to New Orleans aboard the River Queen.

Fearing that Erin might visit the yard while he was away, Brent then rode to collect the books from his private safe and returned home to place them in his bag. Better, he thought, to have them with him than risk her or Gabriel discovering them.

That evening he bid his wife a loving farewell and was driven to the landing to board the vessel, ordering that a bottle of the finest brandy be delivered to his cabin ... and, of course, charged to the company. When the drink was delivered, Brent rested and planned how he would spend the time to New Orleans ... at the card table where he would see if Lady Luck had for once decided to smile upon him.

It was Gabriel who decided the issue of the company accounts, albeit with a degree of unease for he felt, however much he had contributed to the success of the Natchez Mississippi Construction Company, indeed had kept it going after the death of its owner, Mr Riparian, that the decisions regarding its running were for Erin and her husband to make. He was, after all, a hired hand, though one who retained a singular loyalty to Erin.

He knew, or at least greatly suspected, something was wrong and his loyalty called for him to bring it to the attention of Erin, particularly as she had somewhat absented herself from the company in favour of her husband. If she was aware of what was happening there was nothing Gabriel could do about it, but if she did not know...

After much soul searching, Gabriel arrived at the conclusion that he owed it to himself, to Erin and to his workmen to express his concern. With this in mind he took one of the horses and rode to Erin's house.

Erin was sitting in the garden when a maid brought the news that Gabriel had come calling. As he walked to join her, she realised how much she had missed him, how much she had missed the activity and the challenge of the yard. She rose and greeted him with a warm affection and poured him a coffee.

"My dear Gabriel," she said when he had taken a chair at the table, "how delightful to see you. I have been remiss in not visiting the yard of late, have I not? And I realise how much I have missed it."

"Well, Mrs Masterson, I expect you have had other pressing matters to occupy your time. I am sure Mr Masterson keeps you fully informed of developments. But, we have missed you, I confess."

"So, do tell me all the gossip," Erin said. "How are the men, are we busy filling the river with new vessels, how is the dear old River Queen performing?"

And, taking a deep breath, Gabriel explained the reason for his visit and outlined his concerns that things were not as they might currently be presented to her.

Erin, listening in silence as Gabriel went through his litany of recent events that had troubled him, grew increasingly alarmed. She had, she realised, been neglectful of her stewardship of the company and, if what Gabriel was saying was true, it had been a major mistake. She had been naive; she had trusted Brent without questioning the validity of what little he told her about the state of the company.

When Gabriel concluded his report, Erin sat back and considered it.

"What can I do, Gabriel?" she asked.

"I think you should speak privately to Mr Thynne. He has been a great help to you in the financing of the company, ma'am, and he also represents your various backers ... he needs to know."

"Do not misunderstand me, Gabriel, but I have to ask if you are absolutely certain that you have correctly assessed the situation?"

Gabriel nodded.

"I am not an accountant and that is why I urge you to discuss the situation with your brother-in-law. All I can truthfully say at the moment is that I know the boatyard business, I know the amount of work we have successfully attracted and while I do not know what was charged to our customers for that work, Mr Masterson took control of that, I do know that what is showing on the company books is a great deal less than it should be."

Gabriel's unease increased as he realised the distress he was causing. "This brings me no pleasure, Mrs Masterson," he said, "I thought long before coming to see you but I think the company is on the verge of a dilemma ... the figures I have seen simply do not match and I cannot find the reason for it."

"You have done the right thing and I appreciate it," Erin assured him, "But, tell me, are the books you spoke of in the office?"

"Yes, ma'am ... we use them to enter all new orders. But if you were to ask me I would guess they aren't the only books, not the ones you should be looking at."

"No matter. Go and bring me all the books and paperwork you can find. This evening you and I will pay Orell a visit and lay our suspicions before him. As you say, he will be able to help us." Erin rose and Gabriel joined her. "Now, go and meet me here at seven."

When Gabriel had left, Erin sat quietly running what she had been told through her head, devastated at what it meant.

Chapter 26

CAPTAIN VICTOR CHARLES EASED THE River Queen from the jetty into the river and turned her bow south towards Northville Landing and New Orleans, a journey he and his crew were now familiar with. The vessel had lived up to, and exceeded, all of Erin's expectations for she was the finest steamer on the lower Mississippi.

Brent finished the brandy and dressed for an evening of fine food – and more drink – and cards in the gaming room. He had set aside the voyage to clear his head and prepare himself for what he knew would be a delicate meeting with his wavering backers in New Orleans. Nothing must threaten the coming confrontation, he realised, for he needed their confidence to be restored so that his business ventures might still be rescued.

As he made his way from his cabin and along the deck towards the restaurant and gaming room, he noticed that a rising wind howling through the rigging was whipping the river into white-peaked waves, causing the River Queen to groan and creak as it rose and lurched through the angry water.

It promised an uncomfortable night's journey, which made it all the more necessary for him to fortify himself with whiskey – plenty of it – and a successful session at the card table.

In the wheelhouse, Captain Charles steadied himself against

the roll of the vessel and peered out of the rain lashed window. He did not like what he saw, what he could see through the window that was now distorting his view with streaming water, nor did he relish battling a storm in the darkness of such a growing, threatening night.

He unrolled a chart of the river, seeking a haven into where he might steer the vessel for shelter until the storm passed. He knew the river well and even as he studied the chart he knew that no such haven existed within an hour's journey. He doubted he would make it and had no alternative but to hold the steamer to her present course and pray all would be well.

Captain Charles thought of the safety of his passengers and decided to curtail their dining and gaming by getting his crew to order them, with as much reassurance as was in their power that all was well and it was simply a precaution, to return to their cabins.

Thunder was rumbling across the black sky and streaks of yellow lightning sizzled and cracked across from the distant hills, bathing the lurching vessel in ghostly shape as it ploughed through the bubbling water. Steam was hissing and billowing up from the engine room.

A boy, struggling against the waves washing along the decks, reached the gaming room and found it empty save for a single table at which sat Brent and three other men still playing cards and seemingly oblivious to the turmoil and noise raging outside.

"You gotta get back to your cabins, its Captain Charles orders," the boy shouted.

Brent glanced up from the cards he was holding and poured his companions another round from his whiskey bottle.

"Go tell Captain Charles I seem to have a strong hand here, boy, and a lucky streak ready to pay off," Brent said. "You might also remind him that I am the owner of the River Queen and I will decide when to retire to my cabin ... so I guess my friends and I will remain. You might do us the great service of bringing another bottle ... on the house."

The others laughed and resumed their game.

The wind was now ripping branches from the riverside trees

and spiralling them into the path of the vessel. They crashed onto the decks, bouncing and spinning. In the wheelhouse, Captain Charles fought with the wheel as it shuddered and jerked and suddenly a thick spar crashed through the window and showered him and his crew with shards and slivers.

Wiping the blood from his forehead and cheeks, Captain Charles realised he could not reach the safety of the haven and debated his decreasing options. He could hardly see either bank except when a flash of lightning threw them into brief view.

As he debated running the steamer aground on the starboard bank a man pulled the wheelhouse door open and staggered inside.

"Captain, Sir," the man shouted. "We're breached in the engine room and taking on water ... don't figure we can keep her running for much longer."

"Gentlemen, I see no other option than to turn her towards the shore where we might find a better means of saving the vessel and our passengers," Captain Charles called above the shrieking wind.

In the gaming room, deserted by all but the four men still playing cards, Brent dealt his hand and laughed as he leaned across the table to scoop up the pile of notes and coins.

"Gentlemen," he said, rising unsteadily against the pitching of the steamer, "it behoves us to go and demand of our gallant captain that he compensates us for all our whiskey he has spilled."

The others laughed and followed him from the room, heading along the deck to the wheelhouse. The water was now swirling around their feet, surging and foaming along the deck. They clawed their way along the rail but the storm made it impossible for them to reach the wheelhouse.

"I shall make it my duty to severely admonish the captain in the morning," Brent said. "But for the moment I shall return to the gaming table and retrieve what he has left of my drink. Come, will you join me in another hand?"

Two of the players declined but one accepted the invitation and the men parted. As Brent and his companion groped their way back along the deck they heard from one of the cabins a woman calling for help and the crying of a baby.

"It is just a silly woman who cannot find the child's comforter," Brent said, dismissing the calls. "We, my friend, have much more important matters to attend to ... we have a bottle of whiskey to dispose of."

Captain Charles ordered the crew to abandon the engine room and to assist the crew not required in the wheelhouse to gather the passengers and have them prepared to leave the steamer when he gave the order.

In the wheelhouse, he reached above him head to the rope and pulling it he sent the mournful boom of the vessel's horn across the river and the banks beyond to summon assistance.

The storm grew in intensity and it became more and more difficult to control the steamer and turn her against the flow of the river towards the bank. The vessel tilted to one side and was swept broadside across the river, water cascading over the lower deck and flowing along it to the stern where the great wheel churned and whined. A sudden gust of wind sang through the rigging and one by one the cables holding the stack twanged asunder sending it crashing down on the upper deck cabins, the soot and smoke swept across the vessel into the night.

Captain Charles and two of his officers fought to turn the wheel and slowly the stricken River Queen swerved towards the bank and, carried on the rolling river, thudded into the levee. From behind him, he heard the screams of the terrified passengers and the shouting of the crew trying to maintain calm so that they could herd them to safety.

He ordered his companions in the wheelhouse to go to the assistance of the passengers and to save themselves. Alone in the wheelhouse, he grabbed what documents he could and stuffed them inside his tunic.

He stood for a moment in silence and looked about him. Finally he patted the wheel and turned for the door.

"Sorry for abandoning you, old girl ... you were a fine friend," he said and ran to make a final check on his passengers.

Brent and his drinking companion had joined the milling, panic stricken passengers. The vessel was stuck fast, its bow had furrowed deeply into the river bank. Waves were washing over the stern but the steamer was held secure enough for the crew to calm the passengers and line them up to be helped from the deck to the land.

Brent pushed his way through the crowd and jumped to safety. As he stood watching the unfolding drama, the hysterical men and women struggling through the water and clawing their way up the river bank, the steamer being slowly torn apart by the relentless wind, he resolved to have Captain Charles dismissed ... for ruining what had been a most successful night at the card table.

Captain Charles was still on board and the River Queen was beginning to break up as it was pushed against the levee. He was wading waist deep through oily water pouring through a long gash in the vessel's side and had to heave aside floating debris as he searched to assure himself all the crew had made it to safety. He found, to his relief, that no passengers remained and made his way to the deck from where he jumped into the river and was pulled to the bank by crew members.

"Do a roll-call of the passengers, make absolutely certain they are all safe," he told one of his officers.

As dawn broke the storm blew itself out – a hot sun was now climbing defiantly into a cloudless sky – Captain Charles surveyed the bedraggled groups around him. He figured he was near Northville Landing, though he did not know exactly how near, and he prayed that the sound of the steamer's horn in the night had raised someone's curiosity. The passengers needed warm, dry clothing and medical attention.

He waved to an officer who joined him.

"Take a couple of the fittest men you can muster and go find us help, we have to find these poor souls food and shelter," he said.

To his amazement the River Queen was still afloat, though still stuck deep in the mud of the river bank. She was in a poor condition, her decks broken and strewn with broken branches and glass, the cabins on the top deck smashed beyond recognition by the stack, the wheelhouse demolished.

Carriages had started to arrive as the daylight took hold, alerted by the horn, and the passengers were ferried to Northville

Landing where they would get hot food, clean and dry clothing and medical attention. From there, too, Captain Charles would be able to send news of the disaster back to Natchez and make arrangements for the passengers to continue the journey to New Orleans if that was what they wished or to return to Natchez.

Brent, meanwhile, had plans of his own. He returned to the vessel and searched his flooded cabin for the books and documents, and any clothing worth retrieving. He would telegraph Erin to assure her of his safety and would then continue to his meeting in New Orleans.

Chapter 27

ERIN RECEIVED THE NEWS OF the destruction of her beloved River Queen in the early afternoon and burst into tears, both of grief for the loss of the vessel and relief for the safety and rescue of the passengers.

She was also angry and confused at Brent's decision to continue his journey to New Orleans as though nothing of importance had interrupted it.

Indeed, he had scarcely mentioned the River Queen in his message, had not at all touched on the condition of the crew and passengers, had merely informed her of his plans. There was not only the matter of the books that Gabriel had brought to her attention, and about which she was shortly to meet with Orell, there was the dismissive manner of his message. He was, after all, her husband and as such, she felt, he would have desired to be with her at such a traumatic time.

She could not bear to be alone in the house – Amelia was still attending college – so she went each morning to the yard, where the Natchez newspapers and periodicals clamoured for whatever snippets of news they could find regarding the River Queen and how its fate would affect the Natchez Mississippi Construction Company.

Had they known of her growing concern over the financial

state of the company and her husband's possible implication in it they would have clamoured with even more vigour.

Meanwhile, Gabriel took it upon himself to contact Captain Charles and together they arranged for the passengers to continue on to New Orleans on another steamer or to return to Natchez. In Northville Landing a Board of Enquiry was set up to consider all that had happened during the storm and both men had agreed to attend along with Erin. He had also sent a team of the most skilled workmen to assess the damage to the River Queen and to determine if it was able to be saved.

Erin sat at the desk in the yard office mulling over in her mind how she was going to conduct that afternoon's meeting with Orell. She had a feeling it would be an awkward one for she felt responsible for what, if it turned out to be accurate, had overtaken the company her brother-in-law had done so much to encourage and attract finance to. It was a company that now appeared to face ruin.

Gabriel was sitting on the boardwalk outside the office watching the men building two barges. Around him there was the thumping, banging, hissing and clanging of the workshops. He read the letter he had recently received from Matthew, who had by now crossed into the Colorado Territory and was enjoying the temptations of Denver.

Gabriel did not notice Erin standing in the office doorway.

"Gracious, Gabriel," she said. "You were engrossed in your letter. I trust it did not contain news of an upsetting nature."

"No, ma'am," he said, folding the letter and tucking it into his shirt pocket. "Just a letter from an old friend, nothing to worry your head over."

"I am delighted to hear that. I think I have more than enough to cause me, to cause us all, a great degree of anxiety. You are quite clear what you need to tell Orell when we meet him?"

"That I am, ma'am, though you must understand it is just speculation. We have the company books, to be sure, but Mr Thynne must interpret them to his own satisfaction. If there are any other books or bills or contracts I have not been able to find them. Truth to tell, ma'am, I hope such things do not exist."

Erin and Gabriel met with Orell in his office and he had

asked his chief accountant to join them. He listened in silence as Gabriel revealed his suspicions and showed him the books, supporting his conclusions with what documentation he had been able to find at the yard. There was, in addition, Gabriel's considerable experience and previous long service with the company, which Orell considered to be of equal value to what the books indicated since he agreed with Gabriel that they were probably not the real accounts.

When he had completed his story, Gabriel sat quietly beside Erin while Orell and his accountant thoroughly examined the books, making copious notes as each column of figures was totted up several times over.

Finally Orell looked up from the books and papers scattered across his desk.

"I fear," he said gravely, "there is every likelihood, Gabriel, that what you have said has been substantiated ... the figures simply cannot be matched. Money charged to the company's customers has been entered in the books as less than they paid; in short, large sums of money have been diverted from the Natchez Mississippi Construction Company to ... well, I cannot for the moment say exactly where, but elsewhere.

"My colleagues, your backers, must be informed of this as swiftly as possible and the matter must be rectified ... your company, my dear Erin, faces complete ruination."

Erin, while accepting the seriousness of the situation, was adamant that she first wished to discuss it with Brent. She could not believe, even in the face of such strong evidence, that the fault lay at his feet, that he had so betrayed her. It could not be possible; he would not do such a terrible thing.

She had to wait with growing concern until her husband returned from New Orleans and occupied her time trying to keep the company going, trying to keep what might lie ahead from the men.

Brent reached New Orleans three days after boarding the Delta Pride and booked into one of the city's finest hotels. After the ordeal of the River Queen and still anxious about the approaching meeting with his backers – his damned backers – he nonetheless found time to purchase a fine wardrobe of new clothes and boots and wined and dined in the best restaurants.

Was he not, he told himself, a man of success and substance? Did he not control one of the river's most thriving of companies?

His recent setbacks were merely temporary, he would grasp his doubting backers in the palm of his hand and restore his ownership of the Lynchburg hotel as well as establish a new one in New Orleans ... against all of which the Natchez Company would pale into nothingness.

Gabriel walked through the yard. It was late and the men had gone home, leaving the workshops silent and deserted. On the slipway a barge was nearing completion and work was progressing in the carpentry shop on furniture for a vessel on order from a company in Vicksburg.

All this gave him hope for the future.

He returned to the office and closed and locked the door against the chill air. He lit several candles, brewed himself a coffee into which he tipped a substantial whiskey and drew a sheet of paper from a cabinet beside the desk.

Matthew had finally been able to provide an address in Colorado to which Gabriel might return news of events in Natchez. As he reached for a pen and a pot of ink, Gabriel smiled: he sure got around, did his young friend.

Gabriel dipped the pen in the pot, shook off the excess drops and began his letter. There was a lot to tell Matthew.

The meeting between Brent and the backers did not go well. They were utterly opposed to putting finance into a hotel in New Orleans and certainly not of providing assistance for the retention of the hotel in Lynchburg. Indeed, they informed Brent that far from providing money for his schemes he owed them a considerable sum for work previously promised but undelivered ... and they demanded satisfaction as quickly as possible.

Brent cursed them, told them that they were fools not to support him and would greatly regret their lack of faith, assured them of certain success. It was to no avail and they departed, their demands for recompense ringing in his ears.

That night, Brent comforted himself with several bottles of brandy and the company of a woman picked up in a saloon.

He also made arrangements to take passage on the Delta Pride back to Natchez where he was confident the future turnaround in his diminishing fortune lay.

Chapter 28

HAVING TIRED OF DENVER AND harbouring the feeling that something more worthwhile and rewarding lay elsewhere, Matthew sat in the shabby boarding house his resources had reduced him to and searched his pockets and saddle bag for whatever cash they might contain. Satisfied that he had retrieved every single note and coin in his possession, he spread them on the bed and began counting.

His fortune, which he conceded was stretching the description beyond credulity, came to $46. If he put his charms to good use he could pay for the room and purchase a mule, having long since sold the mounts he had when he left the Tennyson Station several months past. All he required was a mule that would live long enough to take him to ... well, to take him out of Denver.

He had heard from a man he had met in a nearby saloon, a man whose cousin knew a man who had been told by a man who had maybe read about it in a newspaper, such being the usual means of picking up useful information, that gold was plentiful in the Rocky Mountains and all a man was required to do was stoop down and pick it up.

Anything, Matthew figured, was better than feeding the bed-bugs in a run-down Denver boarding house and, anyway, another town over another mountain or along another road was always worth exploring. He packed his belongings into a saddle-bag and a blanket roll, paid for the room and went in search of that mule, maybe even a horse if his luck – and charm – held out.

Eventually he found a horse, a creature that eyed him suspiciously and even appeared to be sneering at what it saw. Matthew figured he had not exactly found his best friend but it would have to do. He patted its flanks and the horse looked around at him in what appeared to be disgust. Not his best friend at all.

He rode north from Denver, the snow capped mountains rising into a shroud of hanging cloud off to his left. He had studied a rough map of the area and was intrigued by the name of Breckenridge, a town on the Blue River.

The town, he discovered, had a curious history and a connection with his own past for it had been created in 1859 and named in honour of John C Breckinridge, the Vice President of the United States. Only when Breckinridge threw in his lot with the Confederate States the citizens, somewhat miffed, altered the 'i' to an 'e' ... Matthew had admired Breckinridge and since he might as well go there as anywhere else he turned his unfriendly horse towards the town.

He rode for most of the day, stopping only to light a fire on which he brewed a pot of coffee and heated some bacon and beans. As the afternoon moved towards evening he came upon a narrow, shallow river and followed it through a thick forest of aspen. It was September and the leaves were shimmering in a great yellow, golden curtain above his head. As he rode he felt the air getting thinner and though the sun was still in the sky, drifting slowly to the west on a cushion of white clouds, thinner and colder.

The river, clear as crystal, was dipping and tumbling and bubbling over rocks and his horse, clearly possessed of a mind of its own, veered from the bank and lowered its head to drink. Matthew eased the ache in his back and stretched, lifting himself in the stirrups.

To his left he spotted a clearing and when the horse had satisfied itself he pulled it around and trotted to it. It was carpeted in brown dry leaves and pine cones. He took his saddle from the horse and threw his blanket on the ground before gathering a pile of cones, fallen twigs and an armful of broken branches for a fire.

He lay in the clearing and kept the cold away by stoking the fire into an explosion of crackling sparks. He finished the coffee and food and swished the remaining hot water over his tin plate. He lay and watched the stars twinkle and glimmer through the creaking branches above his head.

From far away he heard a coyote howl gloomily at the darkness.

He pulled his jacket tighter around him, his collar up around his ears and his blanket tucked under his chin, and Matthew figured Colorado was the right place to be. A cloud dimmed the brightness of the moon and he threw several more spars onto the fire before settling back to sleep, his hat – for a moment he allowed himself a smile at the memory of how it had bothered Erin – over his face.

He slept soundly and with dawn breaking he was awakened by the snorting restlessness of his horse. Matthew stretched and rubbed the sleep from his eyes. He got up and walked to the river to splash water on his face and neck. He filled the coffee pot and returned to the still glowing fire to make himself a drink and to throw a handful of grass and oats into his hat for the horse.

As he waited for the water to boil he pulled his saddle bag nearer and took from it a letter. It was from Gabriel in Natchez and it had been delivered the day before leaving Denver. He unfolded it and read.

He reckoned it would take him another day, maybe two, before he reached Breckenridge. The thing was that he did not know if the river he had been following was the Blue; he doubted it for he thought it to be too far away. Maybe on his travels he would come across civilisation and find out which way his destination lay ... not that it mattered, anywhere would be good in this display of such magnificent beauty.

For the rest of the morning, thankfully warmed by a bright sun, Matthew followed the river until he found a shallow ford he could cross. On the opposite bank he saw a small, wooden jetty to which was moored a flat ferry that looked as if it had not been used for some time. Indeed, the river was so shallow he wondered why anyone had thought there had been a need for a ferry ... somebody who went broke, very quickly, he guessed.

He splashed across the river and cantered along a plank road and presently to his surprise, came upon a board with the painted legend WELCOME TO PATTERSON ... HEART OF THE MOUNTAINS. He spurred his horse along the road and as he crested a rise he saw below in a wide, green valley a one street town.

Matthew patted his horse's neck.

"Welcome to Patterson," he said and guided the animal down to the street.

It was a tidy looking town, albeit in the middle of nowhere, with a river running to one side of the street into a small, blue lake at the far end. There was a combination of timber and stone buildings, indicating to Matthew that Patterson intended to be around for a long time. At the end of the street there was a row of trees lined along either side and even, just before where the river ran into the lake, a small square park that reminded him of the Plaza he had seen in Santa Fe.

There was a briskness in the air as people went about their business or stood talking in groups. He saw further along the street a two storey red-brick building proclaiming itself to be the Patterson Hotel. Several horses were tethered to a rail and beside the hotel a cart was being unloaded outside Benson's General Merchandise Store. A white painted church stood opposite the hotel and beside it was a small, stone building with Sheriff's Office painted in black on the wall.

As he travelled along the street people stopped to see who the stranger might be, but their curiosity held no hint of unfriendly menace.

Matthew wished he had enough money left to test the comfort and hospitality of the hotel – he also felt in the sudden need for a bath and a shave, neither of which he could currently enjoy – but figured that if he rode through the town and found a secluded corner of the lake, far from prying eyes, he might manage to wash and grab a shave, might even find in his saddle bag a shirt that would, if not considered in detail, pass for clean. If he was successful in all of this he planned to take a closer look around Patterson and see what it offered.

He found what he was looking for and tied his horse to a tree while he lit a small fire – he was getting good at lighting fires – and boiled a pot of water. He used one of his shirts to wash himself and shaved.

He checked his financial assets – all of $14 – and decided to speculate it on a drink in the saloon he had noticed. Such establishments were usually ideal for discovering what opportunities might be available.

It turned out to be more civilised than Matthew had expected, more of an inn than a saloon. Inside there was an inviting log fire and instead of rowdy cowhands, painted ladies and a tuneless piano tinkling in a corner there were tables around which sat men engrossed in conversation. He walked to the bar and bought a beer.

He turned from the bar to survey his fellow imbibers and was approached by a rotund gentleman dressed in a frock coat and holding a large hat. The man extended a hand and Matthew shook it.

"Good afternoon, sir," the man said, easing towards the bar with an expectant look. "Allow me to introduce myself: I am Mortimer Hedges, and I have the honour of being the Mayor of Patterson ... and you, sir, are?"

He certainly seems to take being Mayor of Patterson seriously, Matthew thought and provided the requested information.

"Newly arrived, I may safely assume?" Mayor Hedges said.

"Yes, just passing through," Matthew said and, realising Mayor Hedges was hinting broadly that he was absent a drink, nodded to the barman to pour a whiskey. Matthew hoped he could afford it.

"But why?"

"Why?"

"Yes," Mayor Hedges said, "Why are you just passing through? By that I mean Patterson is a quite excellent place in which a young man such as yourself might settle. We encourage such things, you know. Indeed, I challenge you to find a more promising town in all of the Rocky Mountains than Patterson. You should consider staying."

"I had my mind set on Breckenridge, I came across Patterson by accident," Matthew explained.

Mayor Hedges dismissed Breckenridge with a flap of his hand.

"A fine enough place, to be sure," he said. "But not fit to polish the boots of Patterson."

"What is there to do in Patterson?" Matthew wanted to know. He was running out of money and was in desperate need of work.

"A great deal, young man," Mayor Hedges seemed on the verge of rapture. "Why, we are a growing community. Gold has been found in great quantity in several nearby rivers. Our stores are blossoming with trade. There are several growing ranches within easy reach of the town. We will ..."

Matthew, as politely as he could, raised a hand to stop the litany of Patterson's delights.

"I have to be honest with you, Mr Hedges; I am almost devoid of money and in need of a job. I am not against finding a fortune in gold but I could not at this moment afford to purchase a pan in which to discover it."

There, Mayor Hedges said, he might be in a position to offer assistance. Matthew looked interested.

"You might have noticed the Sheriff's Office," Mayor Hedges said and Matthew nodded. "We do not at present have a man of law ..."

Matthew instantly stopped him.

"I am hardly the man to fill the vacancy," he said. "If you are seriously offering me the job of Sheriff. I am totally not the man you are seeking, believe me."

"Young, fit, personable," the Mayor said. "And we are a peaceful town aside from the odd drunk or marital dispute. Patterson is no Dodge City or Chicago ... you will never find yourself fatigued by over work."

Matthew began to consider the offer more seriously. It was, to be sure, the most ridiculous offer he had ever been given and yet it would, for a short period of time, provide him with money and perhaps somewhere to rest his head.

Mayor Hedges was clearly in a determined mood and decided to outline the advantages of Matthew becoming the Sheriff of Patterson. "We can offer you $215 a month and bed and breakfast in the hotel. Why not try the job for, let us say, two months and see how it fits you?"

With his finances reduced now to less than $10, Matthew figured his choices were limited. He considered the proposition carefully. *A damned lawman*, he thought, *am I mad to even think of it?* Finally, if still reluctantly, he nodded. He would become the law in the town in the heart of the mountains, and God help him for it.

Mayor Hedges shook his hand and turned to face the others, calling for a moment's silence. "Gentlemen, please allow me to introduce Mr Matthew Morgan, he has just accepted the post as our new sheriff."

To his amazement, Matthew was greeted by wild cheering and clapping, his shoulders thumped in enthusiasm. More amazing still, he found himself facing a row of brimming glasses lined along the bar.

"Drink up, Sheriff, and we will go to my office where I will swear you in," Mayor Hedges said.

Ah, thought Matthew, therein lies a problem. "I do not take oaths," he said. "I made only one in my life, to the Army of the Confederate States of America ... and it did me no damn good. So I don't take oaths."

Mayor Hedges waved aside his objection. "A trivial matter," he said. "I, myself, supported the noble cause of the South, so we will dispose of the oath."

The following morning Matthew awoke in a comfortable bed in the hotel and with a splitting headache. On the table beside his bed lay a silver star with 'Sheriff' etched across its centre. He clutched his head in his hands. God almighty, what had he gone and got himself into?

When he got around to it, he would have one hell of a letter to send to Gabriel.

Chapter 29

ERIN WAS DETERMINED TO BE composed when Brent returned from New Orleans. There was so much she needed to know regarding the running of the Natchez Mississippi Construction Company and in particular the alarming discrepancies Gabriel had discovered in the yard's financial standing. But she did not desire an outright confrontation with her husband, fearing what it might lead to.

Answers, she simply wanted answers and prayed that they would banish all thoughts of wrongdoing on his part, prayed that there was a quite reasonable explanation that would result in a return to the stability she had experienced in recent weeks.

She was, too, anxious to hear his first-hand account of the loss of the River Queen. She had, meanwhile, dispatched Gabriel and a team of the company's most skilled men to meet with Captain Charles and ascertain if the vessel might be saved. Much depended upon it.

Her sister, Olivia Julianne, had been a regular visitor and welcome comfort in such trying times and Erin, fearing she would not be strong enough on her own to face Brent, asked her to stay until things had been settled.

Olivia Julianne willingly agreed and together they prepared for Brent's return.

Returning on the Delta Pride, Brent planned his strategy, assuming that Erin was unaware of either his pressing financial plight or of what he had been doing at the yard. He felt, with confidence, that his behaviour towards her in the past weeks would be to his advantage, would remain the saving of their future together. Notwithstanding the disaster that had overtaken the River Queen, the future of the company and his continued influence in its running were the keys to his personal future.

Erin sat in the carriage watching the Delta Pride edge its way to the Natchez landing. She scanned the decks in search of Brent and eventually saw him. He waved and blew her a kiss before pushing his way through the other passengers to the gangway that was being readied by several crewmen.

As he walked briskly from the steamer and along the jetty to greet her, Erin got out of the carriage. She thought him still a handsome man while noticing that he looked tired and his face was etched with lines of worry. She held out her arms and embraced him turning her lips to his. Together they walked arm-in-arm to the carriage and he helped her in.

When they drove up the driveway and stopped at the steps leading up to the front door of their home, Brent saw, to his annoyance, that Olivia Julianne was now standing on the porch. His strategy had not taken account of anyone else being there but, on alighting from the carriage and assisting Erin down, he forced as warm a greeting as he could muster and the three turned into the house.

Erin talked to the housekeeper and asked if a meal could be prepared and set for them in the dining room while Mr Masterson retired to the bedroom to change his clothing and freshen up after his long river journey. While they waited for the meal, Erin had a maid bring coffee and bon-bons to the drawing room for herself and her sister. There, they sat awaiting Brent.

Presently, Brent joined them, having washed and shaved and changed into more informal attire. He poured himself a brandy and sat beside Erin on the couch at the fire. Olivia Julianne sat in a high-backed leather chair and occupied her time with a book, which she was clearly not reading.

She was quite relishing the outcome of the approaching conversation between her sister and her husband, even if Erin had told her she would not witness it at first hand.

Erin asked Brent about the events surrounding the wreck of the River Queen, about how his business meeting had gone in New Orleans, about what life was like in the city, if he had met any of their friends. All of which he answered in as serious, light and casual a manner as he felt necessary.

The maid appeared to inform Erin that their meal was ready to be served in the dining room and Brent, taking Erin's arm in his, escorted her and Olivia Julianne. He held out Erin's chair at the table and moved to assist Olivia Julianne before taking his place at the end of the table.

All was calm and very civilised.

The meal became a pleasant if somewhat strained affair of inconsequential gossip that Olivia Julianne considered a waste of time given that, in her opinion, more pressing matters required attending to. She longed to raise the subject of the differing company accounts but, sensing this, Erin discouraged her with a stern look ... the time was not right. Erin would select the ground if, as increasingly seemed likely, a battle, or at least a skirmish, was to develop. Olivia Julianne fumed in frustrated silence.

The meal finished, they returned to the drawing room where the talk followed a similar pattern, and after a short time Olivia Julianne closed her still unread book and said she would take a stroll around the garden to catch the last of the evening warmth.
Erin's silence as she and Brent sat in the drawing room eventually prompted him to reach across and take her hand in his.

"You are quiet, my dearest," he said, squeezing her hand. "Is anything troubling you? I am here for you, you must know that, and what troubles you troubles me. Is it the awful thing that has overtaken the River Queen?"

"Yes, of course I am concerned about that, it was so important to my – to our – lives and future success," Erin hesitated for she did not want to risk hearing the answers to her many unasked questions, did not want to have to face the truth they might reveal.

"But, my dearest," Brent said, "has Gabriel not gone to see how the vessel might yet be saved, surely we must remain confident in his abilities to restore her?"

He placed his arm around her shoulder but felt her resist his embrace. Erin knew she must broach the subject of the company books but she found it difficult.

She was about to ask her husband if he had been stealing money, if he had been cheating their customers, and she was terrified of the outcome.

"There are other matters that trouble me," she said, struggling to find the right words to find and maintain a rhythm of calm reasonableness that would carry her to a satisfactory conclusion. "They concern things which have been brought to my attention relating to the company books ... I simply cannot reconcile what I have been shown ..."

"And yet you seem to have made up your mind to believe what you have been told and condemn me for it. It is hardly the action of a loving and supportive wife, would you not agree?"

"I have not condemned you, nor have I accused you of anything," Erin said. "I am your wife and I love you. I merely wish to have what I have seen in the company books explained to me ... and that will be an end of the matter."

"Will it, will it really, my dear Erin? I can see in your eyes that I stand accused ... and I will not have it."

Erin considered for a moment for she realised the situation had moved into dangerous waters and there was no going back, no retrieving of her words that would calm him.

She began to get up, seeking to diffuse the growing tenseness between them, but Brent grabbed her arm and pulled her down.

He pushed his face close to hers, still holding her arm and anger flashing in his eyes.

"You will sit quite still and listen to me," he said coldly, "I am your husband, and what you have is mine to do with as I like, my dear Erin. You will not question in any way the manner in which I conduct our business ... and never forget that the Natchez Mississippi Construction Company is now as much MY business."

Erin struggled free from his grasp but he lunged towards her, grabbing her dress. It ripped and she spun around in fright, staggering back across one of the fireside chairs and crashing against the stone fireplace.

Brent got to her and hauled her roughly to her feet. Blood was trickling from her forehead and she tried to pull the frayed edges of her dress together. She slapped his hands from her and turned towards the door but he caught her and struck her. Blood gurgled between her teeth and she gagged as it trickled down her throat ... and he hit her again.

She fell to the floor and screamed. In the garden, Olivia Julianne was startled by the cry. She ran to the house and watched in horror as Brent crouched over Erin and struck her once more.

Olivia Julianne yelled for him to stop and, surprised at the intrusion, he stood up and took from the side of the fire a long, metal poker.

"Get out!" he yelled. "This is none of your business ... get out!"

He stepped away from the still prone Erin and, throwing aside the chair she had fallen over, he crossed the room, the poker raised. He swung it and struck Olivia Julianne on the shoulder. She quickly gathered her scattered thoughts and picked up a bronze statuette from a table. She backed towards the door, holding the statuette for protection.

He was on her, vainly trying to strike her. Olivia Julianne threw the bronze figurine at his head. It hit him and he stumbled to his knees. She tore the poker from his hand as he attempted to get up and brought it down on his head. He groaned and slumped into a frightening silence.

Olivia Julianne steadied herself and suddenly vomited violently. To her amazement she could think only that it was such an unladylike thing to do. She wiped her mouth with the back of her hand and picked her way through the scattered furniture to take Erin in her arms. She began calling for help and a maid came running.

"Go quickly and bring a doctor, send someone to my home to get my husband," Olivia Julianne ordered, adding as an afterthought, "and find an officer of the law."

She was joined by another maid who screamed at the disorder and the blood splattered trio. Olivia Julianne still holding her sister, told the girl to be quiet and bring her hot water and towels so that she might clean Erin's wounds. The maid, still crying, scurried off.

Presently a man was shown into the drawing room and introduced as a constable and shortly after a doctor, a near neighbour, arrived. He gently took Erin from Olivia Julianne and with the assistance of the constable lifted her to the couch and began to examine her cuts and bruises.

The constable went to Brent and after testing his pulse declared him still alive but in need of medical attention. The doctor, satisfied that Erin was comfortable, moved to tend to Brent and when he had completed his examination stood up, wiping the blood from his hands with one of the towels.

"In the name of God," he asked, "what happened?"

"My sister was attacked and struck repeatedly by that foul brute," Olivia Julianne said, pointing to Brent. "And he then attacked me ... so I threw the statuette at him."

"Quite hard, I would safely say," the doctor said. He turned to the constable. "If what Mrs Thynne says is true, you had better remove the blackguard to the nearest jail and press charges."

"I fully intend to, sir," the constable said and pulling Brent to his feet he helped him from the room.

"Your sister has been hurt but, thankfully, not seriously," the doctor said to Olivia Julianne. "I suggest we get her to bed where she can rest and I shall come first thing in the morning to further attend her."

It was a tragic event that could not be kept a secret for Brent had been formally charged for his attack on Erin and Olivia Julianne and remained incarcerated pending a trial. Such could not be hidden from a curious public that was fully satisfied by lurid stories, many exaggerated and many simply untrue, in the newspapers.

Shortly after the incident, Orell had arrived at Erin's home and demanded of the constable that Brent be charged with every available crime on the statutes.

He hinted at additional charges that he was in a position to bring several more.

Erin, distraught at the loss of all she had worked for, at all she had hoped her future would be, remained in bed for several days at the insistence of the doctor, until her injuries eased ... but only they would ever heal, her heartache would last.

At the yard, Gabriel was told of what had happened by Orell and in the privacy of the office he took a sheet of paper from the desk and wrote a letter to Matthew.

Chapter 30

MATTHEW ATE A HEARTY BREAKFAST in the dining room of the Patterson hotel. He had been the town's sheriff for two weeks and, as Mayor Bridges had predicted, he found it an easy job. There had been a couple of drunks to escort to the cells to sleep it off and be released in the morning but any crime of a more serious nature did not disturb either him or the town. He was quite enjoying himself.

He had a now established routine and, wiping his mouth, he pinned his silver badge onto his waistcoat and walked from the hotel. He strolled up one side of the street as far as the lake, talked to as many of the citizens as he could, which meant most of them, and crossed to repeat the exercise down the other side. And that, basically, was that, the sole extent of what was required of him.

He returned to the Sheriff's Office where he brewed a pot of coffee and sat with his feet lifted to the desk to leaf through the newly delivered letters, notices, wanted posters and newspapers. He had a quick glance at the two newspapers – the Rocky Mountain News and the Colorado Transit – and set them to one side to check the mail. To his delight, there was a letter from Natchez.

It did not contain good news for Gabriel had written about discovering the parlous condition of the company, as revealed in the books and subsequently confirmed by Orell and his accountants.

The Natchez Mississippi Construction Company was on the verge of going bankrupt.

Even more disturbing to Matthew was the news of the attack on Erin and the arrest of Brent. Matthew had thought often of Erin – almost every day – and came to realise she meant more to him than he, perhaps, cared to admit. Yet their lives had drifted apart, from even the tenuous relationship they had, and there was nothing he could contemplate that would bring them together.

He sat quietly and remembered, with a smile, all the things he missed about Erin and he felt a fury within him at what Brent had done.

He arose and walked from the office. He unhitched his horse and turned it towards the hill from where he had first looked down on Patterson. In addition to his morning walk through the town, Matthew had started to explore the surrounding countryside, which was included in his jurisdiction. It allowed him to get to know what lay beyond the town and to show the ranchers and miners that the law had returned.

He also wanted to come to terms with what Gabriel had written about the company, the loss of the River Queen and of Brent's cruelty to Erin. It angered him that he was so powerless to offer her any assistance.

The morning was freshened by a rising breeze that heralded the coming winter. The aspens were still shimmering with their gold and yellow while a light cloak of snow lay on the shoulders of the distant mountains. It was a morning in which a man could clear his head, could organise his tumbling thoughts and come to level headed conclusions. It was a good morning for a man to be alone with his destiny.

He rode along across a meadow dotted with bobbing, untroubled wild flowers. To his right a stream meandered through the trees and curved towards a small, quiet canyon. It was the early afternoon so he stopped and dismounted to lead his horse to the stream and to allow it to feast on the grass along its banks.

He sat with his back against a tree and with his knife sliced pieces of dry beef to eat. When he finished eating he walked to the stream and stooped to scoop water onto his face and slosh around his mouth. As he wiped his bandana on his face he saw something glinting in the stream.

Matthew bent forward and saw what looked like a yellow stone. He picked it from the stream and shook the drops from it, holding it up for a closer look. It looked like a gold nugget ... he had never actually seen one before but it sure looked like a gold nugget should look. He spread out his bandana and placed the stone in it.

He walked slowly along the bank, peering intently into the stream. He saw several more nuggets of varying size and lifted them from the water to place in his bandana. He continued exploring for several hours and when he stopped the bandana was filled with nuggets.

He returned to the tree he had rested against and sat with the bandana between his legs. He did not want to believe what he had found. He had the feeling that with his luck it would turn out to be fools gold. To be sure, he had been assured that all a man was required to do was stoop down and pluck a fortune from the ground ... but that was other men, such things never happened to him and he did not want to find himself a fool by thinking otherwise.

He tied the corners of the bandana together and placed it in his saddle bag. He still believed he would be found sadly mistaken when, indeed if, he took his find to be judged but he decided to take one last walk along the stream, just for the hell of it.

An hour later Matthew returned to his tree with his pockets full of nuggets. He looked around him. The valley was completely deserted, so much so that he guessed few, if any, had ever set foot in it.

He took from his bag a graphite stub and the envelope containing Gabriel's letter and began pacing out a wide area around and along the stream, on both sides. When he had marked out what he felt would constitute a claim he searched for several thick, straight branches which he pushed into the ground to form a square. He drew the square on his makeshift map and, using the remains of the envelope, wrote his name and the date on four pieces. He placed each piece of paper under a pile of stones at each of the branches.
He mounted and rode quickly back to Patterson in search of a lawyer and, if it existed, an assay and land grant office. The feeling

still, nevertheless, nagged at him that it would all turn out to be a hollow illusion.

He came upon a lawyer as he was locking up his office opposite the hotel and persuaded him to open up and explain to Matthew how, or even if, he could register a claim and establish it as legally binding.

The lawyer indicated a map of the territory that hung on the wall behind his desk and together they studied it. The lawyer asked Matthew to indicate where he wished his claim to be and again they studied the map.

"Thing is," Matthew said, "it lies in a canyon around a morning's ride west from town and I do not know if the canyon has a name."

He began tracing the route he took that morning from Patterson and eventually came to where the map showed the stream running into a narrow – and unnamed – cut between two hills. "I guess that is where I laid out the claim."

The lawyer turned to his desk and took a thick folder of documents from a drawer, placing it on the desk and unrolling the documents. He filed through them and finally found what he was looking for.

"Well, Sheriff," he said after a moment's consideration, tapping the document, "you appear to have a larger claim than you at first imagined. Let me explain." He beckoned Matthew to look closely at the map. "The way I see it, and I believe the document supports me, is that nobody has ever owned your canyon ..."

"Damn me," Matthew said.

"Well I would say you have not been damned but rather you have been blessed. Large swathes of the territory remain uncharted or, indeed, claimed by anyone. Large swathes of territory around these parts remain completely unexplored ... and you, I am certain, have found such a place. If you like, to satisfy you, I can look into the matter in greater detail and get back to you."

"What exactly are you suggesting?" Matthew asked.

"I am suggesting that you should not merely claim your small square of land around the stream but claim the entire meadow and valley ... nobody else appears to have done so."

Matthew sat down, amazed at what he was being told. Could it be possible that he had found, and could claim as his own, such a beautiful place?

The lawyer sensed his shock.

"Do not get your hopes up just yet ... but as I say, I do believe the valley is yours to claim."

"Then, by all means explore the possibilities and claim it," Matthew said.

The two men shook hands and Matthew, his saddle bag slung over his shoulder, asked where he might find the assay and land office. At the door of the office, the lawyer directed him along the street to a stone, single storey building.

Matthew entered the building. A man, with his sleeves rolled to his elbows and a green shade tied around his head, stood behind the counter. There was a set of weighing scales on the counter, with brass weights stacked in two columns beside it. Matthew pulled his bandana from the saddle bag and clunked it onto the counter.

"Is this what I think it is?" he asked, doubt still heavy in his voice.

The man peered at the nuggets and looked up.

"Depends if you think it's gold," he said.

"Is it?"

The man lifted a nugget and tested it in his hand.

"Mister, I would hazard a guess that it is," he said and lifted the rest of the nuggets still wrapped in the bandana. He took them and set them in one of the scale's bowls, balancing them with weights set onto the small flat plate.

He turned and brought a square of paper to the counter. On it he wrote down the weight of the nuggets, Matthew's name, the date and added his own name at the bottom. He handed the paper across the counter.

"I have to take a closer look, but I don't reckon I am wrong ... it's gold, and good quality gold. One other thing, mister: guard that paper with your life; it's your proof that you brought the gold."

Outside, Matthew took several deep breaths ... it had been one hell of a day, and no mistake. He figured, even if he was the sheriff, he was entitled to get disgracefully, falling down, rip roaring drunk. And he did.

He spent the following days recovering from his indulgence and trying not to think of the reasons for it, if reasons even existed. The frustrating silence from both the lawyer and the assay office seemed to Matthew to indicate he was after all a fool.

He was making his morning rounds when he glanced back along the street and saw the lawyer crossing from his office to the jail, holding a sheet of paper. Matthew shook his head – guess this was where he became the fool for thinking his luck had changed – and walked slowly to the Sheriff's Office, prepared for the worst.
As he reached the door he was met by the lawyer coming out.

"Thought you were inside," the lawyer said and returned inside.

"Just doing my duty," Matthew said as he pulled a chair to his desk and slumped into it. "Guess you got some news for me?"

"Indeed I have," the lawyer said and slapped the paper down in front of Matthew. "You are now the legal owner of 15,000 acres of prime Colorado territory, and there is a river thrown in for good measure. I took the liberty of naming your new spread Morgan Canyon Ranch, that was for legal reasons so if it does not suit you can call it whatever you like ... I still like my choice."

Matthew read the paper twice. It showed that he had staked a successful claim on the meadow, the valley, the canyon, the river within his land and whatever he found in it: sludge, stones, fish, fowl ... or gold, silver and copper.

"There is one minor problem," the lawyer said. "You owe the United States Government a fee, to be negotiated. I guess by your hat you might find that sticks in your craw."

"Not if you do it on my behalf ... as my lawyer. I guess I will just have to learn to live with the embarrassment. I am a forgiving soul."

The lawyer laughed and they shook hands. When the lawyer left, Matthew sat at the desk and tried to get his thoughts in order.

He was now the owner of 15,000 acres of Colorado ... and he had no idea what he was going to do with it. Indeed, he realised, he did not have enough money to pay the fee the lawyer mentioned so any whoopin' and hollorin' would be a tad premature.

Later in the day, as Matthew did his second check of Patterson for the day, mainly because he could not sit and brood over what had happened, the man in the assay office saw him pass and stopped him.

"I was coming to see you, Sheriff," the man said. "I got the final word back on the nuggets you found. Seems you found yourself a mother lode ... you got yourself a damn river of gold."

It was not happening, Matthew thought. He would wake up in some rat infested hotel in some nowhere town and find it was all a damn, miserable, tormenting dream. He closed his eyes and then opened them ... no, he was standing in the street of the town at the heart of the mountains. And he was a wealthy man

Chapter 31

GABRIEL, WHO HAD BEEN WITH a team of workmen from the yard to examine the damage to the River Queen, returned to Natchez from Northville Landing. And he came home with heartening news for he was certain the vessel could be saved and returned to service on the river.

He found Erin to be in buoyant mood which surprised him, given her recent tribulations. He feared it was a false optimism but decided his job was to ensure the continuation of the company and the restoration of the River Queen, for all their sakes. This Gabriel knew would be a difficult, if not ultimately impossible, task, given the financial cloud that hung over the company.

What he did not know, nor would know for some time, was that Erin had considered her situation with a strength that surprised even herself. The school ma'am had discovered much about herself since first, in what now seemed another world, being told that she had been left a broken-down Mississippi paddle steamer and, in addition, a boat building yard. She had turned it all around, and with the loyal help and skills of her men had turned the River Queen into the pride of the Mississippi.

She had entered into what she thought would be a loving marriage ... and had been betrayed. Worse still, she and her sister had been physically threatened and attacked.

She had resolved to lay down strict conditions that would govern the rest of her life, to which end she steeled herself for a most difficult confrontation with Brent, who remained in jail pending a trial.

She sat with her husband in a dismal room at the Natchez jail and laid out her ultimatum, from which there would be no deviation.

She told Brent that neither she nor Olivia Julianne would press the charge of assault, nor would she press charges on his financial dealings at the company. She would seek, if possible, his release for she confessed she did not wish to suffer the ordeal and obvious embarrassment of a trial – a trial she knew all of Natchez was awaiting with mounting excitement – and for all this she sought a divorce on the grounds of cruelty.

She had, as she expected, to brush aside Brent's pleading and assurances of reform, promises of a fresh start, and continued. He would, she further demanded, leave Natchez and go to ... well, to wherever he chose, it mattered nothing to her for she was finished with him.

When she had concluded, Erin rose and left the room. Outside, the world was going about its business, the sun was shining, the sounds of the river came to her ... and she wept, dabbing the flood of tears suddenly unleashed down her cheeks. She wept for a love that had turned so sour, so heart breakingly bitter and empty. She allowed her grief to flow, to cleanse her, to strengthen her resolve for the future.

She wiped the tears from her swollen, red eyes and blew her nose. The world was still going about its business, the sun was still shining, the sounds of the river were still drifting around her. She squared her shoulders and, without looking back, took the first steps into the rest of her life.

"You have been quite wonderful, Gabriel, and I want you to know that I owe you, and the men, more than I can truly convey."

Erin and Gabriel were walking through the yard. Difficult as the situation of the Natchez Mississippi Construction Company was, the workshops were alive with activity on a number of orders from the Vicksburg shipping company.

"I must point out, ma'am," Gabriel said, "that we're still in a mess of trouble. I hate to remind you that we're doing this work on contracts negotiated by your husband ..."

"I no longer have a husband," Erin said.

"Forgive me, ma'am ... but that doesn't alter the facts. We will make some money on this Vicksburg job, but not much and we need to find money, lots of it, from somewhere, and quick."

"I am well aware of that," Erin said, "But I will not, simply not, lose the company. I will speak with Orell as soon as possible and see if his people will assist us. You can trust me in my determination: the company will survive, survive and prosper. And we will get the River Queen back on the water, better than ever."

Gabriel nodded. He never doubted they would. Erin was one hell of a woman!

The problem was that Erin had no idea how she was going to do it.

She did go to meet with Orell and two of his associates, who had already invested in the company, to seek finance for the work to be done on the River Queen. Orell proved to be, once again, her great advocate for he did most of the talking and so eloquent was he on behalf of their continued support that they had no hesitation in providing what Erin required.

"My dear," Orell said when the men had departed, "what they have agreed to invest, while it is a substantial amount, is not enough to guarantee the future stability of the company. You need more orders, perhaps even to consider other outlets not directly connected with the trade of the river ... you need to rationalise your entire business philosophy, to find other commodities to manufacture and sell."

Erin agreed and said she would return immediately to the yard and discuss it with Gabriel. She had learned to trust Gabriel's judgement and wealth of experience for he more than anyone else had been instrumental in the reopening and success of the company. When she had finished telling Gabriel of the outcome of her meeting with Orell and of his advice for diversification – which Gabriel had also been putting his mind to – Erin felt more confident about the yard's future. A large order had been received from New

Orleans and she was determined to find other means of making money.

Several weeks after her meeting with Orell, Erin received news of an event that shocked her and threatened to open up old wounds and cause her more anguish. It was Gabriel who, after some thought, brought it to her attention, having read of it in a New Orleans newspaper that had been given to him.

The item had been taken by the New Orleans newspaper from a dispatch from a newspaper in Virginia – the Lynchburg News – and referred to the arrest of a local businessman for a 'vicious and unprovoked attack' on an associate and to the subsequent revelation that both the attacker and the victim were involved in the 'foul and despicable deeds' of a gang of carpetbaggers in the Louisiana and Mississippi states.

The victim had, it was reported, confessed to several attacks on property and the burning of a building in Northville Landing as well as the murder of several people in Sutton County in Mississippi, including 'the much loved and highly respected former Colonel James Reid Sinclair, late of the Army of the Confederate States' on the instructions of his attacker, who had ordered all the acts described.

That man was named as Brent Masterson, 'former owner of a hotel in Lynchburg and declared bankrupt, of no fixed abode.' The report concluded with the prediction that all concerned would eventually 'face the full and stern retribution of the law.'

Erin read the report in silence and when she had finished she folded the newspaper and returned it to Gabriel. It mattered nothing to her, though she resolved to visit Lydia, Brent's sister, and the girls, Charlotte and Mary, for throughout her ordeal and unhappiness she had never been in conflict with them.

Enough additional finance had been placed in the company's account and Gabriel returned to the River Queen, where the workmen who had remained had done much to remove the wreckage, smashed furniture and broken branches and glass that littered the decks and wheelhouse. The major task now facing them was the examination of the still waterlogged engine room and the paddle.

He picked his way along the cracked and broken deck and clambered inside the remains of the cabins, the cabins where Erin had first set eyes on the sleeping, gun-toting Matthew. He smiled at the memory and wished his young friend was with him now. He would find the time to write to Matthew.

Erin continued to run the yard and to put her mind to what additional work might be generated. She decided to run a contest among the men: those coming up with the most interesting suggestions would receive a $100 bonus. She had the carpentry shop build her a box with a slot in the lid, paint IDEAS on its side and have it nailed to the side of the office door.

When Erin did pay a visit to Lydia and the girls, for the first time since Brent had attacked her and fled north, she found his sister to be supportive, distraught at what he had done. They embraced and Erin assured Lydia she had nothing to be embarrassed or ashamed of, that she would always cherish the friendship they had.

Chapter 32

THE CABIN WAS TAKING SHAPE. The frame had already been erected and men he had hired from Patterson and Breckenridge were bringing to it carts laden with trees that would be trimmed of their branches, run through a large saw and nailed in place. Eventually, according to the plan he held in his hand as he surveyed the activity, Matthew would be the owner of a fine timber home on a small hill overlooking the stream and the valley.

He was, indeed, now a wealthy man for having successfully claimed the 15,000 acres as the lawyer had suggested he planned to have a ranch while at the same time stoop down at regular intervals and pluck a gold nugget from the stream. It was still scarcely to be believed: the Morgan Canyon Ranch, a name he had retained in acknowledgement of the assistance the lawyer had provided. The more he said it, the more he liked the sound of it.

All of this, of course, lay in the future. The cattle roaming the valley, his valley and the gold from the stream, his stream, and even the half-constructed home, his home, would have to wait for Matthew had several other things to do.

Such things had increasingly been gnawing at him for he harboured the feeling that he needed more in his life, much more than the wealth, the land, the cattle, the river with its gold, the home.

As he sat with his back against what he now considered his guardian tree, the one he had rested against before discovering the gold, he considered the life he had recently led, the years of war, the aimless drifting, and what fate had decided he would now become. He knew that he wanted to become what fate had decreed with someone at his side.

He was not a lazy man so he had remained as the Patterson Sheriff, a job that certainly did not tax him for it was still a town that took care of itself and its citizens. Thus, when he was not watching the men work on his home or was exploring his land, Matthew could be seen walking up one side of Patterson's street and down the other, greeting and talking to, as was his regular custom, the people.

He had also entered into several business deals with partners, guided and advised in the ventures by his always cautious lawyer friend. He was now a partner in a freight hauling concern, the town hotel and a lumber yard.

He was not a religious man but he had donated funding to the town church as well as to the school. It was his way of thanking Patterson for being the place it was.

He was troubled, deeply so, in one respect. He had in his pocket the latest letter from Gabriel and he took it out and unfolded it. It alarmed him to hear of the plight of the company but he was happy to learn that the River Queen was being restored. He trusted Erin would find a way to overcome her troubles.

Damnation, he thought, he was so far away from all that was happening in Natchez and there was nothing he could do about it, even if Erin was prepared to overlook the manner in which he had disappeared from the yard. He doubted she ever would, she had no reason to, and there was nothing he could do about it.

He rode back to town, he was still staying in the hotel, and in his room wrote back to Gabriel with the very latest news of the ranch, adding the customary invitation to come for a visit or even to stay since he could always use a good, honest, hard-working foreman when he started to build his herd and work the spread. After some thought, he added one last message seeking news of Erin. It was something he had not requested in any of his previous letters. Anyway, Gabriel always included plenty of news about her since he felt she would not be interested in what he thought.

It was Olivia Julianne who came up with a suggestion for developing more work for the yard, though she still wondered why Erin would wish to keep it going. Indeed, she had caused a minor falling out with her sister by expressing a long held feeling that Erin should seek a purchaser for the company and the River Queen and live the life of a wealthy lady of leisure on the proceeds. Happily, Erin's reaction to this was to dismiss the notion with laughter ... the very idea!

Olivia Julianne's more useful suggestion was certainly a good one.

One afternoon, while the sisters were walking around Natchez, Olivia Julianne stopped to admire some magnificent wrought iron around the balcony of a town house and remarked how excellent similar work would enhance her own home.

"Your little company could make it for me," she said.

Erin looked at the balcony with an interest she had never previously shown when passing the house in the past. Natchez, indeed most of the towns along the river, were adorned with fine examples of such iron work, where it had not been removed to be turned into more deadly materiel during the war, and she thought the Natchez Mississippi Construction Company could quite easily provide it.

"What a splendid idea," Erin said, embracing her startled sister. "I will have your ironwork made as quickly as it is possible. You do come up with wonderful suggestions."

Of course I do, Olivia Julianne thought, *if only other people realised it*. She was quite pleased with herself.

"May I claim my $100?" she asked.

"No you may not. But you can have your railings for nothing; I shall use your home as an experiment."

The work of restoring the River Queen was, alas, causing Erin and Gabriel a major headache for it was proving to be more expensive than they had initially calculated, money the company simply did not have. She faced the terrible prospect of having to abandon the work and, if it was possible, which she doubted, find someone to purchase the vessel. It was a prospect she did not wish to contemplate for the steamer meant a great deal to her, it held so many memories.

"Oh dear, Gabriel," she said when he had returned once more to Natchez with alarming news of all the work that the River Queen required, "I cannot lose the Queen, surely there is a way to save her? We did it before and was she not then in an even worse condition? We cannot just leave her to rot, she was magnificent, she does not deserve such a terrible fate."

"I understand," Gabriel said. "She was everything you say, and more, but we do not have the money to complete the work. To do so would place the entire company in danger ... it is, surely, a matter of sacrificing the River Queen to save the company? I can see no other solution, and I have discussed it in detail with Captain Charles. You must decide, ma'am."

"I will, Gabriel, I will. I will discuss it with Orell."

"If you pardon me, ma'am," Gabriel said, "you cannot keep asking Mr Thynne to find more backing, he will simply run out of willing assistance."

Erin knew he was right. Orell had done so much for her and the company and she knew there would come a point beyond which he could not, would not, venture. She feared that point had now been reached ... she was about to lose the River Queen.

The snows of early winter began capping the mountains, flurries drifting like delicate lace across the valley. Matthew was now to be found more regularly working alongside the men he had hired to build his cabin for he wanted to be in it before the weather took its tightest grip.

It would be the first thing he truly owned, the first true roots he would ever have. On a more practical level he realised he could not leave a half constructed cabin to the unrelenting ravages of a Rocky Mountain winter, he wanted to be there, to spend the coming months turning it into a home.

Matthew and the men finished the roof and made the cabin weatherproof, certainly enough for him to move in. He celebrated the event by bringing from Patterson a cartload of food and drink and a party of friends. Another cartload of essential furniture followed several days later.

And, contentedly alone in a breathtaking landscape of white brilliance and tall, creaking trees cloaked in costumes of glistening snow, he set about laying the foundations of the rest of his life.

Chapter 33

GABRIEL STOOD IN THE SHATTERED wheelhouse of the River Queen. He had returned with a determination to see, perhaps for the final time, if there was any solution to be found to the saving of the vessel, to the saving of Erin's dream. He had brushed away the broken shards of glass and planking and was now gazing at the original plans for the steamer spread across a table.

Orell had returned to Natchez that very morning, having accompanied him to see the condition of the vessel for himself, with an equal determination to find the finance Erin so desperately needed.

Gabriel had, indeed, provided several possibilities – albeit, Orell felt, slim in the extreme – and he promised he would at the very least put them to the test.

In Natchez, Erin steeled herself for a momentous decision, one she had been putting off for many weeks: she would go to see for herself, perhaps for the final time, the River Queen. She must, she told herself, go as a level headed businesswoman, not as a woman who viewed it as more than a mere assembly of broken timbers and iron but as a lost love. Had she not anyway lost much more than a mere boat?

She had not been in Northville Landing for some time for it held so many happy – and now departed – memories for her but she resolved to find within her the courage to make the journey. She also, in case her courage faltered, decided to ask Amelia if she would care to accompany her since her young ward, now a beautiful and sophisticated, indeed often infuriatingly spirited, young woman had not been there since the death of her father.

Amelia, who was still being courted with increased ardour by her young Yankee lieutenant, agreed to travel with Erin. The lieutenant had been sent on military business to Washington for six months and Amelia was delighted to have her thoughts diverted from him, somewhat, and, of course, to escape from the college she was attending.

Amelia was always ready for what she called a Great Adventure ... and what tales she would have for the friends she had left when Erin had opened her home and her heart and brought her to Natchez.

They travelled, as they had at the beginning of Erin's own Great Adventure, aboard the Delta Pride, with Erin issuing a stern warning to Amelia that if either of them were to meet a handsome gentleman during the trip they were to be led swiftly from the encounter and locked in the cabin, with the key thrown in the river for additional safety.

Of course, in the case of Amelia a number of men – gentlemen or no – found themselves drawn to the ladies' table. All were politely entertained with cool indifference and sent on their disappointed way ... to much contained mirth on the part of their hostesses.

"I intend to glide as gracefully as I can into a realm of contented spinsterhood ... men are a downright nuisance, my dear Amelia," Erin declared, but added as an afterthought, "I suspect, however, that you have chosen a vastly different glide."

On reaching Northville Landing, they were met at the jetty by Gabriel and driven to the home Erin had so happily shared with dear Jessie. Brent had not been allowed to sell it, as he had so often insisted he should be ... for Erin's sake, of course. A housekeeper had been employed to maintain the house and it proved to be a warm and welcoming return.

While Amelia selected a room and unpacked, Erin and

Gabriel, who had brought the plans of the vessel with him, walked out to the garden and sat at a table under a willow tree.

"Well, Gabriel," Erin said as she poured him a coffee, "I trust you have some news of the River Queen for me ... I trust it is good news."

"It is, shall I say, bad news and terrible news."

It was what Erin feared, all terrible news.

"Of course," Gabriel began as he unrolled the plans on the table, pinning the ends down with the coffee pot and his cup, "the Queen can be saved, the men have done a great job in cleaning up most of the mess and surveying the damage to the engine room and the wheel, but to have the old lady back to her best still remains prohibitive ... so much so that ..."

"That we could not afford the work."

He nodded. There was little he could add that Erin had not already known.

"There is, or may be, a small sparkle of optimism," he said. "I had, as you know, Mr Thynne looking over the River Queen and I made some suggestions regarding the finance we would require for the vessel. He returned to Natchez with the promise of doing all in his power to obtain it."

"But in the meantime, can we keep the men working on the boat? Are we simply wasting their time and what money we have left to keep the yard in business?"

"Until we hear from Mr Thynne that he has reached the limits of his search and there is absolutely no further financing to be found I think we should continue with the work. In the end, if you have to sell the River Queen then she will be in as good a shape as we could make her."

"Then we shall keep the work going and trust in Orell to ride to our rescue," Erin said.

The following day her visit to the River Queen did little to strengthen her resolve for what she saw was a once beautiful vessel still stuck in the levee, its hull breached, its wheelhouse and cabins torn apart, the engine room flooded and the paddles broken and twisted. All of this Erin viewed in silence, tormented by the knowledge that the money for the work did not exist.

Gabriel made the only suggestion possible in the circumstances. There was, he pointed out, nothing Erin could do, he would keep the men working to clear away the wreckage ... and she should try, however difficult it may be, to enjoy her return to Northville Landing by seeing old friends, host a dinner party, do what was necessary to take her mind off what she had seen.

It was a suggestion she took to heart, though he had been right in saying it would be difficult, and she and Amelia embarked on the campaign.

And at the end of the week Orell contacted her and Gabriel with remarkable news: he had found a backer who promised him whatever funding was necessary to return the River Queen to the river, faster, more luxurious, more spectacular than she had been before. And if the Natchez Mississippi Construction Company required money to remain in business it would also be made available. The finance had been provided by an investment company in one of the northern states, a company that guarded its privacy with the strictest of terms.

Erin could not believe such a change of fortune and wanted to know all about her benefactors but Orell assured her that he had investigated the company and was fully satisfied that it was a company to be trusted, that the offer was genuine and the money guaranteed. That, he stressed, was all the investors required her to know. He had, on behalf of Erin and the existing backers, taken the liberty of accepting the money and the conditions governing it. He advised Erin to do the same, which she did.

She and Amelia prepared to return as quickly as they could to Natchez. Erin left Gabriel to continue the work on the vessel, work she knew would be done to the perfection she wished for and would return it to service in a condition, as stipulated by her new investors, that would be faster, more luxurious and more spectacular.

Her task upon reaching Natchez would be to expand the company and the yard for she had received, in addition to the one from Olivia Julianne, quite a collection of ideas from the men. As she sat on the small balcony of her cabin on the Delta Pride, she thought how proud of her father and Mr Riparian would be of what she had achieved. Through their curious friendship it had all been possible.

The company did indeed thrive and expand for not only did orders come from the river but from several of the companies now criss-crossing America with their railroads ... carrying their passengers in comfortable coaches built by the Natchez Mississippi Construction Company. It was said that if you sailed in it or rode in it, decorated your home with it or cooked your dinner on it, sat on it in your garden or ploughed your fields with it, it had almost certainly been made by Erin's company. Well, such a statement may have been lavishly generous but there was more than a grain of truth to it.

It took seven months but eventually the River Queen was restored and Captain Charles, who had rejected several offers of employment from other companies to remain with Erin, brought her back to Natchez to prepare for the resumption of the service to New Orleans.

The arrival of the vessel in Natchez was greeted with enthusiasm by the citizens and Erin – with the usual contribution from Olivia Julianne, always willing to be involved in a celebration – organised a ball for all those who had made it possible.

She also arranged an additional treat for many of those closest to her – Olivia Julianne and Orell, Gabriel, Mrs Charles, Lydia and her daughters, Amelia and her Yankee lieutenant – who were invited to travel to New Orleans on its first run.

Gabriel wrote to Matthew with all the news.

Chapter 34

SPRING HAD COME TO MATTHEW'S valley. He rode through it, following the stream as it meandered through the growth and renewal all around him, stirring and stretching in the warmth of the warm sun.

He had achieved much in a short time. He was now the Mayor of Patterson, an honour he had initially been reluctant to accept but had been encouraged to do so by Mayor Hedges upon his retirement, and his home was the centre of the town's growing social scene. To his amusement, Matthew had been described in several periodicals as the most eligible bachelor in Colorado.

He rode, as he always did, to where a hill provided a panoramic view down across the valley and dismounted. Below him was part of his herd of Hereford cattle, their red and white heads turned to the sun.

Fate, the Gods, call it what you will, had certainly been kind to Matthew ... and yet. He was strangely restless, he harboured a feeling, he could not quite explain it, that there was something not right with his life. He had so much, but not enough. The lack of it did not include wealth or prestige, of which he had in abundance, but he was not sure what it was.

He found himself increasingly thinking of Natchez, of Gabriel, of Erin. He wondered if she ever thought of him, if she even remembered who he was. He very much doubted it and told himself not to be so stupid as to think she would.

He turned back to his horse and mounted. He returned to the house where, sitting with on the veranda with a brandy, he decided to put his thoughts into action.

The River Queen, now even more successful than she had been before the storm, was plying the Mississippi and, even more importantly, earning the company a handsome profit. People lined the river banks whenever they heard her calliope heralding her banner bedecked arrival.

It was now four months since her return to service and Captain Charles and his crew had set several records for the speed of the vessel's journey between Natchez, Northville Landing and New Orleans.

Olivia Julianne, now won over completely to the success of the company, had established herself in numerous functions: the interior designs and furnishings, the enhancement of the catering and the programme of entertainments the River Queen offered. Erin was quite content to allow her sister to get on with it, though she did on more than one occasion have to caution her towards modification.

Erin's standing comment was that if she did not exercise such caution, Olivia Julianne would have elephants imported from India for the further delight of the passengers but a minstrel troupe and a fine orchestra would have to suffice. Olivia Julianne countered with the argument that she had not, of course, contemplated elephants but secretly reflected that it might not be such a ridiculous notion.

She might look into it.

The River Queen was approaching its berth in Natchez and Gabriel was waiting on the jetty to oversee the loading of equipment purchased in New Orleans for the yard.

He watched as the passengers disembarked and listened as they passed to their comments of delight and praise for such an excellent experience. Several businessmen, regular passengers, saw him and came to shake his hand and clap his shoulders ... she was, they declared, quite the most magnificent boat on the river.

Gabriel modestly thanked them for their support and loyalty ... well, of course the River Queen was magnificent, had he and his men not made her so?

He returned to the yard with the equipment in a cart and when it had been unloaded and distributed around the various workshops he walked to the office where he found Erin sifting through a pile of new contracts. She looked up and smiled. She opened a drawer in her desk and removed a glass and a bottle of whiskey, held it up and Gabriel nodded and sat down.

"We have come a long way, have we not, Gabriel?" she said, pushing the contracts to one side and pouring herself a coffee. "It has been quite an adventure, I do declare. I have to pinch myself for assurance that it has not been all a dream ... but it is true, we have come a long way."

"We have that, ma'am," Gabriel agreed. "You have been quite wonderful."

Erin, feeling the colour rise to her cheeks, brushed his praise aside. All of what the Natchez Mississippi Construction Company had become would not have been achieved without the faithful Gabriel and her workmen. She would never forget that.

"You have been working night and day, ma'am," Gabriel said. "I have a suggestion to make, if you will allow me: why do you not take a trip to New Orleans? You might ask your sister to accompany you."

"That is actually a splendid idea," Erin said. "I do so love New Orleans and have many good friends there who I have not seen for some time. You know, I will speak with Olivia Julianne and make the arrangements."

That evening while in her sister's home for dinner, Erin received the enthusiastic response to her invitation and the two agreed to make the journey to New Orleans during the first week of June, three weeks hence. Erin now had one other thing to attend to and asked Orell if he might see her in private.

Orell asked a maid to bring them coffee and he and Erin took chairs in the garden to catch the day's lingering heat. When the coffee came he poured her a cup, added sugar and cream and handed it to her.

"You have something on your mind, my dear," he said. "If there is something troubling you ..."

"No," Erin said after some thought. "It is merely something that has occupied my thoughts for some time. It concerns the mysterious investors who saved the River Queen, indeed saved the company. I have never been told who exactly they are, only that they have consistently guarded their identity."

"I do not know the answer to your dilemma," Orell said. "I will tell you what little I know. I was given the name for a possible source of money and through my contacts in the north I was assured that the source was a genuine one. I even employed a detective agency to independently verify what I had already been told. They too confirmed the complete integrity and suitability of the investors. When my agents made contact they were told of the conditions of strict privacy ... other than that you know the rest: the finance was provided and proved the saving of us."

"It is all extremely mystifying, is it not?" Erin said. "And it has now been repaid with interest ..."

What Orell did not tell her – again on the instructions of the investors – was that a repayment was not required. He merely nodded.

He had, of course, his own thoughts on the matter, thoughts he felt it better not to reveal to Erin. He was strongly of the opinion that the funding had come from Brent, by way of atonement. The knowledge would not have brought her pleasure.

That evening Gabriel and some of the men from the yard rode into Natchez for a sit-down meal and a spell of cards and a drink. But first he had something important to do. He stopped off at the telegraph office and had a message wired to Matthew. Gabriel had nurtured a plan for a long time and he figured the time had come to add some reality to it.

Matthew travelled to Baltimore, a city he had never set foot in before. It was a long way from Patterson and his valley but on the advice of his lawyer friend, who on his behalf was searching relentlessly for investment opportunities, he had purchased stock in the Baltimore and Ohio Railroad since he realised it offered a solid investment in an expanding network. It was an opportunity to see if he could shake off his feeling of restlessness, an uneasy thought that he was being lured back to his old life of drifting aimlessly from one nowhere town to another.

Matthew was well aware of his good fortune and he had put it to good use. At heart he knew he could never leave his valley yet those feelings of wanting something more would not be banished. A long trip to a big city, with all its discomfort and fatigue and, upon arrival, all its noise and bustle, would dispel further thoughts of green pastures being more rewarding elsewhere.

He had given his instructions to his foreman, a tall, gangling Texan who knew more about cattle than Matthew thought it possible to know, and he departed with a sense of optimism, a sense that something extraordinary was about to happen to him. His lawyer had, anyway, stressed that while in Maryland he should look out for more investment potential.

And in Baltimore he certainly found such potential for he invested in property and a shipping line. He had been in the city for just over a week and one evening he found himself exploring the Fell's Point district across the inner harbour from the rush and scurry of the city.

He had taken greatly to Baltimore and as often as he could he escaped from the endless procession of business meetings and mind numbing dinners, all of which simply made him richer but bored to tears and did not subdue his restlessness. He had taken to walking around the city using what he considered quite an ingenious method of finding something new and interesting: walk until he came to a corner, turn left or right and walk until he came to another corner, turn left or right and walk ... a man could find himself in some intriguing places.

Thus he was walking and turning, left on this occasion, around Fell's Point when he came across an inn with the most amusing name he had ever seen: The Horse You Came In On.

He stopped and looked up at the sign swinging and creaking in the light breeze and decided no one who ever stood outside an inn with such a name should simply pass on. He pushed open the door and entered.

A lively crowd, a good many of them sailors, was lined

along the bar and he eased himself through it and ordered a beer and a whiskey. He listened to the talk around him, to the sailors' tales of adventure and danger, to the wild and wanton women they had encountered in bars from Londonderry to Liverpool, Bristol to Boston, Sydney to San Francisco, from ... well, from hell to high water and back.

Four sailors to his right were talking about their next voyage and Matthew listened with growing interest: in two days time, he discovered, they were bound for New Orleans. He had a letter in his pocket that hinted towards it being just such a journey he should himself make.

He excused his intrusion and bought them a round of drinks. He asked the name of their ship and if it took passengers. It was, they told him, the Maine Packet and it did take passengers. The following morning, though suffering from a raging headache from what had become an overly jolly evening with his sailor friends, Matthew booked a cabin on the Main Packet bound for New Orleans.

Olivia Julianne was beside herself with excitement. She simply loved being anywhere that offered stores brimming with the finest apparel from New York and Paris, anywhere that offered the finest food and wine from every corner of the world, anywhere that offered culture, sophistication and refinement ... anywhere that underlined to her how she saw herself. New Orleans offered it all, and more.

Erin enjoyed the city in equal measure but more particularly for the many friends she had there. It also, as the wise Gabriel had predicted, offered her a welcome diversion from all that had happened to her and to the company.

It was now her time, her moment to embrace the fruits of her labour and to begin to enjoy life afresh. She was not yet certain in what manner this would be but when it came she would be open to it.

She and Olivia Julianne had finished a morning of shopping and were sitting under a tree draped in dangling Spanish moss in a small square. A humid heat drifted off the river and they fanned it off.

"I do declare, Olivia Julianne, I shall trickle to the ground in a pool of moisture with this heat," Erin said as she flapped her wide brimmed bonnet to cool her cheeks.

"It is alarmingly hot, to be sure," Olivia Julianne said, adding with a note of disapproval, "But please Erin, it is most unladylike to be waving your hat like that, you are not a Gandy Dancer on the railroad. Do compose yourself."

Erin smiled. Her sister never failed to surprise her. Where she had once thought of Olivia Julianne as a stiff backed harridan forever gazing down her nose at a world of constant disappointment, she had discovered her to be wise, industrious, loyal and funny.

"Why, Olivia Julianne, you never cease to amuse me ... the very fact that you have even heard of a Gandy Dancer brings a smile to my face. Anyway, it is my face and my hat and I shall do ...." She stopped suddenly and for the first time in a long time she remembered a long ago conversation involving a hat.

The memory surprised her, unleashed a flood of recollections and questions whose answers troubled and confused her.

Olivia Julianne observed her with a puzzled look.

"Why, Erin ... are you feeling faint?"

Erin broke from her trance and smiled.

"No," she said. "I was merely recalling someone I once knew, someone who at the time meant more to me than I was willing to acknowledge."

"A man? Gracious, you had a secret admirer before you married that scoundrel Masterson ... do tell."

Erin shook her head and placed her hat back on her head. She had, of course, thought often of Matthew, wondered why he had left so suddenly, wondered what had happened to him. And increasingly she came to realise how much she missed him ... for all that he had constantly infuriated her.

"There is nothing to tell, it was merely a passing memory. Indeed, I do not know if the gentleman is alive or, if he is, where he lives. He was something of a vagabond and I would not be surprised to discover he has remained one to this day. Truth to tell, I am astonished that I even thought of him just now. He is gone and that is the end of the matter."

The sisters remained in New Orleans for two weeks and at the start of the third week Erin arranged for their passage to Natchez when the River Queen made her return journey. Until then the energetic Olivia Julianne spent a fruitful day in arranging for the company's wrought ironworks to be represented and sold throughout the city.

With relentless persistence, she also tried to prise from Erin more information about her 'secret admirer' ... to no avail, though being Olivia Julianne she determined to discover who it was by her own means.

Matthew had, upon arriving in New Orleans from Baltimore, telegraphed Gabriel with the address of the hotel he was staying in and had received the news back that Erin and Mrs Thynne were also in the city but booked to return to Natchez.

Of course, such a coincidence had been part of Gabriel's plan for on learning the dates for the sisters' visit he had written to Matthew in Colorado with the news.

Matthew made his way to the office of the Natchez Mississippi Construction Company in the French Quarter and booked a cabin for the journey to Natchez. As he walked back to his hotel, he wondered if he had done the right thing. Perhaps he had been rash, perhaps if he met Erin she would not welcome it, would snub him for his conceit in thinking she would do otherwise. He had left Natchez without summoning the courage to tell her why, to tell her how he felt about her.

The River Queen approached the jetty, its horn booming in the afternoon heat. A crowd was already gathering along the riverfront to see her arrival for the vessel was, indeed, the Queen of the Mississippi. Matthew walked along the levee and sat to watch her ease to her mooring.

As he took in the activity, the passengers preparing to disembark, his thoughts turned to a day – a day in a distant past that belonged in a different world – when he had first set eyes on her as a broken hulk. He remembered finding shelter on her and he remembered first seeing Erin. He would always remember that moment and, with a sigh, he wondered if he would ever see her again, if he had the courage to even try.

"Damnation!" he said and rose to walk back along the river to his hotel.

He waited in the shadows of the evening as the passengers hurried along the jetty to board the steamer. He had chosen to get to the jetty before the other travellers started to arrive since he did not wish, not yet, to run into Erin and Olivia Julianne. From his hiding place he hoped to see the sisters arrive and safely install themselves in their cabin, then he would board and figure out what to do.

Nothing he had ever faced during the war, no dangers he had ever encountered from the Yankees, were as daunting as those he now foresaw. And then he saw them, driving along the riverfront in a handsome carriage that pulled up at the gangway of the River Queen. The driver assisted Erin and Olivia Julianne from the carriage and called for help to take their luggage and boxes aboard.

Matthew watched all this and could not take his eyes from Erin: she was beautiful. And in that glorious instant he knew what he had been missing, what the feeling of emptiness in his life had meant. He waited until he saw Erin and Olivia Julianne safely deposited to their cabin and, picking up his bag, he walked from his hiding place and boarded the vessel.

In his cabin, he poured himself a drink and stood at the window to watch the River Queen pull slowly from the jetty and listened as the wheels churned her into the river and turn northward for the journey to Northville Landing and Natchez. He listened as the crew called the depth of the water and scurried around in a whirl of activity. He stood to watch the city glide past the window until the vessel reached the open countryside beyond its limits.

From outside his door he heard the footsteps of passengers hurrying in eager anticipation to the restaurant and gaming room. It suddenly came to him that he had never actually seen these rooms, not prior to or following the storm for he had left the yard while the initial work was still being completed.

He turned from the cabin window and sat on the bed. He was not, in truth, certain what he should do next and the thought came to him that he feared what his next move might lead to ... that he lacked the courage to even make it. He wondered what he was doing there, why he had embarked on such a fretful venture.

Erin and Olivia Julianne were settling into their journey, unpacking their dresses and hanging them in the wardrobes, setting aside the clothes they planned to wear to dinner. Olivia Julianne, though, had to positively forbid her sister to go on an inspection tour of the steamer.

"For the journey," she instructed firmly. "You are not the owner of the River Queen. You are a valued customer and you will relax and enjoy the experience. Do I make myself clear?"

Erin smiled. She felt like a small schoolgirl caught and admonished for being naughty by a stern teacher – gracious, had she ever been as formidable when she was a school ma'am? – but she did, reluctantly, agree with Olivia Julianne that it would be unsettling for the crew if she began stalking the vessel. She would fight the temptation and enjoy the journey for its own sake. Well, perhaps when her bossy sister was not looking she might make the odd note of what she found wanting and mention it to Captain Charles and Gabriel in Natchez.

Matthew washed, shaved and dressed ... still unsure of his next move. He was hungry, which he felt was a good start since he knew he could not undertake the journey in a state of starvation and would at some point have to go to the restaurant.

When he had finished dressing he poured another fortifying whiskey and took several deep breaths.

The enemy lay in waiting – not the lady herself, or so he hoped, but the moment when he would come face to face with her, the moment itself was the enemy – and he must not flinch from the confrontation.

What am I doing here, he asked himself as he squared his shoulders, ran his hands through his hair and opened the cabin door.

He reached the door of the restaurant and glanced around it, checking the tables. He did not see Erin or her sister and stepped inside. At the far end of the restaurant he saw an empty table and as a young waitress came towards him he pointed to it and she guided him through the other diners. He pulled out the chair and moved it to where he could see the door. He requested the waitress to bring him a beer and sat down to read the copperplate, hand written menu.

The waitress returned and set the beer on the table. She stood holding a small notebook until he finished scanning the menu.

"If I might suggest the fish, sir, fresh up from the coast this afternoon," she said, tapping the menu with a pencil.

"Well now," Matthew said, "if someone as pretty as you suggest it then it must be good ... so the fish it is, with all the fixings."

The waitress blushed and hurried away. He sipped at the cold beer and stared at the door.

He almost missed them when Erin and Olivia Julianne eventually arrived at the restaurant for the waitress had brought his dish and was placing it on the table. It was only when she stepped away that he saw them being shown to their table just to the right of the door.

He tried not to stare but could not take his eyes off Erin. She was dressed in a gown of white silk and from around her shoulders she took a blue shawl. Her hair, longer than Matthew remembered it to be, curled down her neck. And not for the first time did he think her quite the most lovely and intriguing of creatures.

He toyed with his fish and watched a waiter fuss around their table, pointing out, as his waitress had, the best the menu had to offer and holding a bottle of wine for their approval. He watched Erin nod and smile and when the waiter had poured he watched her raise the glass to her lips ... he could not stop himself from watching her every movement.

Olivia Julianne was now looking around the crowded restaurant and she caught Matthew's interest in her and Erin. She stared him down and leaning across the table she tapped Erin's arm with her fan.

"My dear," she whispered, "I do believe you have found yet another secret admirer for there is a gentleman, and a quite handsome one, who appears unable to take his eyes from you."

Erin laughed.

"Then, if what you say is true, the gentleman's eyes are

sorely in need of spectacles. Really, Olivia Julianne, you can be foolish at times. I am sorry I ever mentioned anything about what you will insist was my secret admirer."

"And yet ..."

"And yet nothing. There was no admirer, secret or otherwise, there was merely a person I knew briefly ... indeed, I found him quite infuriating and I expect wherever he is today he is even more so."

Olivia Julianne maintained her scrutiny of Matthew who was now expending more interest in his meal than it warranted. He was tormenting himself over what he should do. He concentrated on his meal and sneaked glances at the sisters. He ordered another beer, simply to have something to keep him at the table. If he did not do something more positive he feared he would spend the entire journey at the table.

Finally he pulled several bills from his pocket and folded them to slip under his plate. He finished his drink and rose from the table.

"My dear," Olivia Julianne said, "the gentleman is about to leave, he is coming this way ..."

"Then we will not embarrassment the poor creature by staring at him," Erin said, looking up at the poor creature. She gasped. "Dear God..." she said, her hand covering her mouth.

And when the moment arrived, Matthew's courage failed him, he did not stop. He saw how she had reacted and took it as the bad omen he had feared ... Erin had no desire to see him back in her life.

As he walked towards the door of the restaurant, he smiled and their eyes met. Outside on the deck he leaned against the rail and stared down to the water lapping and bubbling along the vessel. He was a fool, he thought, a damn fool.

Olivia Julianne reached out to Erin, concerned at her strange behaviour. Erin sat silently, her hand still covering her mouth. Olivia Julianne poured a glass of water and handed it across the table.

"Are you feeling better?" she asked.

Erin nodded.

"Yes," she said, sipping the water. "I just ... I thought I saw someone from my past."

"That gentleman who passed," Olivia Julianne said. "The one I had pointed out, the one who kept looking at you ... do you know him?"

"No, he merely resembled someone I did once know, but I was mistaken. If you do not mind, I think I will return to the cabin. I fear our visit to New Orleans has fatigued me more than I imagined."

Olivia Julianne assisted Erin to the cabin and saw her safely tucked up in bed. She remained until Erin slipped into a peaceful sleep and, pulling her cloak around her shoulders and the hood over her head, she walked to the deck to gather her thoughts. There was, she suspected, more to what had occurred than Erin was revealing. There was, she realised, only one way to obtain the information and that was to find the man and have him, indeed if necessary make him, tell her. She turned and went back to the cabin, determined to solve the mystery in the morning.

The River Queen was making good time. The river was running slow and smooth and a bright sun was painting the promising dawn in purple, red and yellow splashes.

Erin stirred and stretched ... and the memory of the previous evening came back to her. She pulled the quilt to her chin and chided herself for being so silly. To be sure, the gentleman in the restaurant bore a resemblance to Matthew but he was much better dressed than she had ever remembered him to be. And, anyway, why would Matthew be on the River Queen? If he was anywhere, she decided, he would be on a horse drifting aimlessly from place to place.

And yet she wished it had been Matthew. She had found herself increasingly thinking of Matthew and wondering what had become of him. He had been the infuriation of her life, with his twisted, knowing smile and his too easy going ways ... oh yes, and that battered, infuriating Rebel hat he insisted on wearing. She wished it had been Matthew for she missed him, missed him very much.

She turned to see if Olivia Julianne was awake so that they

might plan the coming day's activities. But her sister was not there, her bed was empty.

Gracious, Erin thought, what had roused Olivia Julianne so early? She plumped up her pillow and settled down again. With Olivia Julianne it was never wise to question the working of her mind.

Olivia Julianne had found a seat at the far end of the deck, the better to see if the mysterious gentleman who had so clearly shocked Erin appeared. The morning was building its heat and she pushed open her parasol to shield her eyes from the glare, and to hide beneath.

Around her the passengers were coming from their cabins and walking along the deck to the lounge for morning coffee. And eventually she saw Matthew step from his cabin – nine doors from where she sat, she counted – and stretch. He was, she thought, certainly a handsome man, in an outdoor sort of way. If she wished Erin to have had a secret admirer before her disastrous marriage to the scoundrel Brent then such a man as she was looking at fitted the bill.

As Matthew turned to join the promenade to the lounge, Olivia Julianne suddenly realised what a curious sight she presented, a woman sitting on her own. She realised how out of place she looked.

Matthew reached her and smiled. To her surprise, for he was otherwise smartly and expensively dressed, he wore a grey slouch hat that had clearly witnessed much in a long life. On seeing her, he raised the hat and bowed.

"A fine morning, ma'am," he said, his eyes twinkling roguishly, and passed on.

Olivia Julianne flushed. "Well," she muttered. "I never!"

She sat pondering what to do and finally decided that boldness was her best strategy. She rose and followed him into the lounge.

Chapter 35

THE LOUNGE WAS ALMOST FULL, most of the tables occupied and being attended to by several busy waitresses who moved briskly from the kitchen with pots of coffee and hot pancakes.

Olivia Julianne scanned the lounge in search of her mystery man and in search of an empty table. She had realised on entering the lounge that she could not simply approach him, they had not been introduced and she did not wish to act in an unseemly manner by imposing herself upon him. She saw him being served by a waitress at a table to the right of the room. She could see no other table at which she could sit and turned to leave, to await another opportunity to talk to him.

Matthew looked up and saw Olivia Julianne. He rose and smiled, catching her attention. He indicted an empty chair at his table and after a brief hesitation she nodded and walked to join him. He pulled the chair out for her and she slid into it.

"I was about to leave," she said. "I did not realise the lounge would be so full so early in the morning."

"I am delighted you decided to join me," Matthew said.

"I do not make a habit of imposing myself upon strangers," she said.

"Well," Matthew said, "I am not entirely a stranger. We

have never met but my name is Matthew Morgan and I worked for your sister in Natchez ... I know who you are: you are Mrs Olivia Julianne Thynne and your travelling companion is Mrs Erin Mast."

"Goodness me, Mr Morgan, I confess I had a feeling there was a great deal more to you than met the eye. And by the way, my sister is, I am delighted to say, no longer Mrs Masterson. That person has met his deserved comeuppance in a Lynchburg jail."

The waitress brought Olivia Julianne a cup and a plate of scones and Matthew poured her a coffee.

"I noticed you looking at us last evening and I had a feeling you knew Erin," she said. "And now I insist you must tell me all about it for you quite discomforted my sister."

And Matthew told her everything: how he and Erin had first met, how he had left Natchez when she married Brent, how he had drifted from one town to another until discovering his valley and his river of gold in Colorado. He told her he was now a wealthy businessman and rancher.

Olivia Julianne listened in fascination to his story and as she listened a great many things became clear to her.

"You are, I believe I am right in saying, the benefactor whose money helped save the River Queen and the company. Come now, Mr Morgan, you cannot deny it. My husband contacted you and you rescued Erin."

Matthew nodded but added that she must never tell Erin. The knowledge must remain a secret between them.

"But why did you do it, and why are you here on the River Queen?" she asked.

Matthew looked at her and smiled.

"Because I love her. I realised some time ago how much I loved her, how something had long been missing from my life and that something was Erin ... because I love her."

"Oh, my goodness! You are my sister's secret admirer," Olivia Julianne had an overwhelming desire to smother him in an embrace.

"Alas, I have a feeling it is not something your sister wishes to reciprocate. I fear my journey has been a futile one."

"My dear Matthew, I am alarmed at your lack of faith and

courage and I think you are very much mistaken. My sister, I am convinced, has exactly the same regard for you. Indeed, though she has never revealed your name, I know she has thought of you often."

"So what can I do to convince her?"

"You will do exactly what I suggest, my dear Matthew. You will place yourself in my hands and it will work out to perfection ... you will see."

She winked, raised her cup and clinked it against his. Olivia Julianne was about to do what she did best: organise things.

They finished their coffee, during which he told her more about himself and when he finished Olivia Julianne rose.

"Come to our cabin; we are in 12 on the upper deck, in thirty minutes time," she said.

He walked from the lounge and strolled nervously to kill time by watching the stern wheel foam and churn through the river. He checked his pocket watch constantly, alarmed that the minute hand seemed hardly to move.

When she arrived back at the cabin, Olivia Julianne found Erin dressed and preparing to go in search of her.

"Well," Olivia Julianne said, "I could not sleep and went for a morning stroll. Now, if you will compose yourself and stop pacing about like a caged tiger I have a surprise for you."

"A surprise? What sort of surprise?"

"Do sit down, it will be here shortly."

"But what is it?"

"If I told you it would no longer be a surprise, now would it? Remain calm and ..."

She was interrupted by a knock on the door and she went to open it. She ushered Matthew inside and stepped outside, closing the door behind her. Erin could not believe what she was looking at. One thing alone convinced her. She smiled and rose.

"I see you still have that infuriating hat, Mr Morgan," Erin said.

"We are, as you know, quite attached. It is something you will have to get used to ... for the rest of your life."

"Oh, Matthew ...," Erin said and ran to embrace him.

About the Author

Colin McAlpin is one of Northern Ireland's best known journalists/broadcasters having been an award-winning Sports Editor, Features Editor, Arts/Entertainments Editor and columnist for the three Belfast daily/Sunday newspapers. He is a long-established travel writer and an authority on the American Civil War.

He co-hosted with his daughter, Heidi, a weekly magazine radio programme on a Belfast station and headed a team that established a museum for Crusaders, one of Northern Ireland's premier football clubs.

He was a co-founder of the Northern Ireland Film Commission (now Northern Ireland Screen), the UK Guild of Regional Film Writers and he is a former Chair of Dance Northern Ireland.

Also by Colin McAlpin

Julia

The much-anticipated sequel to the highly-acclaimed SANTA FE SISTERS sees the past calling to Georgina, now happily married in New Mexico, and drawing her back to her beloved Glens of Antrim for revenge and a final settlement.

But the past demands a cruel, heartbreaking payment and for Georgina's friend, the poetess Julia O'Malley, there is a flight from a deadly deed to a new life of danger, adventure, choices ... and a lost love.

Another epic story from author Colin McAlpin set in the aftermath of the American Civil War and the development of the American West, with the author's customary cast of strong female characters facing an uncertain future with courage, faith and hope.

Santa Fe Sisters

It is the late 1880s. Sisters Georgina and Violet Sophia Devonshire live in the village of Glenscullion in the beautiful Glens of Antrim in Northern Ireland enjoying a life of good fortune, until misfortune befalls them and they are forced to leave for a new, yet uncertain, life in America.

On the voyage from Londonderry to Baltimore they befriend an elderly gentleman who unfortunately dies during the journey. It is an encounter that changes their lives forever. Along the way, the sisters meet a collection of weird and wonderful characters, including a deadly business rival, a colourful vaudeville singer and an enigmatic preacher man. And romance may be on the cards too. But will their dreams turn to reality in the face of opposition, danger and betrayal?

SANTA FE SISTERS is a carefully researched story featuring strong female characters who will keep you enthralled until the very last page; it's a tale that will linger long in the memory and leave you wanting more.

The
Midnight Star

Their reasons for making the journey were all different but the dangers and the hardships were the same for everyone on the wagon train as it blazed a new trail.

For Alicia Henshall and her young daughter Louise Jane it would be an epic and unforgettable journey into the unknown.

Those who survived the adventure would not only find new challenges, but discover that love and hope can blossom in the toughest of conditions. Their lives would be forever changed.

From the author of the highly acclaimed SANTA FE SISTERS, this is a story of courage and discovery set in the years immediately after the bloody American Civil War, combining real events and strong fictional characters.

Made in the USA
Columbia, SC
25 June 2018